ATTENTION
ALL
SHIPPING

Also by Kathy Biggs

The Luck
Scrap

ATTENTION ALL SHIPPING

KATHY BIGGS

THE BOROUGH PRESS

The Borough Press
An imprint of HarperCollins*Publishers* Ltd
1 London Bridge Street
London SE1 9GF

www.harpercollins.co.uk

HarperCollins*Publishers*
Macken House, 39/40 Mayor Street Upper
Dublin 1, D01 C9W8, Ireland

First published by HarperCollins*Publishers* 2025

1

Copyright © Kathy Biggs 2025

Kathy Biggs asserts the moral right to
be identified as the author of this work

A catalogue record for this book is available from the British Library

Hardback ISBN: 978-0-00-873690-3
Trade Paperback ISBN: 978-0-00-873691-0

This novel is entirely a work of fiction. The names, characters and incidents portrayed in it are the work of the author's imagination. Any resemblance to actual persons, living or dead, events or localities is entirely coincidental.

Sea Fever by John Masefield © 1902

Typeset in Adobe Garamond Pro by HarperCollins*Publishers* India

Printed and bound in the UK using 100%
Renewable Electricity at CPI Group (UK) Ltd

All rights reserved. No part of this publication may be reproduced, stored in a retrieval system, or transmitted, in any form or by any means, electronic, mechanical, photocopying, recording or otherwise, without the prior written permission of the publishers.

Without limiting the author's and publisher's exclusive rights, any unauthorised use of this publication to train generative artificial intelligence (AI) technologies is expressly prohibited. HarperCollins also exercise their rights under Article 4(3) of the Digital Single Market Directive 2019/790 and expressly reserve this publication from the text and data mining exception.

This book contains FSC™ certified paper and other controlled
sources to ensure responsible forest management.

For more information visit: www.harpercollins.co.uk/green

*This book is for my brothers,
Michael and James
and in memory of our Dad,
Michael Sammon (1930 - 2017).*

PROLOGUE

November 1999
Off Milford Haven

The boat went down like something swallowed whole: the deck there, then gone – simply vanished from under his feet. He gripped the rail with hands he could no longer feel and struggled towards the wheelhouse.

'Joseph, Joseph!' he screamed. But the wind swooped down and whipped his voice away and before he knew it the water was at his knees, his waist, his chest: a cold malicious thing that leached the very life from his bones. He held his own against it for a few moments or minutes, until all he knew was the weight of his waterproofs and the tug of the ocean bed and the only thing he could hear was the panicked rasp of his own breathing. He lay on his back and looked up at a sky that hung, like a dark spill of lead, over the thrashing waves. Spears of lightning rained down and broke on the surface of the mountainous sea, illuminating nothing but his hopelessness. Eyes closed, he gave his face to the rain. He shut out the noise of the storm and thought of his mother and da, Grace – Joseph.

'I'm sorry,' he shouted, as his throat filled with salt water. 'I'm sorry.'

CHAPTER 1

November 2019

She was late again but there could be no rushing, not in the dark, with the weather coming at her from all sides, the trees along the lane up in arms, struggling to hold their own against the battering wind. Grace twisted her head to get the hair off her face, heaved the gate up an inch and released the latch, trying not to hurry but unable to stop herself. He would be watching out for her now, standing in the open doorway, his small face screwed up, peering across the yard. She pushed the gate open, caught it back with the length of rope and picked her way back to the car, trying to keep to the edge of the track to avoid the worst of the mud, feeling the hem of her coat – her good coat – whipping wet against the back of her legs. She put the car in gear, aimed it through the gateway and slewed into the yard. The headlights were struggling to penetrate the slicing rain but she could see the place was running with water: great sheets of it flying off the barn roof, snatched skywards by the wind before it could reach the ground to join the river that had somehow appeared between the barn and the house. Six feet wide, charging through the yard, making off with things she'd have to go and look for later – feed bowls, plant pots, the clothes pegs. She crawled the car through and parked as near to the house as she dared.

'Da, I'm here.' The wind took her voice and hurled it away. He was at the lip of the porch, one hand steadying himself against the post box.

'Is that you, hinny?'

His voice trailed through the dark towards her.

'Yes. Hang on a minute.'

She pulled her coat tighter and opened the boot, one eye on him as she wrestled with the shopping. 'Wait there, Da,' she shouted, but there he was, coming towards her, his hair dancing around in the wind, his thin trousers and shirt soaked already. She abandoned the bags and slammed the boot closed.

'Where have you been?' His hand was on her arm, clutching at her through her coat sleeve. She could smell the urine on him.

'At work, Da. At work. Then I got a bit of shopping in. Come on.'

She prised his fingers off her arm and linked him across the yard, steering him around the worst of the water, her mind already working through the evening ahead.

The kitchen was freezing. She wrapped a blanket over his shoulders, rubbed a towel over his wet hair and sat him at the table while she started on with the stove.

'There was a young girl here,' he said, as she knelt down, teasing bits of wood into the grate.

'What?'

'A young girl.'

She pushed the wood basket to one side and looked at him.

'The post woman, you mean?'

'Naww. Not the post woman, the girl. A girl.'

She bent to the grate again and added more wood. She had two choices. This is what her life had come down to: she could go along with him or she could stand her ground and prove him wrong. She'd learned there was no victory in proving him wrong, no pleasure to be had in seeing the light go out of his eyes, confusion slackening his face.

'What did she want then, this young girl?'

'Michael,' he said. 'She was looking for our Michael.'

She sat back on her heels, her hands loose in her lap. 'Michael?' She felt his name drop from her lips and onto the floor. *Michael's dead,* she wanted to say, but held it back, closed her mouth tight against the shape of the words. She waited for him to say more but he got up, the blanket off his shoulders and on the floor, and picked his way across the room, his hands clutching at everything he passed: the sofa, the chair, the door frame. She could see the stains on the seat of his trousers.

She pushed another couple of sticks into the grate, then heaved herself up and flicked the switch for the hot water. 'Shower tonight, yes?'

He didn't say anything. He was bent over the dresser, running his hands over its cluttered surface. She watched him for a minute, then went over and put the palm of her hand on his back. She needed to get him out of the wet clothes.

'Da, what are you doing?'

He cranked his head round to look at her. It bobbed a couple of inches above the dresser: a dandelion on a stalk.

'Looking,' he said. 'I'm looking for it.'

'For what?'

'I don't know. She left something. That girl. She left an envelope.'

'What about Shirley? Did she come at dinner time?'

'Yes.' Jack saw her from the corner of his eye, folding her arms across her chest. He'd answered too fast. This was the problem with it: answering too fast or too slow. There was a line between the two but he could never find it. She always rumbled him.

'I'm going to have a word with her,' Grace said. 'If she's going to keep letting us down, we'll have to get someone else.'

'Yes.' He had forgotten why he was at the dresser. 'Have we had our tea?'

'No. I'll get it on when you've had your shower, yes?'

He pulled his monkey face at her. 'Tomorrow,' he said. 'I'll have a shower tomorrow.'

'That's what you said yesterday. And the day before.'

She went into the bathroom before he could say anything else and switched the wall heater on. She stood listening to the electric bars clicking as they heated up, then reached behind the shower curtain and turned on the shower.

'Here it is.' He was behind her, holding a small white card towards her. 'I've found it.'

She took it from him. It was Delyth's calling card. 'This is from the district nurse,' she said.

'Yes.' He shuffled past her, lowered himself onto the bathroom chair and started unbuttoning his shirt. 'She was looking for our Michael.'

She pulled a towel out of the airing cupboard. 'She was, was she? So what did you tell her?'

'I told her he was out on the boat.' He was stepping out of his trousers now. She bundled them up before he could see the mess of them.

'The boat.' She let that land a moment. 'So did she do anything while she was here? Look at your legs? Take your blood pressure?'

He looked at her over his shoulder as he hoisted his foot over the shower tray. 'Look at my legs?' he said. 'For goodness sake, Grace, why would she look at my legs? She was nothing but a girl.'

* * *

Afterwards, Grace wrapped him in the towel and sat him back on the chair. Jack watched her rinsing out the shower, bundling up the wet towels, his heap of stinking clothes.

There was weariness in her every movement. She had been such an easy child: content to be busy, content to be quiet. It had driven her mother to distraction. The girl was too biddable, according to her. No backbone, no grit. He'd never disagreed – not openly – because Wenna was not the kind of woman to tolerate contradiction. Instead he'd quietly tried to prove her wrong. Making a great deal of Grace's small achievements was what it had generally boiled down to: some success at school or Young Farmers, her way with bringing on a new sheep dog. But it had cut no mustard with Wenna.

What would she say now, he wondered, because here that girl was, a grown woman, on her knees on the bathroom floor and here he was, his thoughts lined up straight one moment and gone awry the next. He looked down at the top of her head, at the broad streak of grey marking the centre. She sprinkled his feet with talc, then stood him up and tucked his balls into a plastic nappy.

'Have we had our tea?' he asked. She was fitting him into his vest.

'No. We'll be having it now. I've brought some boiled ham.' She cinched his dressing gown belt round him. 'Here,' she said and passed him a comb. 'You do your hair while I go get the shopping out of the car, yes?'

The weather was still flinging itself around the yard: bold gusts of wind hurling rain against her face in cold handfuls. The dogs came to the barn door and looked out at her.

'Later,' she called and hooked the carrier bags over her arm, put her head down against the pelting and ran for the house. He was already on the porch, his foot hovering over the step.

'Go back in, Da,' she said. The cold water off the porch roof lashed down her neck while she waited for him to totter round and square himself up.

She got him sat at the kitchen table, opened the stove

door to put some more wood on and glanced at the clock. Nearly two hours in and nowhere near a cup of tea. She filled the kettle and slid it onto the stovetop, then turned to the shopping.

'Here, Da, you can give me a hand. Pass me the tins, why don't you.' She crouched down by the cupboard and held a hand towards him. A flutter of panic crossed his face. 'It's all right. It doesn't matter which one first. Here . . .' She knelt up and put a tin of peas in his hand, then took it off him again and put it in the cupboard. 'That's it, now another one the same.'

The kettle was boiled by the time they were finished, then all that was left to do was cut a slice of bread and lay the ham out. She cut it in squares for him, speared the first one on the fork.

'Did you feed the dogs yet?'

'No. I'll do it after. After we've finished.'

She knew what was coming. He put his fork down and worked the piece of ham around his mouth. His throat clicked like a trapdoor when he swallowed.

'Always see to the animals before you see to yourself. That's the proper way, Grace.'

She gulped a mouthful of tea. No point in saying there were no animals, just the two dogs and an uncertain number of cats.

'That's the best way, the farmer's way, always see to the animals . . .'

She tuned him out, got on with her bread and ham, made the most of the tea while it was hot. He'd keep going now till it was time for bed. Or until the needle suddenly jumped tracks and he'd be off on something else. On and on until, hopefully, he fell asleep.

'Come on, then.' She'd cleared the table and stoked the stove. The next step was to get him upstairs; upstairs and ready for bed. Not *in* bed, because she'd learned that didn't work. No point doing that until she was finished outside.

'Right, Da. In position.' The bedroom was chilly, but it was too late to do anything about it.

He nodded and settled himself into the small armchair by the bedroom window. His watching post. She hoisted the curtains out of the way so he would have a good view.

'Now stay there, Da. Stay there and watch for me coming out. I'll be quick, all right? I'll put the torch on. Look out for the signal, yes?'

'Yes.' He was wiping the glass with his dressing gown sleeve. The rain was drumming on the slates above their heads.

She was only halfway down the stairs when he shouted her name.

'What, Da? What's wrong?' He was already getting out of the chair.

'Oh,' he said. 'There you are.' He gave her a toothy grin, his face slack with relief, and sank back into his seat. 'I just remembered. Don't forget to put your coat on, hinny. And your scarf.'

She clattered back down the stairs, grabbed an old waterproof, flicked the torch on and hurried out into the yard. She looked up at the bedroom window: his face beamed down at her like a small moon. She flashed the torch at him twice, then bent herself against the hammering rain, waded through the streaming water and headed for the barn. The dogs were waiting. She fussed them for a minute. They needed to be loosed, let run. She looked back at the house: he was still there, but he was on his feet, his hand up against the window. She put the food down and lurched back through the rain.

'All right, Da?' He was on the landing, peering down at her.

'I didn't know where you were. There was someone outside in the yard. I was shouting for you.'

'It's all right,' she said. 'I'm here now. So . . .' She took a deep breath, peeled off the wet jacket and hooked it over the bannister rail, shrugged off the weariness that was bending her in two and started up the stairs. 'What's it to be, cocoa or tea?'

His face lit up. This was the start of it – the bedtime routine. A tip she'd filched from her other life: the life she had before – a husband, a house . . . a child. She'd packed it away and brought it with her without knowing. A bedtime routine was the secret of a good night's rest. Dr Spock or . . . she couldn't remember.

'Oo, cocoa,' he said, smacking his lips.

'Come on, then. Let's get you tucked in, then I'll go get the milk on.'

She unwrapped him from his dressing gown and sat him on the edge of the bed.

'Slippers.'

He smiled: his party-trick moment. He flicked his feet in the air and sent the slippers flying across the room. He'd done it one time and knocked the lamp over.

'Teeth.'

She held the denture pot open and he plopped them in, then wiped his mouth with the back of his hand.

'Specs.'

He unhooked them and handed them over, his eyes suddenly adrift in his face.

'Right, hop in.'

He leaned back as she lifted his legs and swung them round.

'Lovely,' he said, as she tucked the sheet and blankets round him.

'Lovely,' she said back, and switched the radio on.

'Is it time, yet?' he asked.

'Not yet,' she said. 'You listen to the news while I make the cocoa, then it will be time.'

CHAPTER 2

Grace filled the milk pan, threw another log on the stove, then, satisfied that all was quiet upstairs, got the newspaper out of her bag and settled in the armchair by the stove. Five minutes. It wasn't long, but it was hers. Some nights he fell asleep. She'd get upstairs with the cocoa and he would be curled up, the pillows on the floor. But not tonight; she could hear him talking back to the news presenter.

'Here we go then, Da.' She fussed the pillows into a better shape and handed him the beaker. Beakers with spouts: that was another tip she'd brought with her. 'I'll get my pyjamas on and then it will nearly be time.'

'Good. Best to know,' he said. 'Best to know before we turn in.'

She ran a hot flannel over her face and neck, brushed her teeth and pulled her pyjamas on. They were damp and cold against her skin. She'd certainly be talking to Shirley in the morning. Leaving him on his own all day, letting the stove go out.

'Gracie.'

His voice trilled across the landing.

'Coming, Da.'

'I think it's time.'

She looked at her watch. He was right.

'Okey-doke,' she said. She switched off his bedside lamp, then climbed into her own bed. She'd done it months ago, worn ragged with the endless trekking from her bedroom to his: taken the small bed from the spare room and set it up a few feet from his. *Not ideal*, the woman from the council had offered, as she'd handed over a small pile of information leaflets. Care homes. Grace had watched her teetering back through the muddy yard, then slung the lot in the Rayburn. *It's important you don't give up on your own life*, she'd said. Grace had smiled and said nothing. No need to tell the woman she'd done that a long time ago.

'Rightio,' she said. 'Ready, Da?'

She glanced over. He was ready, his hands primed in front of his face, his scraggy wrists loose out of the ends of his pyjama sleeves. She pressed PLAY on the cassette recorder. The music struck up and so did he, eyes closed and a gummy smile on his chops, swaying this way and that as he conducted the orchestra, changing course every now and then to do a few bars on the violin or a short trill on the piccolo. *Sailing By*. When she was young, he'd waltzed them round the kitchen – her and Michael taking turns to balance on the tops of his slippered feet as they swirled past the kitchen table, the dresser. One, two, three; one, two, three. As the music approached the final few bars, he spread his hands on his lap and composed his face.

'Attention all shipping,' he said, in a BBC wartime broadcaster's voice: the crisp consonants blurred owing to his lack of dentures. 'This is the *Shipping Forecast* as issued by the Met Office at twenty-three hundred hours.'

Then they were off into the thick of it: Jack's head cocked on one side, gripping the sheets like he might be thrown off balance at any moment, while Grace recited the names under her breath: Viking, North Utsire, South Utsire, Lundy, Fastnet, Irish Sea, Shannon, Rockall, Malin – each one lighting a picture in her head. It was the same picture every night: towering waves, dark skies, her father tucked inside the leaky wheelhouse, *veering slowly, losing identity*, water dripping from his eyebrows, as she rowed towards him, shouting his name above the black midnight roar, willing him to see her, to know that no matter what, she would get to him, she would not leave him stranded. It was wearing her out, she knew this, but the only solution she could think of was to keep going – and to avoid the mirror at all costs. She'd clocked the note of disbelief in the council woman's voice when she'd given her date of birth. *Oh, so you're only forty-four, Grace?* She might have defended herself, explained that she didn't have the money – or energy – to make the effort any more. Instead, she'd offered a weak smile, hoisted her grubby jeans and smoothed down the front of her sweatshirt.

She looked over at him – he had his finger poised over the bedsheet, as if to take notes. Cromarty, Forth, Tyne, Dogger . . . he bent his head and sketched hurriedly, then looked up at her.

'Good news, girl, good news,' he said.

'Good news indeed, Da,' she said. 'We can sleep safe in our bunks.'

She used the same recording every night, not daring to take the chance of some real-life peril suddenly dropping into the quietness of their room, robbing him – and her – of any chance of respite. She clicked the machine off and then the bedside light.

'Night, Da.'

'Night, hinny.'

She listened as he shuffled himself further down the bed. She pictured his head on the pillow and wondered what he was thinking. Whether he thought at all now. Whether it was still possible? When she was young, he had shown her how to make pom-poms. A sailor's invention, he'd said, as they unravelled wool from an old jumper and wound it round a pair of cardboard circles. It had made no sense to her until he'd cut round the edges, tied the centre with a stiff knot then slid the cardboard away. She'd let out a gasp when he'd shaken the wool out into a perfect ball. All those threads that had been joined together in one perfect continuous length, cut free – their loose ends frayed and leading nowhere. Yet, somewhere in the centre, something was still holding it firm: the *Shipping Forecast*, the farm – her.

She could feel the tug of sleep on her eyelids and the familiar melting sensation that always started when her head met the pillow, like a pool of liquid creeping into her brain, dissolving thoughts, worries, memories. Somewhere on the edges of it, she could hear him creaking round the bed, arranging himself this way, then that, like his bones had forgotten how to rest. She willed him to stop. To find a spot that would magically allow him – and her – to sleep.

'Is it time, girl?' His voice warbled across the room.

She put out her hand and switched the cassette back on. She fell asleep to dreams of being waltzed on her da's slippers: the big stove lit, the food in the oven, Michael clapping his hands as he waited for his turn. Michael. She dismissed him from her thoughts before he had her snagged.

'Attention all shipping.' Her da's voice crossed the room like a searchlight in a stormy sea.

* * *

Grace woke sometime in the night: a noise that had her lifting her head from the pillow and surveying Jack's bed. It wasn't him – his small hunched shape was still beneath the blankets. She set her ears to listen for what it might have been: the dogs, maybe, unsettled by some night-time noise, or something blowing loose across the yard. The rain had stopped but the wind was still rattling the roof tiles. The place was coming apart. It had been a shock when she'd first arrived back but now she was as used to it as he must have been and found herself overlooking the leaning fence posts, the peeling window frames, concentrating instead on the pleasing way the back paddock swept down to the stream or how the sun caught the barn window on a morning and sent spears of gold across the kitchen table. Little things. Things you could keep hold of and rely on: like a firm knot in the centre of a ball of loose wool.

One of the dogs started barking. Taff. She recognised the catch in his throat. She pushed back the blankets and, keeping an eye on her da, slipped out of bed, unhooked her dressing gown from the door and padded down the stairs. She went to the kitchen window without turning on the light and peered out into the yard. It was pitch black. The lights were long broken – something else she'd got used to. There was nothing to see, but Taff was still barking up a storm. She pulled her jacket over her shoulders, went out onto the porch and shone the torch across the wet ground, tracing its beam towards the car, then over to the barn, sending it as far down the track as it would reach. She switched it off and waited in the dark, trying to hear above the sound of the dog and the rattling roof tiles, straining her ears for some explanation or some false move. She waited a few minutes more, letting the wind whip her hair into her face, knowing that she'd get no more sleep that night, then went back into the kitchen, slipped another log on the stove and waited for the kettle to boil.

* * *

She was at the kitchen table, head on her hands, asleep when Shirley arrived.

'Christ almighty, Grace. What in God's name are you doing there?' She had her hand clamped against her bosom. Dramatic. 'You gave me the fright of my life.'

'Shirley.' She pushed herself up from the table. 'What time is it?'

Shirley pulled the sleeve of her coat back. 'Not quite half-seven. Is he up?' She jerked her chin towards the ceiling.

'Oh God, I'm . . . I'm not sure,' Grace said. The realisation had her up and off the chair. God knows how long she'd been asleep, whether he'd been up shouting for her, whether he'd fallen in the bathroom . . . She ran up the stairs and pushed the bedroom door open. Jack was still huddled on his side, his nose tucked under the blankets – the same position as when she'd gone down the stairs to investigate Taff barking in the night. Something inside her chest balled tight.

'Da?' He didn't move. She stepped carefully round the side of his bed, one arm stretched out in front of her like she was sleepwalking. 'Da?' She put her hand on his shoulder and drew the blanket off his face. This was how it always played out in her imagination: that some lapse in concentration, some unintended neglect would steal him from her, leaving her guilty, leaving her alone.

His eyes pinged open, bright as a blackbird's. 'Is it time?' he said, working his heels against the mattress, trying to haul himself upright.

'Morning, Jack.' Shirley was in the doorway, tying a plastic apron across her belly. 'Ready for action?'

'Ready and waiting, Captain.' He snapped off a smart salute.

Grace smiled as he slid into his morning routine, the one he shared with Shirley, not her. She went down to the bathroom and left them to it, his voice chirpy as a sparrow as the pair of them lumbered around, shaking the floorboards.

'Well, come on then, let's get cracking. Shake a leg or two. There's work to do . . .'

'And fish to catch . . .'

'Cows to milk . . .'

Another double act. She could hear the smile in his voice. It was part of the problem, of course – his perkiness in the morning. He'd always been a lark and somehow that hadn't altered. The first couple of hours in a morning and you wouldn't know there was a thing wrong with him. By lunchtime though – when Shirley was supposed to come back and cook his food, do the fire, encourage a bathroom visit – he started to slide, the threads of his day fraying loose. You could watch it happening; see the slippage on his face. She learned that it was better if you could keep him going with something – their Sunday jigsaw, a bit of a play on the radio – because if he nodded off he woke with a look in his eyes that she couldn't bear: panic, like a child who wanders off in a shop and suddenly realises his mother is not there.

She glanced up the stairs and saw them crossing the landing to the small toilet, his fingers clasped round Shirley's arm. He gave her a cheery wave with his free hand.

'Are you off, my dear?' he trilled.

'Any minute now, Da,' she said. 'I'll be back at teatime. Shirley will be here to keep an eye on you, won't you, Shirley?'

Shirley busied herself with his dressing gown belt. She didn't catch her eye.

'You're back at twelve, Shirley, yes?'

'What? Oh, yes.'

Grace waited. 'It's just that . . .'

'Oh, yesterday.' Shirley was still making a meal of the dressing gown. 'Yes. Sorry. I had a bit of bother with Ryan again. Had to go to the school. I . . . was everything all right?'

Two options. She could go with the truth or just keep the

peace. 'More or less,' Grace said. 'But the stove had gone out. He was cold.' She could have said more – that he was in wet trousers; that he was out in the rain waiting for her; that she couldn't keep letting them down like this – but she didn't. If she lost Shirley, she wouldn't be able to work and if she couldn't work, there'd be no money.

'You've got my number? Just in case, you know . . . anything unexpected comes up again?'

That was no real solution and they both knew it. The first time she'd had to leave the office early, 'for family reasons', her boss, Thackley, had been understanding. The second time, she'd sensed his uneasiness and wasn't surprised when he'd taken her to one side and explained what didn't need explaining: he was the only solicitor in town, they were a small team and, well . . . Joy. To his credit he stopped there, because Joy (Grace had never met a woman so ill-named) was a thorny problem for them both. In short she was rude, disorganised and, despite any lack of qualifications, saw herself as a solicitor's assistant; a partner. She had been vigorously opposed to the idea of appointing an extra team member and, from day one, had never missed an opportunity to prove herself right. Grace had tripped over herself with apologies and reassurances that it would not happen again. But now . . . rocks and hard places – that seemed to be her only lot these days.

She pulled her good coat off the hook and stepped into her shoes.

'I'm off now, Da,' she called.

He didn't hear her, so she left it, slipped out of the door and pulled it shut.

That's what she would remember later – she didn't say goodbye.

CHAPTER 3

Her phone rang just after twelve. She saw Shirley's name and felt her heart drop. Joy peered over her glasses as Grace got up and headed for the bathroom.

'Shirley,' she fumbled the phone to her ear. 'What's wrong? Is my da all right?'

'I'm not sure,' Shirley said. 'I've got back just now and he's not here . . .'

'What?'

'Your da. He's not here.'

Grace couldn't line the words up in any order that made sense. Her da wasn't there? He had to be there.

'Did you hear me?' Shirley was breathing hard into the phone, short gasps like she was running.

'Yes, I . . . what do you mean, he's not there?' Grace grabbed hold of the cold edge of the washbasin. Her face stared back at her from the mirror.

'I'm checking the barn now in case he's gone to see the dogs . . . ah, no,' Shirley's voice faded, she could hear the dogs kicking up a fuss in the background. 'No, he's not in here. Oh, hang on a minute . . .'

Grace pressed the phone hard against her ear. 'What is it? What is it?' Her heart was a small knot pushed tight against her ribs. She could feel the tears welling hot in her eyes. 'Is it him?'

'No, it's OK. No, it's just some tarpaulin. A roll of tarpaulin.'

'I'm on my way,' Grace said. 'Can you wait till I get there?'

ATTENTION ALL SHIPPING

* * *

Thackley was out on a farm visit, but Joy had wanted to make a meal of it. She removed her specs and placed her fussy little hands on the blotter like she was about to run off a piano medley. 'But it's Tuesday, Grace. I'm assuming the weekend correspondence is complete?'

'Yes . . .' It wasn't. 'Look, I'm sorry. I'll be back as soon as I can.' Grace grabbed her coat and bag and took off.

Shirley was at the end of the lane waiting for her. She was alone.

'Have you found him?'

'No. I didn't know whether to call the police. I . . .'

'Jump in.' Grace hit the accelerator, hammered the car up the track and hurried towards the house. 'Tell me,' she said. 'Tell me what happened.'

Shirley shook her head. 'Nothing happened. I got here at twelve and he wasn't there. In the kitchen I mean – or the sitting room. I knew he couldn't be upstairs because of the stairgate, but I still went up and checked. Then I thought maybe he'd gone outside, so I went out to check the barn, then I phoned you.'

Grace stood a moment in the hallway. The emptiness of the house wrapped itself around her and she knew, even before she'd gone into the kitchen – the kettle ticking on the warm stove, or up the stairs – his bedclothes flat and tidy. He was gone.

'He's not here, Grace.'

'I know, I know,' – but nonetheless she kept searching: the cupboard under the stairs, the pantry, the small shed by the back door. She could feel Shirley's eyes on her the whole time.

'What was he wearing?'

'His corduroy trousers, the blue shirt and his jumper. The one with the zip at the neck . . . and his slippers.'

Grace went into the hall and ran her hands across the line of coats. 'His overcoat's not here.'

Shirley nodded. 'I know. His shoes are gone too. Grace, I think we need to call the police.'

'Not yet,' Grace said. 'We might find him. We might find him ourselves. He could have taken himself off for a walk, he could be up the top field, he could . . .' She could hear her voice climbing. The emptiness of the house was drawing the air out of her. 'The barn,' she said. 'Let's check the barn again.'

'There's no point, Grace. He's not there. Come on, we've waited long enough.' Shirley's fingers were already tapping the buttons.

* * *

As far as Grace was concerned, the police officers were on a bad footing from the get-go. She watched from the window, and the way they pulled into the yard – leisurely, like they were maybe on a sightseeing tour, then ambled towards the porch, exchanging some small piece of conversation that had them both grinning – had her back up before she'd even answered the door.

'Grace?'

'Col.'

She stood back from the door to let him in. Colin knew her name, of course, just like he knew his way into the kitchen.

'I don't think you've met Constable Halliday,' he said.

She considered the second officer as he parked himself by the Rayburn.

'Erm no, but . . .' It was not his face she recognised, but his name.

He gave her a small nod. 'We knew each other at school, I think . . .'

'Yes, that's it.'

'Back home from your adventures in the Met now though, Dan eh?' Col said. 'Anyway, Grace . . . can you tell us what's happened . . .' He paused and she wondered if he was going to say it. *This time.* But he got out his pocketbook and smiled at her again. She should have told them to sit down, offered them a cup of tea but she didn't. As soon as Shirley had made the call a sense of urgency had come over her. Like she was at the start line – running shoes on, listening for the starter's gun – and her da was at the other end of the track, waiting for her. She wanted to be off running, not sitting in the kitchen drinking tea.

'. . . anything unusual this last few days?' His pen was poised above the page.

She shook her head. There were a hundred things she might have said, like how he'd tried to light the stove with the bread board, how he'd removed all the pictures off the wall and piled them on the spare bed, how he'd taken to unpacking the cupboards.

'No,' she said. 'Nothing unusual.'

'OK, then.' They got up to leave. 'We'll be in touch. Keep your phone on, yes?'

'Yes.' She was already following them out. Dan Halliday stopped at the door.

'Which way will you go?'

'Town,' she said. 'I'll start in town.'

'OK. We'll go to the park. We'll ring you when we have him.'

We'll ring you when we have him. The words lit a flare of hope in her.

The first time he'd done it she'd not taken it seriously. They'd not taken it seriously. *Remember the day you absconded?* It had become a shortcut to a good laugh – how she'd got home from work and scoured the farm for him, eventually come across him on their neighbour's land on the other side of the river. He was standing on the wrong side of the bridge, his two arms outstretched like a man about to walk a tightrope. The thing that had frightened her most, the thing she had most trouble forgetting, was that she was more than halfway across the bridge before he recognised her. Nonetheless she'd managed to explain it away: he probably hadn't eaten enough, maybe he was coming down with something. But then it happened again. And again. He'd made it into town one time: frightened the life out of her. She'd happened to look out of the office window and spotted him scooting past the post office. She was off her chair and down the stairs without saying a word to Thackley.

'Da.'

He was haring down the high street, his shirt flapping behind him. He didn't hear her.

'Da.' She pulled level with him and put her hand on his arm. He pulled up and turned to face her. He didn't have his dentures in.

'Grace, you're here.'

The loose swing of his mouth made her want to cry. She wrapped her arm round his shoulders. 'What are you doing in town, Da?'

'Town?'

There was no explaining it away after that. After that it was a slippery slope that landed them at the feet of the GP, Social Services and, eventually, Shirley. It was the thought of what lay waiting at the foot of that slope that kept her awake at night: medication, care homes, losing him. Being left on her own.

* * *

Grace rolled the car slowly along the high street, twisting her head left and right, checking shop doorways and alleyways.

She parked outside the library and set off on foot, asking in every shop, every office, trying to stay hopeful, ignoring the mounting sense of shame. *Grace James. Her father's missing – again.* No one said it, of course, but that was surely what they were thinking. But there was no sign of him. She sat on the bench by the bus stop and tried to swallow down the panic in her throat. She closed her eyes and sent a silent message to him. Where are you, Da? Where are you?

He didn't answer.

CHAPTER 4

Jack didn't answer because he was miles away in the middle of what had started out as an adventure but was fast becoming something of an ordeal.

He had no idea where he was, or how he'd got there.

He told himself this was a small price to pay for a day that had turned out to be a sight more interesting than a slow morning looking out the kitchen window – which was where he'd been, poring over an old copy of *Farming Today* when a flash of colour caught his eye. He'd put the paper on one side and watched as a blue van pulled into the yard and parked in front of the barn. By the time he'd shuffled to the door and turned the latch the girl was on the porch step.

'Oh, I remember you from yesterday,' he'd said, and she'd smiled.

He'd asked her in, maybe opened a packet of digestives and then . . . the next bit – the part that had conveyed them from the farm to wherever they were now – well, that was something of a puzzle.

He looked out of the window for clues – but when were fields, sky and sea ever a clue to anything? He swallowed down the knot of anxiety that had lodged in his throat.

'Where are we?' He offered up the question lightly, as if inattention alone had robbed him of his bearings; as if the warmth of the sun through the windscreen was the only reason for the familiar blurring at the edges of his thinking.

The girl leaned forward and inspected a small screen on the dashboard.

'Hmm. Not sure how you say it. Blaen . . . erm . . .' She considered the small screen again. 'Nearly at Aberporth,' she said, and smiled. There was some note in her voice that suggested he ought to recognise the name. He didn't.

'Where Michael used to work, remember?'

'Michael?'

'Yes. You thought that's where he might be. On his boat?'

'Oh, yes, I remember.' He remembered nothing of the sort.

'Are you feeling all right, Jack?'

Jack? The girl knew his name. He wasn't sure if he knew hers. He rubbed his hands on his knees and searched his brain. Nothing opened up.

'Sorry,' he said, eventually. 'I must have dozed off . . . I'm a bit . . .' He circled a bony finger at his temple. 'I'm a bit befuddled.' He embroidered it with a loose laugh that sounded – even to his own ears – thoroughly unconvincing.

But the girl let herself be convinced. She glanced at Jack – the skinny stalk of his neck as he watched out of the passenger window, half-turning in his seat every now and then when something caught his eye – and told herself he was fine. She kept catching sight of herself in the rear-view mirror – the smile on her face she thought might never wear off – as she steered them through winding roads lined with twisted trees and edged with tall grass that brushed the side of the van as they passed. She wound down her window and pulled the air deep into her lungs. She wanted to remember everything about this journey because it was one she'd never dreamed of making – not until she'd found the envelope – the envelope that had led her to Jack – and her world had suddenly opened up.

It had happened three days earlier.

***

Her mother had phoned to say she was going away for a week, that the house would be empty so she, halfway through cleaning the kitchen *again* – the sink piled high with every piece of crockery in the place – had peeled off the Marigolds, packed a few things in a rucksack and headed home. She'd arrived with no particular plan in mind other than enjoying a break from the general squalor of her student digs and doing some research for her latest coursework.

The first morning at home she'd woken feeling queasy: a greasy feel to her stomach that put her off breakfast and gradually got worse until she ended up heaving her guts into the toilet bowl. It relieved the nausea but in less than half an hour she was back on her knees again, holding her hair out of her clammy face. It would have been a lie to say she'd thought nothing of it, or that she'd dismissed it as some stomach bug, because she hadn't. She'd *wondered*. Not whether she was pregnant – because getting herself a prescription for the pill had been one of the must-dos of freshers' week, and she'd joined the queue, aware it was more about wanting to fit in than wanting contraception – but whether this was what pregnancy would feel like at the beginning. This was something she thought about a lot but never talked about. She couldn't think of a single soul who would understand. Definitely not her mother, Vee, who would most likely fix up some counselling session with one of her right-on buddies, then rope her into one of her mind-expanding ventures: rescuing dogs from Romania, welcoming Afghan refugees – anything rather than acknowledge the mortifying fact that she'd spent almost twenty years raising a daughter whose main ambition was to get married, settle down and start a family. A proper family – not a version that had involved some clinical arrangement with a man she barely knew.

Her mother had told her three things about the man who'd fathered her: his name was Michael, he'd been a fleeting friend – happy to play his part in the procedure that had resulted in her conception – and he was dead. Dead before he'd even seen his baby girl. That was all the information Vee would give up. That and the fact she knew nothing about his family. She'd asked for more over the years, of course, questions generally sparked by some conversation at school, or maybe after an evening at a friend's house – a bewildering revelation of how her home life differed from the one she and Vee had cobbled together.

After a light lunch – her stomach settled by then – she'd climbed onto a chair and scanned Vee's bookcase until she saw the title she was after – *Women in Irish Politics* – slotted between *Marxism: the Female Perspective* and, bizarrely, *The Reader's Digest Home Maintenance Manual*. She'd pulled it out and taken it to the table under the window. Google, she'd discovered, only told you so much – Vee's books on the other hand often provided her with material that no one else on the course seemed able to access. Her tutors liked it.

She'd not seen it at first. She'd been scanning the chapter headings, searching for something that might help her essay – about two ordinary Northern Irish women awarded the Nobel Peace Prize – and was making notes, when she noticed something tucked between the pages near the back of the book. She slid out an envelope, yellowed with age, bearing her mother's name and an address she didn't recognise. She'd held it to her nose, then slipped the contents out and laid them on the table: a postcard, a strip of black and white photographs and a newspaper clipping. It wasn't much to look at, she thought afterwards, as she sat in the dark – the daylight long gone and the curtains still open, the room lit only by the light from the computer screen. Definitely not much, but enough to suggest the information Vee had given her was not entirely truthful – and enough to spark a small hope that had, by the following morning, set her on the road to Wales.

CHAPTER 5

The drive had been a slow and careful one – not only because she didn't have Vee's permission to take the camper van, but because of the distracting drift of her thoughts. The miles went by in a tantalising stream of what-ifs, which, by the time she reached the farm mentioned in the newspaper article, had woven themselves into something more solid than hope; something that was expanding inside her, unlocking doors she thought were closed forever.

Her first visit to the farm had left her breathless. Jack was older than he'd been in the newspaper clipping, of course, but she'd recognised him straight away. He'd welcomed her in as if he knew her – walked her through a hall crowded with old boots and coats, into a small kitchen that smelled of wood smoke. She showed him the newspaper clipping first. Explained how she'd found it with some old papers and was wondering – she left this part as open as she could – if he could remember sending it to anyone. He bypassed the question entirely and launched into a long story about showing sheep at the Royal Welsh Show. She listened intently, hoping he might suddenly veer into more revealing territory. When he didn't – when he switched to the subject of showing cattle – she got out the postcard. *Ah, Whitby*, he'd exclaimed, and rattled off onto another track entirely. She'd let him run on for a good ten minutes, her ears primed for any bit of information that might bolster her hope. There was nothing until she drew his attention to the name scribbled at the bottom of the postcard – the name that had set the blood pounding in her ears. He held it up to the end of his nose for a few seconds, then handed it back to her. *Can't read that*, he said, and set off again. She took a deep breath and butted in before he got his steam up.

'It says "Michael".'

'Michael?' he said. 'Our Michael, you mean?'

Our Michael. She didn't answer because she couldn't get the words past the swell of hope rising in her throat.

'Well, that wouldn't make much sense.' He took the card from her and considered the picture. 'They didn't like the east coast. Stayed away from it, they did.'

'They?'

'Michael and Joseph – my brother.'

She waited, willing him to go on, willing him to say something that exposed the gaps in her mother's version of events. Instead he gave a loud yawn and she realised he was on the verge of nodding off.

'What happened to him? To Michael?' She said it quietly, preparing herself for a rerun of Vee's story.

'What?' Jack gave another loud yawn. 'Pah. Many a thing happened to that lad. Stories as long as your arm, he has. You'd have to ask him yourself . . .'

It was as though the air had suddenly gone out of the room and taken all sound with it. All that remained was possibility. She leaned across the table and put her hand on Jack's arm. 'Ask him myself?' She could barely breathe. 'What do you mean, Jack? Where is he? Where is Michael?'

'Oh, he's where he always is. He's on his boat . . .' His voice trailed off towards sleep.

She couldn't help herself. She was on her feet, pulling on her jacket. 'His boat? But where . . . could you take me there, Jack? Could you take me to him? Jack . . . ?'

'Mmh?' Jack straightened himself up and wiped his mouth with the back of his hand.

'Michael,' she said. 'Could you take me to Michael?'

'Well . . .' he was nodding off again.

She glanced out of the kitchen window – at the fading light, the lashing rain. It was too late, too wild, and Jack – she considered his drooping shoulders – Jack was too tired. But she could feel it in her legs, in the blood that was coursing through her body – the urge to set off running, to set off running and not stop until she'd found him.

'What if I come back, Jack? I could come back tomorrow?'

'Oh, yes. Tomorrow . . .'

'OK.' She put the newspaper clipping and the postcard back in the envelope and tucked it on the dresser. 'I'll leave this for you – so you don't forget?'

He glanced up at her, gave her a small nod and let his chin fall towards his chest.

She drove a few miles from the farm and tucked the van into a small, wooded layby. The weather grew steadily worse but she barely noticed it. She sat in the driver's seat, replaying the conversation she'd had with Jack.

Michael was on his boat.

She couldn't believe it. Several times she picked up her phone, thinking she would take the plunge and confront her mother: ask her outright about the photographs, the postcard – about Michael. But she didn't. Couldn't.

They were a team of two – that's what Vee always maintained. It was a joke really, because wherever they lived their home always operated like some kind of social hub: a constant stream of people – women mostly – who were either preoccupied with themselves or with some political injustice that necessitated endless, circuitous debate. This was occasionally interrupted by a sudden call to arms, at which point the house would be turned into a workshop: sheets of cardboard, paint and banners taking over the little space they had. Although she'd struggled with the constant drama, she never completely detached herself from it. This was largely due to its flipside – the times that Vee took off on some mission that couldn't include her and she was shipped out to friends or, as she got older, left to fend for her self. The experience had stranded her on some middle ground: overwhelmed in large groups, but afraid of being on her own. Her solution – she had enough self-awareness to recognise it for what it was – was a hankering for an ordinary family.

    She climbed into the back of the van, made up the bed and lay, contemplating the events of the day. Maybe it was the darkness, or her own tiredness, but she couldn't help coming back to the image of Jack before she left: the look in his eyes and the soft droop of him as he slumped at the kitchen table. It had sounded a small alarm. She dismissed it: turned on her side, pulled the covers over her head and concentrated instead on what he had told her and fell asleep to thoughts of Michael, of the farm – and how she was surely within touching distance of what she'd always longed for.

CHAPTER 6

The following morning got off to a good start. The best start. She'd driven to the farm barely able to take the smile off her face, imagining there was something of a new-page feel to the day – like the wild weather of the previous evening had washed everything clean. Jack was already at the door when she drove into the farmyard. At the door and waiting for her.

'Hello again,' he'd said, and ushered her into the warm kitchen. She watched as he made tea and shook out a plate of biscuits. She didn't want to rush things, but she was unable to hold herself back.

'So, Jack – you thought you might be able to take me to see Michael?'

'Michael?' He looked at her, then dipped a biscuit in his tea.

'Yes. When I was here yesterday you said you knew where he was? That he was on his boat?'

'Oh, I did, did I? Well . . .'

She overlooked the hesitation in his voice as he took a last slurp of tea, levered himself up from his chair, then disappeared into the hallway. When he reappeared he had his jacket on.

'In that case, we'd better get cracking, girl. Come on.'

And she'd followed him out, led him to the camper van with visions of small harbours, setting suns and emotional reunions playing through her head.

* * *

A couple of hours later things were not looking quite so positive.

'Aha,' Jack had announced, as they'd approached their destination – rounding a corner and meeting a line of low houses that straggled towards a small beach dotted with boats. 'Here we are. This is the place.'

She'd pulled the van to a halt at the quay side and got out on legs she couldn't quite feel, already scanning the cluster of boats that lined two sides of the harbour, straining for a glimpse of a man with dark curly hair and laughing eyes. But that was the first time. The second time, still buoyed up by his certainty, she'd called down to a bloke who was working on the engine of an old boat, but no, he'd said, straight away, he'd never heard of any Michael James. And so it had gone on, the day dwindling the hope out of her – and the energy out of Jack.

By mid-afternoon there seemed to be an emptiness in his eyes she'd not noticed before. It made her think of turning the van round and heading back to the farm, but their next stop – Aberporth – was only a handful of miles away. She told herself Jack was tired and tried to dismiss the fear that the world she thought was opening up – a world that included a father – was closing down again.

She steered towards the quayside, turned off the engine and gazed over the small harbour. The tide was out and there was something in the way the boats lolled sideways that made her want to cry.

'Are we here?' Jack said. Jaunty, almost, but his smile didn't mask the confusion on his face.

'We are. Are you ready?'

He didn't answer; he was looking at the boats. The tide was creeping in, nudging its way across the seabed: the rivulets it had left earlier, running with fingers of frothing water. In an hour, she knew everything would look different.

'I thought we might have a look for him first.' She paused, watching for some flicker of understanding, but no, Jack's face was slack with not knowing – either the place, or why they were there. 'Maybe we should get a bite to eat, instead. And then . . .' the thought put a hitch in her voice, 'then we'll go back to the farm?'

'Hmm.' Jack made no move.

'Come on.' She leaned across to unbuckle his seat belt. 'Let's stretch our legs and see what we can find.'

The café was small: two tables tucked into the window space of what otherwise would have been a shop. They ate, or at least she did: Jack declined food but sat cradling a cup of tea, his one leg bouncing out a nervous rhythm, his eyes skittering around the café, then at her.

'Everything all right?' the woman behind the counter asked, as they were leaving. Her eyes were on Jack.

'What? Oh, yes. He's . . . he's just a bit tired. We're heading home now. Come on, Jack . . .'

She'd linked his arm and steered him out of the café and towards the camper van, feeling the woman's gaze at her back the whole way. They had travelled further than she'd realised and before they were even halfway back the sky was closing down on them, curtains of cloud that suddenly blotted out the sun setting behind them and obscured the way ahead. The woman's concern had released a pool of anxiety in her chest and she was working hard to contain it.

'How about some music, Jack? Do you like music?'

He didn't answer. He was hunched over in his seat, his chin almost resting on his chest. She let him be and wound her window down an inch. The sea air, the gathering darkness, the disappointment – it had settled on her like a thick blanket. She was aching to sleep. She stretched out her hand to turn on the radio.

'Oh . . . aha . . .' Jack sprang upright. A string of saliva hung from the corner of his mouth. 'Is it time?'

'What?'

'Is it time? Are we tuning in?'

'Er . . . no, not yet.'

'Soon, though?' he said. The sharp edges of his cheekbones were dabbed red. It gave his face a clownish look.

'Yes, soon.'

She looked at the satnav. They still had miles to go. The daylight had all but gone and it had taken the last of her courage with it.

'Should I be getting my pyjamas on then?'

He was tugging at his jumper sleeve.

'No, not yet, Jack.' She put her hand on his arm. He pulled it away.

'Not yet? But it's dark.' He went back to his sleeve, then started grappling with the belt on his trousers.

'Jack . . .' She was scanning the road ahead for somewhere to pull in. The satnav was telling her there was a petrol station a few miles ahead, but Jack was tugging at the seat belt now, trying to get to his feet.

'What about the animals,' he said. 'Have they been fed? Have you finished in the yard? Oh, come on, Gracie, it must be time.' He was clutching at his trousers. He stopped suddenly and turned his face towards her. 'Have I been to the bathroom?'

The bathroom? Oh God.

'No,' she said. 'Not yet, but . . . oh, hang on . . .' She could see lights up ahead: the bright lights of the petrol station. 'I'm going to stop here, Jack. So you can go to the bathroom, OK?' She couldn't bring herself to look at the crotch of his trousers.

'Stop?' His voice was tinny and high. 'There's no time for stopping, girl. We need to get cracking. We need to get ready before it's time . . . oh, blast it.' He was wrestling with the door handle.

'Jack,' she screamed. 'Stop it. Stop it.' She pulled sharply into the forecourt of the station and cut the engine. He looked out of the window and pointed at the brightly lit shop.

'Oh. What's this?'

'It's a petrol station, Jack. There's a bathroom here, so you can use the toilet?'

'Yes,' he said. 'The bathroom. And then will it be time?'

'Yes, yes. Then it will be time. Here . . .' She helped him down from the seat – the bones beneath his clothes were light as balsa wood.

'Oh, it's cold,' he said, rubbing his hands together.

She draped her jacket round his shoulders, linked his arm in hers and set off for the glare of the shopfront.

* * *

He had been in the bathroom a long time. She should have been in there with him, making sure he was all right – but she simply couldn't bring herself to do it. She'd called his name quietly through the door a couple of times, and his voice had trilled back above the sound of splashing water. She paced the aisles, trying to work out what to do, then went to the toilet door and listened again. She could hear Jack humming above the splashing water and suddenly had an idea: he was getting ready for bed so maybe she should go and get the bed ready for him. She could settle him down in the back of the van, he would fall asleep, then she could drive back to the farm, drop him off and . . . she couldn't let herself think further than that. She had a final listen at the door, then walked towards the exit without looking at the counter and opened the sliding door of the van. She was halfway through arranging the bed, laying out the sheets and blankets, when she heard the shouting. She turned and looked back across the forecourt. The attendant was at the door, shouting to her. She left what she was doing and hurried over.

'What's wrong . . . oh my God . . .'

Jack was sitting on the floor, clutching his forehead. Blood was streaming down one side of his face.

'I don't know what happened . . . he . . . I think he must have walked into the door.'

Jack was peering up at her through bloody fingers.

'I don't know where she is,' he said. 'I don't know where she is . . .'

'I think he needs to go to hospital,' the attendant said.

'Yes, yes . . .' Her mind was on fast forward. If she took Jack to the hospital, she'd have to *explain* and how could she do that? How could she explain what she'd done? She'd made a mistake, a huge mistake. It should have been obvious to her from the start: she had launched herself into some fantasy on the strength of a postcard, a photograph, a newspaper clipping – and the words of an old man who, she now realised, was nothing but confused. Jack had never had a clue where they were or where they were supposed to be headed, and the excitement that had him clapping his hands and leaning forward in his seat, his face lit up with recognition, had been meaningless.

CHAPTER 7

Be careful what you wish for. It had been one of her mother's favourites: some kind of tight-lipped braking system – wheeled out at the mention of any fancy idea – that took the momentum out of anything resembling a desire for change. It had more than its fair share of airing when, sparking with excitement, she'd first taken Greg home. God, how ready she'd been then, to break away, to forge a different life; how ironic that the path she had chosen had led her full circle back home.

The kitchen was warm and the radio was playing softly in the background, the dogs were fed and her supper was set out on the table. Grace had dreamed of evenings like this – longed for them – yet here she was, unable to sit or eat, swamped by the emptiness of the house and unable to do anything but think of her da. She had worn a path between the kitchen and the front door; back and forth every couple of minutes, prompted by some imagined sound outside. She'd phoned the office and left a message on the answer machine. She needed the rest of the week off. Unpaid leave, she'd said, shoving the thought of Joy's satisfied smirk – and the council tax and oil bill – to one side. She was on the doorstep looking out into the dark yard when the phone rang.

'Grace?' It was Dan Halliday. The sound of his voice drained the strength from her legs.

'Have you found him?'

'Yes. We've found him. He's . . .'

'Is he all right? Where is he? Have you got him there with you? Is . . .' She had to stop herself.

'He's all right, Grace. Well, a bit shaken up.'

'Can I speak to him? Can you put him on?'

'Well, no.' His voice grew fainter like he'd moved away from the phone. 'They're still patching him up.'

'What?' She was grabbing her coat and car keys now, shoving her feet into her boots, running across the yard without closing the front door. 'Patching him up?' Her voice wailed into the dark. 'Where is he, where are you?'

'Bronglais. A & E.'

'I'm on my way,' she said. 'Tell him I'm on my way.'

* * *

Dan had waited for her. He stood up and walked towards her as she hurried in through the glass doors of A & E.

'Grace.' His face was grey under the lights. There was stubble on his chin.

'Where is he?' The catch in her voice almost had her, but she pulled it back. She wouldn't cry. Not yet. Not till she had him back home, safe, in bed. She'd driven the whole way fuelled by that thought: she would wrap him up warm, put him in the car and they'd be back home with cocoa and 'Sailing By' and he would be all right and she would find some other way to bring the money in so she could look after him better and . . .

'Grace.' He had his hand on her arm. 'Are you OK?'

'Yes, yes. I'm fine, I just need to see him, I . . .' The tears were too close, a rising swell in her throat. She pushed past him and headed towards the empty reception desk.

'You have to ring the bell,' he said. 'Someone will come and let us through.'

'Yes, yes. I know. Look, thanks for waiting, but you can go now. I can take it from here. I just want to get him home, you know?'

He looked at her. 'But—'

'I'll ring you tomorrow.' She was jabbing at the bell, which didn't seem to be producing any corresponding sound. 'You can fill me in tomorrow. I just need—' Her voice cracked. 'I just need to get him back home. Oh . . .'

The door behind the desk suddenly flew open and a woman strode through. She had a stethoscope round her neck and collection of blood samples in one hand.

'Sorry,' she said to Grace. 'It's chaos back there.'

'My father,' Grace said. 'You've got my father.'

'The old chap with the head injury?' Dan was still there, hovering behind her.

Head injury? Grace felt her knees sag. She put her hands against the counter. 'Jack James,' she said. 'Can I see him?'

The woman gave a small laugh. 'You certainly can. He's been asking for you – in between keeping us entertained, that is. He's a bit of a character, isn't he?'

Grace nodded. She didn't trust herself to speak. One kind word now and she would be in tears.

He didn't see her at first. He was busy relating a tale to a young nurse, one hand clutching the poor girl's arm, the other darting this way and that in accompaniment to whatever it was he was describing. He was what she called 'excited'. They would call it agitated.

'Da.'

He broke off mid-sentence and swivelled his face towards her. The dressing on his forehead came down over his eyebrow. He tilted his head back and squinted at her.

'Grace? Where have you been, girl? I've been looking for you. They made me get in here, look.' He grabbed a fistful of blanket. 'And I told them this is the wrong bed, this isn't my bed but they said no, wait here. So I waited and waited and . . .'

He threw back the blanket and flung his leg over the side of the bed.

'Jack, no.'

The nurse was back at his side. He pushed her out of the way and swung his other leg down.

'Da.' Grace stepped forward and put her arm around his shoulders. 'Get back into bed.'

'I can't do that,' he said. 'It's not my bed. They've given me someone else's bed.' He looked at the nurse. 'They'll be along any minute, won't they? They won't want to find me here, messing the sheets up, so . . .'

He inched his bottom forward and dropped his feet to the floor. 'Ooh.' He put a hand to his forehead.

'Jack.' The nurse took hold of his hand. 'The doctor said you have to stay in bed. You've banged your head, remember?'

Remember? Jack didn't remember a damn thing except the lights. Bright lights, blue lights, a man shining a torch in his eyes. And now this – this room, this bed, these people staring at him.

'Grace,' he said. 'I want Grace. Where is she?'

* * *

They were being kind to her; she knew that. *It's most likely the shock*, they told her, as they wheeled him up to the ward, a nurse on either side of the trolley, her da floundering like a landed kipper, grabbing at the safety rails, yanking the blankets and all the time shouting her name.

'He'll be different in the morning,' the nurse crooned, 'after a good night's sleep. You go home. Try not to worry too much.'

'But . . .' She didn't want to go home, she wanted to stay – needed to stay – but the nurse was adamant: he'd had a shock; he needed to rest; Grace didn't need to be there.

So she'd somehow found her way out of the hospital and to her car, then driven back to the farm. She'd walked through the dark and empty kitchen and gone straight to bed where she lay for a long time, telling herself he'd had bad lapses before and come out of them. A few months earlier, for example . . .

It was like he'd suddenly been switched off, that's how she would have described it. She'd steered him through the evening and the following early morning – wound tight with fear, her da wide-eyed and adrift – before abandoning him to Shirley and going to work. She'd managed a few hours at her desk, then driven back to the farm jittery with thoughts of what she might find.

She found the front door wide open and the kitchen window swinging on its hinges. She'd called his name before she was across the yard, her eyes scanning left and right for some sign of him. But there was nothing. The sight of his coat and boots in the hall had given her a moment's reassurance, but that had disappeared, replaced by a picture of him wandering cold and shoeless – looking for her. She'd torn through the house, calling his name, trying to work out what she should do first – comb the farm, call the police . . . when she heard him. A faint cry.

'Da?'

She flew down the stairs and into the kitchen.

'Is that you, hinny?'

He was in the pantry.

'I'm here, I'm here,' she'd shouted, and the pantry door had opened and out he'd come . . . with a cake.

'Ta da!' he'd said, his two eyes dancing over her face. 'Look what I've been up to.'

She watched as he tottered across the kitchen, his eyes flitting from her to the table, and set it down in front of her.

'Now what would your mother say to that?' he said, giving her a toothy grin.

She lowered herself onto a chair.

'It's . . . it's marvellous, Da,' she said. 'Mum would have said it was marvellous.' She was holding back the tears.

'Pshaw! Not on your nelly. "You've forgotten the icing sugar." That's what she would have said.'

She watched as he took plates from the cupboard; the bread knife off the draining board; a couple of forks from the drawer. Then he pulled out a chair and sat down beside her.

'Thought I'd strike while the iron was hot, so to speak,' he said, and it was that that tipped her over, had her mopping at her eyes with her sleeve. Not the fact that he'd been gone, absent, switched off, but the fact he'd been aware of it.

* * *

Grace turned onto her side and looked over at his empty bed. She steadied her breath to the tick of the clock. He'd recovered then – he would recover now. She stretched out her hand in the dark and switched the cassette on.

'Attention all shipping,' she said, in a deep voice. And then she let the tears come.

CHAPTER 8

Grace was on the ward early and found her da sitting up in bed chomping his way through a bowl of cornflakes.

'Hello, girl,' he said.

It was a generic greeting that granted none of the reassurance she was praying for, so she waited – waited for some confirmation that his lapse the night before had been temporary, that he'd not passed some milestone, flung into a place he wouldn't come back from.

'Grace, sit down, hinny.' He waved his spoon at her. 'You look a bit peaky. Want a few cornflakes?' A trail of milk tracked down his chin.

'How are you feeling, Da?' She heard the relief in her own voice.

'Sore.' He tapped the spoon against the dressing on his forehead. 'My head is sore.'

'Have they given you something for it?'

'Medicine.' He puckered his mouth into a tight ball. 'Nasty.'

Grace scanned the room. Four beds. Two were empty and the other one had the curtains half pulled round. She could just make out the shape of someone huddled beneath the sheets.

'He came in last night,' Da said, like he was handing over the nurses' report. 'And what a racket! And that one,' he pointed the spoon at the empty bed opposite. 'That one has mysteriously disappeared. Hmph.'

'Tea or coffee, Jack?' A woman poked her head through the door.

'Tea, thank you, my dear,' he trilled. 'They know my name,' he said, winking at her. 'They all know my name.'

She left him talking to the woman with the tea trolley and went to find a nurse. She'd got her lines prepared and rehearsed – she'd brought him some clean clothes, the care package was already in place, so she was going to take him straight home, because home was the best place for him.

It got her nowhere. More tests were booked, the nurse said. A CT scan, another set of X-rays, the consultant, new medication. The long and short of it was they wanted to keep him in another day. *To make sure.* She watched the nurse's lips moving but her mind was already elsewhere, examining the options. The usual choice: she could stand her ground or simply go along with it.

'How was he last night?'

'Restless,' the nurse said. 'Singing, apparently. Dropped off eventually. Chirpy this morning, though. So . . .' The nurse was rummaging in a tall cupboard. She came out with plastic bin liner. 'Do you a swap?'

'What?'

'I'll take his clean clothes and you can take this lot home for washing.'

* * *

Grace sat outside in the car for a long time, watching the empty car park fill: the bustle of people with places to go, some tiring sense of urgency in the way they hurried from their cars to the hospital entrance. The sky was a jigsaw of blues and greys: a smudge of pink where a weak ray of sunlight, bleached by the cold, leaked through and half lit the hills behind the hospital. She could see sheep grazing. She knew she ought to go – make the most of a Saturday on her own, get things ready for him coming home, but still she sat, trying to celebrate the fact that there had been no confusion in his face when she'd walked in, that he'd known her straight away, but somehow unable to banish the image of him the previous night: clinging onto his hand while he fought her off, frantically calling out her name.

By the time she'd driven back to the farm the sky had cleared and the sun was starting to make a difference. She let the dogs out of the barn, sat with them while they ate, then pulled on her wellies and old coat and set out on the path that wound behind the house towards the top fields. She walked briskly, trying to concentrate on what she could see, what she could hear: the frosted grass creaking under her boots, the steam rising from the forest ahead. It wasn't enough.

'It may soon be time to consider the next step, Grace.' That's what the GP had said last time he'd ended up in hospital. And that time wasn't as bad as this – a minor fall in the yard after he'd followed her out. But this: once they got wind of this they'd be back at the door with their leaflets. The thing that scared her most was that she wouldn't have the strength to kick against it, that she'd become so adept at going along with things she would simply cave in and let them take him away. She shook the thought from her head, pulled her coat more tightly round, whistled the dogs and turned back towards the farm.

She saw the police car in the yard as she was winding down the last field. Her first impulse, fuelled by the fear that something else had happened – a turn for the worse maybe – was to speed up, to get herself down there fast, but try as she might she could go no quicker. She thudded down the path on legs of wood, clumsy and awkward, the dogs weaving around her feet until they too spotted the car and set off towards it, tails up, ears back, the two of them barking up a storm.

'Grace. Hello.' Dan Halliday let the window down an inch or two.

'Has something happened? Is . . . ?'

'No, no,' he said. 'Sorry. Everything's OK. Just coming to, you know, fill you in on yesterday.'

'Right.' She hooked her fingers under the dogs' collars. 'Give me a minute.'

It was an excuse, something to buy her more time, because, although she needed to know how her da had ended up at Bronglais, she didn't need what she anticipated was going to be a lecture on the virtues of better security. She hauled the dogs across to the barn and shut them in. They didn't let up: steady thuds against the old planking, working each other up into a lather.

'You've got a couple of good dogs there,' Dan said. He was out of the car now.

'Yes,' she said. She was too tired for small talk. Whatever he'd come to tell her, she just wanted it told and him gone because all she wanted now was a bath, something nice to eat; some space to think, to get her strength up.

'Is it all right to come in?' He was looking at the house.

'Of course.' She stomped off, leading the way. She'd have to offer him tea now. Answer questions. Talk. All of it using up this bit of time she had.

The kitchen was gloomy and chilly despite the sunshine and the stove.

'Did you manage to get some sleep?'

'Yes. Thank you.' She didn't take her coat off.

'So . . .' He paused, like he was waiting for her to jump in, fill the gap.

She didn't. She waited. Waited for the details, the facts, *the narrative*; ready to log it all and paste it on to the story so far. The account got longer every time she recited it. The doctors, social workers, consultants all nodded sagely as she set it out for them; her father no longer a person but a series of events.

'A young girl took him in, apparently.'

'What?'

'Yeah. A & E staff said a young girl had brought him in.'

Grace lowered herself onto a kitchen chair. 'A young girl? But we don't know any young . . . oh . . .' It came back suddenly. The night she'd got home and he was in a state. *There was a young girl here* – that's what her da had said – and she'd dismissed it. She'd taken it as tiredness and confusion and steered him past it.

'That mean anything to you?'

'No. Nothing.'

'Well, it was good timing from our point of view – I'd only spoken to them half an hour earlier. Flagged him up as missing, you know.'

'Yes . . . right, well . . .'

She stood up from the table. She needed him to go, to give her some room to work out what the hell was going on.

'Well, thanks. Thanks for coming and . . . er . . . letting me know . . .'

He walked to the door, then paused. 'Grace . . . I hope you don't mind me saying . . .'

'What?' She heard the ice in her voice because here, no doubt, it came: some practised speech, prompted by social services, a warning dressed up as concern . . .

'I'm sorry . . .' He was making a meal of it. She could feel the tightness in her jaw.

'Sorry for what?' she said. Her voice was like snipping tin.

'About you and Greg, you know. And . . .'

She took a step back from the door and into the gloom of

the hall so he couldn't see the alarm on her face, because here it was, coming at her.

'And . . . and for what happened to your boy. Harry.' His eyes were seeking hers in the shadow. She turned away. 'I'm sorry,' he said. 'I've been away. I've only just found out . . .'

'No . . . no, it's not . . . it's not an easy thing to . . .'

She needed him to leave. Now. Before it was too late; before the wheels came right off and she couldn't fit them back on.

'Right. Yes. Thank you . . .' She had her hand to the door again. 'I'd better get on. But thanks, thanks for coming.'

Grace shut the door behind him and went back to the kitchen. She filled the kettle, slopping water on the floor as she lifted it onto the stove, then sat herself at the table. She spread her hands out on the old oilcloth and closed her eyes.

Memories were lining up but she wouldn't let them come. Not now, when she was on her own, when her da was in hospital, when there was so much else to think about. She took several deep breaths: in through the mouth, out through the nose. Cleansing breaths, the counsellor had once said – as if you could clean away things like that: the end of your marriage, the death of your own child. But it was the present she needed to concentrate on now.

A young girl had been to the farm; a young girl had taken her da to hospital. So who was she and where the hell was she now?

CHAPTER 9

The journey to the hospital had been a nightmare: her attempt to settle Jack in the back of the camper van had been hopeless, so instead she'd fastened him into the passenger seat, then watched, with alarm, as he'd kicked off his shoes and laid his dentures on the dash board. She primed the child locks and set the satnav. By the time they arrived in Aberystwyth her nerves were shot: he'd ridden alongside her, humming some tune she'd not heard before. He stopped from time to time to adjust the bandage she'd wrapped round his head or to mumble snatches of what sounded like a poem or a speech. She'd tried to blank it out and concentrate on what she was going to say when she got him to the hospital.

She needn't have bothered.

The nurse they passed as they went in through the main doors took one look at the blood on Jack's face and stopped.

'Now who have we got here, then?' she said, resting her hand on Jack's arm. Jack managed a crooked smile, straightened himself up and gave her a shaky salute.

'Jack James, Velindre Farm, Nevern, at your service, Ma'am.'

'Well, Jack James of Velindre Farm, you'd better come with me and let me have a look at what's going on underneath that bandage.'

It was as simple as that. Jack let go of her arm and took hold of the nurse's.

'What shall I . . . ?' she said, as the nurse led them through the packed waiting room.

The nurse nodded towards a reception desk. 'Go and book him in – I'll come and find you. What's your name?'

Her name. Her name was the last thing she wanted to give.

'It's OK,' she said, 'I'll not be far. I'll go book him in now and . . .' She turned and walked quickly towards the empty reception desk. She stood there for a few minutes then, no longer able to stand the heat, the noise – the suspense – found a seat tucked beside a row of vending machines and sat down to wait.

She was searching her pockets for loose change when the policeman walked in. He scanned the waiting room, then went up to the empty reception desk and pressed a buzzer. She dropped all thoughts of coffee and leaned back in the chair so he wouldn't see her. She counted to ten, then peered round the side of the machine. He was still at the empty counter, his back to her. Before she knew what she was doing, she was on her feet and walking towards the exit door. She walked like she was in a dream – the sound of the busy waiting room drowned out by her thudding heart – telling herself it was all right: Jack had given them his name and address, he was in safe hands; she had done the right thing . . . She walked out of the hospital, climbed into the camper van and, without knowing where she was going, drove away.

She'd driven for miles, her eyes flicking from the road to the rear-view mirror – her heart hammering against the possibility of blue flashing lights – until some road sign had caught her eye and she'd turned onto a steep narrow track and followed its downhill wind to a car park, which lay in a small clearing at the edge of the sea. Then she'd switched off the engine, crawled into the bed she'd prepared for Jack and waited for sleep.

When she woke the next day the memory of their outing swamped her with a feeling of shame and embarrassment that, even though she was alone, made her face burn. It was amplified further when she realised it was past noon and, despite the recklessness of her actions, she'd been granted an undeserved night of deep and untroubled sleep.

Jack. The thought of how she'd abandoned him put a knot in her belly. She leaned over and wiped the condensation from the van windscreen, then slid open the side door and let the weather come pelting in. She knew there was some logic in leaving him behind – an explanation that might take the edge off her guilt if she chose to let it. The police had been a constant backdrop to her life with Vee: running from them, outwitting them, ridiculing them. There'd been something gleeful about her defiance of their authority over her which made Vee feel powerful, superior even. It had been different for her though. Without knowing it, the police became substitutes for every fairy-story villain she feared: the wolf, the ogre, the wicked stepmother, and she'd learned to be afraid of the very institution that had been set up to protect her. So from that point of view – a childish point of view – her actions had made sense: she'd delivered Jack to safety; he'd told them who he was, so they didn't need to know how he'd got there – or about her. The problem was . . . she wasn't a child.

She pulled on her boots and sweater, locked the van and, following a sign for the coastal footpath, set off along a small track that skirted a thin band of woodland before turning sharply and heading up a steep incline. She made herself walk without looking back until the path caught up with the fields that sloped down to the cliffs. Then she turned and looked out over the sea. The endless stretch of it, from the craggy rocks below her, to the horizon that was nothing but a trick of the eye – a subtle shift of colour. She caught her hair back, tied it into a loose bundle and set off into the buffeting wind.

By the time she got back to the van the light was already fading – and so was she: a weariness that had woven itself into her very bones. There'd been an allure to the coastal path that had pulled her on, so on she'd gone – trudging up sharp inclines and down clumsy flights of rough-hewn steps, pausing only to get herself out of the wind or to glance over some sharp edge at the waves thundering below. The scenery had been magnificent – she was sure of that – but she'd barely noticed it. She had simply let her feet follow the path and allowed her mind to weave a path of its own.

The first strand took her to Jack, and the conviction that she had to go back to the farm – she needed to make sure he was OK, to apologise and explain herself. The problem was the courage – or recklessness – that had brought her so far had disappeared. This steered her thoughts automatically to phoning Vee – an idea she dismissed immediately – not only because Vee thought she was still at uni, immersed in some lengthy discourse that was going to save the world, but because she knew exactly what she would say. Vee's idea of mothering had been to treat her as if she were an adult, overlooking or simply dismissing anything she deemed childish – like being a child. It was supposed to have strengthened her character, made her independent – along with all the other qualities Vee would reel off at regular intervals – always having an opinion, not running with the crowd and always facing the consequences of your own actions. Oh, she might love the boldness of taking off, but when she learned what had set the whole escapade in motion, she would be livid. Worse than that, she would be disappointed – again. She saw it in her mother's face every time they met up: the disappointment that the eco-warrior baby she'd strapped to her rallying, demonstrating bosom like some kind of figurehead had turned out to be so ordinary.

Women have to be warriors, she'd said one time as they were walking back from school. There'd been an open day – a chance for parents to meet with the teacher, admire the work their child was producing. It was the drawing that sparked it. *My family.* She'd drawn herself in a ballerina outfit, sandwiched between Vee on one side and a tall, smiling man on the other. The ground in front of them was sprigged with purple flowers. *Violets*, she'd said – in front of the teacher – *like your name.* Vee had glowered at her, then, as soon as they were out of the playground, set in on the warrior talk. The next picture she drew was just the two of them: Vee got up in some Wonder Woman outfit – a gold V emblazoned on her bosom. That one got put up on the kitchen wall.

She slid back the door of the camper van and felt the damp air blowing on her face. Thinking about Vee had been a bad idea – it had laced the indecisiveness she was already struggling against with the fear of making the wrong decision. The light was almost gone. She wandered out to the thin strip of pebble beach and watched the push and pull of the waves, grateful for the distraction of the soundtrack – loose pebbles rattling under the surf, her waterproof jacket flapping in the wind. A row of lights on the blurred horizon marked the passage of a large ship.

There had been a third strand to her thinking, of course – one she'd tried to dismiss, because, in the light of what happened the day before, it was inappropriate, selfish. Nonetheless, she couldn't shake it from her mind. Going back to the farm would not only allow her to apologise to Jack, it might help her find out if any part of what she'd imagined was true. *Michael was on his boat.* What did that mean?

She considered the fading sky for a moment – as if the answer might be written there – then went back to the van and took her phone from the dashboard. It was a strange coincidence, she thought, as she scrolled, that her mother's number – the only contact listed in the 'V' section usually – was now accompanied by another: Velindre Farm. She let her finger hover over the two numbers, then took a deep breath and tapped. She thought at first that no one was going to answer. And then – a thin voice trilling across distance, *hello . . . hello . . .* and her phone went dead.

CHAPTER 10

Grace was in bed. It was too early to be there, but the day – its complications and disappointments – had been too much for her. She needed to switch it off, to wake in the morning to a fresh page, one that didn't feel so crumpled and worn thin. She was drifting off to sleep when the phone rang, then down the stairs and in the kitchen before the third ring, her heart bouncing against her ribs.

'Yes?' She had to stop herself from shouting. 'What is it? Is he all right?'

She sat down on the bottom stair, dizzy with the fear of what she was going to hear. But no one spoke.

'Hello?' she shouted. 'Hello?'

There was some slight noise over the line – the sound of the wind perhaps, or the sea – and the line went dead. She waited in the hall, the stone flags cold under her bare feet, willing the phone to ring again. Eventually, when she could stand the silence no longer, she plucked it off the wall and called the hospital. He was having his milky drink, the nurse said, and the thought of it had taken some of the buzz out of her head so she'd gone into the kitchen, made herself a mug of cocoa and taken it up to bed.

She settled herself under the duvet, turned her face to the wall so she couldn't see his empty bed and waited for her mind to slow. It didn't. Before she knew it, she was bowling along a road she no longer let herself travel: a road that led to the past.

***

She had met Greg at school. She'd always known who he was of course, because that was the nature of the place, but their first proper meeting had been one Friday afternoon at the school running track. The town football team were on the pitch training for the Saturday morning match and there he was, unable – he told her weeks later – to take his eyes off her: the easy length of her stride, the loose swing of her shoulders, the bounce of her hair. He was waiting for her as she came in from her final lap, smiling his smile, asking about her running times, her trainers, *her regime*. She'd been dazzled beyond: him three years older and headed, by all accounts, for the Premier League. She had found herself smiling back, his attention lifting her out of her usual awkwardness, reeling off her personal bests, her track records, her modest successes. Smiling as she embroidered a version of herself that she would spend the next twenty years trying to live up to.

Her da had been less dazzled. The boy wasn't from farming, so the fact that he had a promising football career ahead cut no mustard with him. She'd found herself trying to explain how that was an advantage, like it might be something to aspire to. *There's more to life than farming, Da*, she'd said. He'd looked at her like she'd taken her head off and put it on backwards. Her ma had wanted to take it a step further.

'I know you don't strictly believe in all my mumbo jumbo, but I have a strong feeling that . . .'

'Don't, Ma . . .' Grace hadn't wanted to hear some story dredged up from God-knows what century. She'd had no time for the signs and premonitions her mother was so fond of. She'd walked away, but not before hearing her mother's parting shot.

'A very strong feeling that you'll be the one who takes on the farm and *this Greg*, well . . .'

'I'm not interested, Ma,' she'd said. 'I know what I'm doing . . .' And, with the confidence of someone who didn't have a clue, she'd dismissed her mother's words and embraced her new life as Greg's girlfriend.

And what a life it was, at first. Overnight, it seemed, she'd acquired a shine: she was no longer boring Grace James from Velindre Farm, but Greg Fraser's girlfriend; a small-town WAG.

It hadn't stopped there, of course. When she left school (shelving her original plan of going on to university), she found herself thrust into a limelight that should have betrayed her but didn't because, wherever they went, Greg kept her close; there was no need to talk, just smile. She had a photograph somewhere – her, long and sleek in a tight black dress that was too grown-up for her, Greg's arm clamped tightly round her waist. A woman had sidled up to her that same evening while Greg was in the middle of a photo shoot.

'You must be Grace,' she said, raising her glass. 'His latest model.'

Grace had smiled. 'Oh, I'm not a model,' she stuttered – and the woman stifled a laugh and wandered off.

CHAPTER 11

Grace was upstairs packing some fresh clothes into a bag when the dogs struck up. Thinking it was either Huw with the milk, or Glen with the post, she went straight down to the front door and whistled the dogs back. They ignored her: Taff was already at the gate – howling and throwing himself against the metal bars, with Teg behind him, running in tight circles, yipping in anticipation of a good chase. There was no sign of Huw's pick-up or the post van.

'Taff. Teg.' She whistled again. They ignored her again.

She was halfway across the yard when she saw someone step out from the hedge. Grace raised her hand – a wave perhaps, or some cautionary sign and grabbed the dogs by their collars and hauled them backwards.

'Wait there,' she yelled and dragged the snarling dogs towards the barn. By the time she'd shut them in and barred the door the person was at the gate. It was a young woman. A girl.

Grace's heart skipped a beat. 'Can I help you?'

The girl hesitated. 'Yes, I . . . I've come to see Jack?'

Grace said nothing.

'Is he . . . is he in?'

'No. He's not.'

'Oh.'

The girl looked down at the ground. 'So . . . do you know when he'll be back?'

Grace put her head on one side. 'And you are?' It was a pointless thing to say and she knew it because here, surely, was the young girl Dan had told her about. The one her da had tried to tell her about.

'I . . . I'm a friend of Jack's. I was just wondering . . . is he OK?'

Before Grace had chance to answer, the girl suddenly lurched towards her. Her eyes were full of tears. Grace folded her arms across her chest and stepped to one side. 'I think you'd better come inside,' she said, and set off across the yard without looking back, wondering what the hell was coming at her now – what further complication this girl – this *child*, for that was surely what she was – was going to lay at her door.

'So . . .' Grace was fussing with the kettle, rinsing cups that needed no rinsing. Letting the girl compose herself, because she had no energy for tears. She glanced at the clock. The hospital was expecting her at 2 p.m., which gave her roughly an hour. 'You say you're a friend of Jack's?'

'Yes, but . . . well, it's more complicated than that . . . I think.'

'Go on.' Grace banged two cups of tea on the table and motioned for the girl to sit down. But she didn't go on – or sit down. Instead she stood in the kitchen doorway, looking at everything except Grace. Finally, she took a deep breath and said, 'I know this sounds stupid, really stupid, but I thought . . .' The girl gave a small laugh. Embarrassed. 'I thought Jack was my grandfather.'

Grace choked a mouthful of tea over the table. 'Your grandfather?'

'I know. It was . . . probably stupid.'

'Probably? What on earth made you think that?'

'I've been visiting him. Well, not visiting exactly.' The girl stepped into the kitchen and took a seat at the table. 'I came to see him earlier this week, you see. I made sure you and the other carer weren't here . . .'

'The other carer?' Grace didn't know if it was being mistaken for a carer or the fact that she'd dismissed what her da had been trying to tell her, but she was up on her feet now, busying herself at the sink to hide the flush of heat in her face.

'Yes. And he said he knew where he was – Michael. That's Jack's son. He said he could take me there. And I thought . . . well I believed him. Or I didn't disbelieve him, you know?' Grace turned and stared at the girl.

'So it *was* you? Yesterday. You were here and you . . . you decided to take him out for the day?'

'Yes, but . . .'

'Until you realised . . .' Grace was putting nothing in to soften the mix. 'Realised he wasn't quite what he seemed? That he wasn't quite . . .' There was a theatrical note in her voice that told her she should stop. Instead she tapped the side of her head with one finger. 'You realised he wasn't quite the full ticket?'

'No. It wasn't like . . .'

'So you abandoned him.'

'Yes . . . no. Is he all right?'

'No, he's not.' Grace folded her arms across her chest. 'He's still in hospital – where, I believe, you left him?'

Grace ignored the small yelp and gave a loud sniff.

'With a head injury.'

The girl was crying but Grace was on her high horse now, her backside clamped firmly in the saddle. 'So Michael,' she said. 'You thought . . .'

'Yes, I thought . . .'

The girl bowed her head, and her hair – dark curls that, on a better day, Grace might have admired – fell forward, half covering her face. 'I thought Michael was my father,' she whispered.

'Ha!' Grace couldn't help herself. 'That's ridiculous.'

'I know, I'm sorry.' The girl was on her feet, pushing the chair back under the table. 'I should never have come. I'm sorry, I really am. I hope, well . . . could you give Jack my apologies when you see him. Tell him I didn't mean to cause so much trouble.' She got to the door and turned. 'Tell him he can keep the envelope. I don't need it any more.'

CHAPTER 12

She was fumbling with the catch on the gate when the woman called her back. She turned and saw her at the porch, waving. She raised her hand slightly to return the wave but the woman shouted out again, then left the porch and walked towards her. Her face had lost some of its colour.

'Could you come back in please . . . ?'

She stepped away from the gate. 'I need to go, really,' she said. 'I have to get back home.'

She wasn't up to it. All she wanted to do was get back in the van and drive. Drive back to Vee's, maybe bed down for the night, then go back to her flat. Catch up on some lectures, finish her essay, allow herself to be swept along by the various distractions student life offered.

'Please,' Grace said. 'Could you come back? Just for a minute. I . . . I think we need to talk.'

She nodded, and followed the woman back into the house. The envelope, postcard and the newspaper clipping were lined up side by side on the kitchen table. The woman pointed at them.

'Where did you get these?'

'From my mother's house. I found them by accident. Earlier this week. I . . . I left them for Jack.'

Grace nodded. She'd been at the dresser top as soon as the girl was out the door, with her da's words – the ones she'd dismissed – ringing in her ears, and found the envelope straight away. She'd tipped it out onto the table still brisk with anger, snatched up the postcard. Whitby Harbour. Meaningless, she thought, because Michael and Joseph had hated the east coast, they'd always favoured western seas: Scotland, Ireland and beyond. But then she turned it over. Although the words made no sense – *I'm trusting all went well, will you come, please* – the rough scrawl was unmistakeable. There was a sudden looseness in her head, some internal shifting that made her want to sit down. She steadied herself against the chair for a moment, then darted out through the hall and into the porch. She clutched at the door-frame and shouted after the girl, willing her to stop, to come back and explain this thing – this thing that was scattered across the kitchen table, that had suddenly landed and pushed the breath out of her.

'So,' Grace said, and found she didn't know how to continue. The girl had finally agreed to come back into the house, following her across the yard like some reluctant schoolchild – and now she didn't know where to begin. 'I'm not a carer,' she said, eventually. 'I'm Jack's daughter. Grace.' She ignored the sudden flash of colour striping the girl's face. 'I live here with him,' she said, then leaned forward and tapped the newspaper clipping with one finger: a younger Da at the Royal Welsh Show, his arms draped across the backs of a pair of prize-winning rams. JACK JAMES, VELINDRE FARM, NEVERN. 'This is how you found us, I suppose?'

'Yes. I looked up the farm.'

Grace picked up the postcard and made a study of the harbour view on the front. *Whitby.*

'Do you know this place?'

The girl shook her head.

Grace let her gaze drift from the postcard to the window. 'Well, it doesn't make any sense. It's on the east coast: it's not a place they ever worked. My uncle Joseph and my brother, Michael.' She swung her gaze back to study the girl's face.

'Yes, that's what Jack . . .'

'Oh, he did, did he?' Grace gave a mirthless laugh. 'And what else did he tell you?'

'He said he knew where Michael was. That he could take me to him.'

'My God.' Grace shook her head. 'So where did he say he was?'

The girl put her two hands flat on the table and pulled in a long breath. 'He said he was on his boat . . .'

'Hah, well, at least that bit could be right . . .'

She might have taken this as good news except Grace's words were so laced with sarcasm, she knew to wait for the impending punchline.

'Michael might be on his boat,' Grace said. 'But his boat is at the bottom of the sea. He's dead. Long dead. Drowned off Milford Haven. Him and my uncle both. I'd be very surprised if my father remembered anything about it, actually.' Grace glanced at the clock. 'It was a long time ago. Nineteen ninety-nine. November twelfth to be precise. Anyway,' – she started to get up from the table – 'I have to get going now, so . . .'

The girl straightened up suddenly. 'That can't be,' she said and reached for the postcard. She studied it for a moment and handed it to Grace. 'Look at the stamp . . . and the postmark. It says January 2001.'

'Well, that's not possible.' Grace walked to the window and held the card a couple of inches from her face. The girl was right. The postmark was smudged, but she was right. 'Well, there's got to be an explanation,' she said. 'Michael died in 1999, so this—' Grace waved the card at the girl. 'This must be wrong.' She turned it over and examined it again. There was her mistake, surely: the card was most likely written by some person whose handwriting resembled Michael's. Mere coincidence.

'I'm sorry . . .' Grace said, but the girl was no longer listening. She was sifting through her bag.

'There's something else. I've got something else.'

Grace glanced at the clock again and folded her arms across her chest. She could humour this girl for another ten minutes or so, and then she would leave for the hospital.

'Ah, here. It's here.'

She pulled out another envelope and slid out a strip of photographs – black and white, from a photo booth – and passed them to Grace. Michael's smiling face beamed up at her: his eyes creased by the sun, his hair curled wild by salt wind, his broad grin revealing the tooth he broke when he was fifteen.

'Is that him? Is that Michael?' The girl was at her side now.

'Yes,' Grace said. 'But . . .' She felt the need to sit down, to sit down and piece it all together. 'A baby,' she said. 'He's holding a baby.'

'I know.' The girl took the strip of photos from her hand and turned it over. 'Look.'

'Michael at Malin, 2001.' Grace heard herself saying the words but could make no sense of them.

'No, it says Michael *and* Malin . . .'

'But that doesn't mean anything at all,' Grace said.

The girl was smiling at her now. 'Yes, it does,' she said, softly. 'Because my name is Malin.'

CHAPTER 13

Grace drove slowly: there was some dreamlike quality to the way she shifted up and down the gears. Malin stole glances at her from time to time, but Grace either did not notice or she chose not to return them.

Malin Head. That's all Grace had said. *Malin Head*, like it was some secret password she ought to be aware of. Then she'd gathered up the postcard, the newspaper clipping and the photos, slipped them all into the envelope and handed them back.

'We need to go and get my da,' she'd said. 'Jack.'

We. Malin hadn't objected, she'd simply nodded, followed her out to the car and buckled herself in, waiting for another barrage of questions or accusations. But they'd been on the road for twenty minutes and Grace hadn't said another word. Malin could feel herself floundering in the silence. She tried to concentrate on what she could see from the window – gnarly hedges perched above stone walls, clusters of white painted cottages, the occasional glimpse of glittering sea – but her head was swimming with everything she still needed to ask. The questions were lined up and ready on her tongue. She wanted to release them, to know what Grace was thinking, but she kept quiet.

'He died in a fishing accident.' Grace said suddenly. 'But the papers said it was most likely Michael's fault.' She couldn't remember actually speaking the words out loud before.

Malin looked across at her.

'He'd been out drinking the previous night, according to the newspaper.'

She'd gone back to the farm and found her mother at the table, the newspaper spread out in front of her, the phone in her hand.

'They won't tell me,' she'd said, pointing at the headline. 'They won't tell me why they've said such a thing.'

WAS THE SKIPPER OVER THE LIMIT? the headline blared, above a blurred photograph of Michael – and Milford – and a promise of the full story inside.

Grace had turned the page and studied the photographs – the *Laughing Girl*, her name and colour not apparent, but Joseph, bright-eyed and smiling as she remembered him – then read the columns quietly, without comment. They'd said it, she realised, because it was most likely true. Michael had been out the night before, rolling drunk, according to the other customers in the pub. Rolling drunk and getting cosy with the girl who served behind the bar.

I didn't realise he was heading out next morning, the girl said, but heading out he was; unsteady on his feet, according to the milkman, and reeking of booze. A couple of fellas down at the dock vouched the same – Michael was listing to port before he ever got on the rolling boat. Joseph, by all accounts had thrust the yellow oilskins at him, started the engine and aimed the boat out through the harbour walls and into the roiling ocean.

At 2.57 p.m. – seven hours after leaving the harbour – the coastguard received the first Mayday: Joseph's voice straining above the wind and slam of water. A stalled engine maybe, water in the fuel – he was unsure – but they were dead in the water and drifting – the water too deep and the waves too high to weigh anchor. Three minutes later another call:

they were taking on water; they'd released a flare; they were preparing to abandon ship. Then silence. The lifeboat was already out on another call, and by the time they reached the co-ordinates there was nothing to be seen: no life jackets or debris; no sign of the boat or the two men.

The only thing they'd left behind, it seemed, was a question mark.

'Jack thought he was still alive.'

Grace glanced away from the windscreen for a moment. She'd forgotten the girl was there. 'I know.' Her mother and da had refused to accept the obvious for months – years even. 'It doesn't mean a thing. My da thinks we still farm sheep and cattle.'

'He said Michael was on his boat – that day I came by. That's why I . . .'

Grace shook her head. 'He gets . . . confused.'

'I realise that – now. It's just, well . . . the photograph. If it *is* him, surely it must mean that he survived? That he survived and . . .'

'And that my da might be right?'

'Yes.'

And my mother, Grace thought. *My mother and her signs.*

It had been a joke when they were young. 'Oh, watch out, here comes the crystal ball,' her da would quip, as her mother – based on nothing more than how the birds were gathering – entertained them with predictions of rain, drought or snow.

Michael and Joseph's disappearance, however, put an end to all his teasing because, a couple of weeks later, directed by signs that indicated Michael was still alive, her mother and da had all but abandoned the farm and set off to find him. They left everything in the hands of their neighbour, Conway Lewis, took lodgings in a Pembroke guest house and spent their days scouring shorelines and coves – St Brides Bay, Westdale Bay, Freshwater West – the two of them blown hollow by the wind, loss and fading hope. They had given up, eventually, not because they were ready to, but because some newspaper hack suddenly got wise to who they were, forcing them to return to the farm. Empty-handed.

Grace had visited them soon after their return and been shocked – the two of them pale and lifeless. Her da, it seemed, split his time between the farm and the *Shipping Forecast*. She had a vivid memory of him in his waterproofs and wellies, bunched up by the Rayburn listening to the radio, her mother pouring the tea, oblivious to the mess he had trailed in. She'd gone to tell them that she was pregnant but took the news back home with her, unspoken.

They allowed no funeral for either Joseph or Michael – a decision that had surprised Grace, not understanding at the time that a funeral represented acceptance. It made the thing real. That understanding came years later.

CHAPTER 14

Grace rolled down the window and let the wind blow on her face. Malin. The girl's name was Malin. She knew that the rest of it was immaterial – the date, the postcard, the newspaper clipping – because the truth was there in the name. Lundy, Fastnet, Irish Sea, Shannon, Rockall . . . Malin. She let the names slip through her mind knowing they could only lead to one explanation: her mother and da may have been right. Michael had not died. Michael might, in fact, still be alive. The thought set up a wild gallop in her chest. She didn't know whether to rein it in or to run with it. Rein it in – that's what reason should have told her – but she'd lived by the sea too long to give reason full sway.

* * *

In March 2000, a few months after Michael and Joseph's boat was lost – she was six months pregnant by then – her da sent her a clipping from the local newspaper. LOCAL MAN MAKES MIRACULOUS DISCOVERY the headline declared, and she'd scanned the article with her stomach pushing at her throat. A fisherman from Pembroke Dock had found an orange ID tag washed up in the harbour. Nothing remarkable there, because all lobster pots carried such tags, until he saw the name of the boat it had come from. Saw it and recognised it. She had lifted her eyes from the page at that point, fearing the worst, but no, the tag was not from the *Laughing Girl*; it was from a boat called the *Andrea Gail*. In normal circumstances this would not have sparked more than a passing interest, except – earlier that year – Sebastian Jungers had hit the literary big time. His novel *The Perfect Storm* was based on a real-life story about a group of Newfoundland fishermen who pushed their luck too far and paid the price. The tag, it turned out, had been travelling the seas since their boat – the *Andrea Gail* – had gone down in 1991. Not only that, it had made its way across the Atlantic Ocean to Pembroke Dock.

She'd put the article to one side and phoned the farm. Don't get your hopes up, she wanted to say. But she'd just caught them – packing, loading the car, getting ready to set off. She'd thought of them that night, as she lay in bed – Greg asleep and oblivious beside her. She imagined them, walking side by side along some quiet stretch of sand, their heads down, eyes darting for anything that might lead to Michael. A couple of weeks later she'd travelled up to the farm. She'd been hoping for some time with her ma – a couple of hours by the stove, maybe, talking pregnancy and motherhood – but found Wenna busy with her books, seeking out a sign that would point them in the right direction. She had hardly registered Grace's presence.

'A cup of tea by the fire, Ma?'

Grace had laid the tray, stoked the stove, plumped the cushions.

'What? Ah – I haven't got time for that now, girl.'

'But . . .' The words dried up in her throat. The confession that she was feeling at sea herself; that she was nervous about the approaching birth. That she needed some reassurance, some mothering. She'd imagined that her pregnancy might improve things between her and Greg but it had only made things worse. His dissatisfaction with her that had started soon after they were engaged only seemed to have increased. At first she'd put it down to the problems with his career – the promise of a Premier League that never materialised, the place on a second-division team that seemed increasingly tenuous – but the real problem was her. She simply wasn't the person he wanted her to be.

'Come and look at this, hinny,' her da had said, so she'd left the tea and trailed him to the front room. A sprawl of maps lay on the dining table, a web of fine pencil lines criss-crossing a wide expanse of blue. The Atlantic Ocean.

'Nine years,' he said. No preamble, no explanation. 'Nine years at sea it was. Two thousand nautical miles. Any number of routes it could have taken.'

'The tag, you mean?' she said, but he wasn't listening. He was bent over the table, reciting the names like some poem he'd just written: 'The Mid-Atlantic Ridge, Newfoundland Basin. Rockall Trough, Porcupine Abyssal Plain . . .'

'Da.' She'd wanted him to stop, but on he'd gone, outlining the possibility of a different route, a warmer route. She'd left him to it, trudged up the stairs with her suitcase and sat on the edge of her old bed staring out of the window, trying to swallow down the exasperation that was needling at her throat. She'd moved on, so why couldn't they? She knew well enough, of course: they had refused to believe what the newspapers had written – and she hadn't. As far as she was concerned, the papers had it right. Michael was at fault. He'd been drunk when he took the boat – and his uncle – out in rough seas. He was looking for trouble and that's what he got.

She spent another couple of days with them, nodding at the various hypotheses, and went back to her own empty house to wait for Greg to return. He was away on some training camp, an expensive two-week intensive – guaranteed, apparently – to get him off the reserves' bench and back onto the pitch.

A further newspaper clipping had arrived a couple of weeks later. The body of a fisherman lost off Conwy half a year earlier had come ashore in Liverpool – and off they went again: another wild goose chase that bleached the life out of them. She knew what they were looking for, of course: closure of some sort. Their own orange tag, maybe, to mull over, as they hovered above their maps, tracing the final journey their son had made.

She'd scoffed at the idea at that point because the portion of blame she'd dealt Michael was still stuck sideways in her gullet, lodged too tight to let anything like sympathy trickle past.

She had a change of heart the following year. Hormones. That's how she'd explained it. A natural softening that had come with the responsibilities of motherhood. But there had been more to it than that.

* * *

They were having a rare night out. It was an invitation they couldn't turn down because, a month earlier, Greg's contract had been terminated. After the initial shock – and indignation – he'd thrown himself into a new venture and set up as a private football coach. *It's a chance to get out together for once*, he'd said, as if Harry was ten years old rather than ten weeks; as if it wasn't simply an opportunity to drum up some business. So she'd gone along with it and there she was – her breasts stinging with milk, a table full of people she neither knew nor wanted to know.

'So, what do you say, Grace?' Greg's voice suddenly cut across her thoughts.

'What's that?'

He smiled away his annoyance. 'Andie's suggestion,' he said, nodding across to their hostess – some agile-looking woman who'd recently moved to the area. Blonde. Affluent. Her two boys already enrolled on the town football team.

She turned her head towards the woman, hoping for some clue as to what piece of important conversation she'd missed.

'*The Perfect Storm*,' Andie said, showing her perfect teeth. 'The film? We're all going on Saturday night?'

'Oh. Well . . .'

'If you're too busy with the baby, of course . . .'

Greg had somehow found her foot with his own. 'I'd have thought it would be right up your street, darling,' he said. She was the only one who recognised the warning in his smile. 'Fishing, the sea.'

'Not to mention George Clooney,' Andie offered.

'Oh. Right,' she said. 'Of course, yes.'

* * *

She'd been unprepared, that's what she told herself afterwards: unprepared and anxious. It wasn't until they were seated in the cinema and the lights dimmed out that she managed to relax.

That was her first mistake.

Her second mistake was that she hadn't taken herself off as soon as she felt the tears coming. Instead she'd cleared her throat, swallowed them down – only to have them rise back up, bringing with them some involuntary groan that had them all turning to look at her. She excused herself and stumbled off to the toilets, half blinded with tears.

'What the fuck was all that about?' Greg had snarled on the drive home. 'What a fucking embarrassment.'

'Sorry,' she'd said. 'It was . . .'

She didn't trust herself to explain, to tell him that it wasn't the funeral scene in the church, nor the doomed boat groaning its way up the face of an impossible wave. No, what had undone her was the image of the lone man, adrift in an impossible sea, smiling up into a sky he would never see again, then simply disappearing from sight.

CHAPTER 15

'Grace!'

Malin was trying her best to keep up. The hospital car park had been full and they'd parked by the university. Grace had locked the car and set off like it was a race.

'Grace . . .'

'What?'

'Your phone . . .'

Grace fumbled in her pocket, pulled out the phone and looked at the screen.

'Oh bugger,' she said. 'It's the hospital.' She stabbed at the screen, then held the phone to her ear. 'I'm on my way,' she shouted, but the line was dead. She was late. She'd spent more time at the kitchen table than she'd intended, then she'd driven too slowly, distracted by thoughts of the past. She tried to pick up speed but couldn't: the heat in her head, the bags, the thought of her da waiting for her.

'Are you all right?' Malin was alongside her now, pink in the face.

'All right? Of course I'm all right.' It wasn't true – she could feel the blood pounding in her temples. 'I just need to get to the hospital and pick him up before . . .' She didn't have the energy to finish but the words reared up in her head: *before the social workers gather, before the consultant gets his medicating oar in – before someone decides I'm not coping and refuses to let me take him home.* She was almost at a jog, her hair plastered to her forehead, the bag of clean clothes jostling her leg at every stride. She marched on. The hill was never-ending, her head was buzzing, she was too hot – the girl was calling her name again . . .

'Grace, are you OK?' Malin, for some reason Grace couldn't quite work out, was standing above her, peering down.

'Are you . . . No. Wait, don't get up . . .'

Grace scrabbled her feet back under her. 'I'm fine,' she said, looking back at the pavement for the thing that had tripped her and put her on the floor. There was nothing.

'I caught my legs in the bag,' she said, brushing her knees down and lurching off again.

She'd done no such thing. Something in her was off balance: some spinning sensation that was working its way up from her chest and into her head.

'Look—' She dragged the car keys out of her pocket. 'Go back to the car. Wait for me there. I can't do this, I . . .'

She hurried away before the tears got going. *I can't do this.* She was half running now, the pavement blurry beneath her feet, the strap of her handbag slipping from her shoulder. She charged through the automatic doors, now noticing at least three empty spaces in the car park, and set off up the long corridor. People were looking at her, she knew it, probably conjuring up scenarios to explain the state of her: a daughter in labour, perhaps. She let out a half-choked laugh at the irony of it.

Jack was ready and waiting, parked by the nurse's station in a wheelchair, his coat buttoned up to the neck – something of a shrunken Paddington Bear about him. She took a deep breath and tried to steady herself.

'Now then, Da.'

He peered up at her from under the peak of his flat cap. The bruising on his face took her breath away.

'Ah, here she is, Jack. I told you she wouldn't be long.'
Grace turned towards the voice.

'Is . . . is he all right?' Grace asked. 'The bruising is . . .'

'Superficial.' The nurse's voice was aimed at deterring discussion. 'The X-rays were fine. The consultant's seen him this morning – he's good to go. But social services want a quick word. We're expecting someone shortly, so if you could wait in the day room, I'll let her know you're there.'

Grace glanced at Jack's bruised face. There was no way she could let the social worker see him like that.

'It'll be easier if I just give her a ring. My father . . .' The lie dropped neatly into her lap. '. . . has an appointment this afternoon . . . hearing clinic, you know. I don't want to miss it, so . . .'

Some sudden commotion further up the ward drew the nurse's attention. A tiny woman, sporting a pink bed jacket and nothing else, shot out from a side room and made a run for it. The nurse took off after her.

'Edith!'

Grace steadied Jack to his feet. 'Tell the social worker I'll give her a ring later,' she called. 'Come on, Da. Let's get you home.'

* * *

'I'm sorry about earlier.' Grace found herself reluctant to say the girl's name – the familiarity and unfamiliarity of it.

They were back at the farm, Jack was dozing in his chair by the stove and Grace was at the table with a mug of tea, feeling like she'd woken up from a bad dream. A nightmare even – that's what the walk back to the car had felt like: her da's footsteps getting shorter and shorter until they were almost walking on the spot, until he was almost dangling from her arm.

'It's all right.' Malin was hovering by the sink.

'I got myself het up. It's so . . .' Grace left it. The girl didn't need to know what it was like – what she felt like. 'I guess we need to talk,' Grace said. The thought of it had her heart revving in her chest. Talk had never been her strong point. Living with Greg had mostly been about listening.

So they talked. Or mostly Malin did. She explained how she'd found the envelope in her mother's house, how she'd sat with her back against the bookcase daring to piece together a story that differed from the one her mother had always recited; one that involved a living, breathing father, not some obliging 'friend' who'd handed over a specimen tube, then buggered off. Grace could see how much the girl had wanted it to be true: her face was lit up with the telling of it. She suddenly regretted the bluntness with which she'd burst the girl's bubble.

'So, who is your mother?' she asked.

'Her name's Vee. Vee O'Connor.'

Vee O'Connor. Grace had not known any of Michael's girlfriends – he'd been too far away by then for her to have any dealings with his life. He became part of her old life, like her mother and Da and the farm. She'd visited occasionally – half-heartedly – but her real life was with Greg. Or so she'd thought at the time.

'Violet,' Malin said, 'but she prefers Vee.'

Violet or Vee, neither rang a bell for Grace.

'O'Connor, not James?'

'Oh, definitely O'Connor. . .'

Grace nodded. Changing her name back had been one of the first things she'd done when she'd resurfaced from the fugue of grief and depression.

'So where is she now?'

'Some refugee camp in Calais – I think.' She gave Grace a

small smile. 'I know. It's not what you were expecting me to say. But that's my mother for you – likes to do the unexpected.'

'So when is she coming back?'

It was a good question. An important question bearing in mind the fact that her camper van was parked in the farmyard.

'I'm not really sure.'

'Oh. So does she do it a lot, then, refugee camps in Calais?'

'Yes. Well, that sort of thing, you know. Campaigning, protesting, direct action . . .'

'She's not one of those people who glue themselves to the road, is she?' It was a poor attempt at humour. Some compensation, Grace hoped, for her earlier sourness.

Malin gave a small smile and nodded and recounted how Vee had returned home from her first M25 escapade – triumphant, but with no skin on her palms. Vee the activist, the adventurer.

'So what did she tell you about your . . . your father?'

'She told me nothing . . . just . . .' A flush of crimson lit up the girl's face. 'It was done, you know . . . artificially.'

Grace pondered for this a moment. *Artificially.* That didn't sound particularly like the Michael she remembered: the boy who, from the age of fourteen, had had the girls queuing up for him. There'd been something about him they couldn't resist. His looks were part of it, of course, but not all of it. No, it was the way he'd made people feel. Like some bright current flowed from him, some easiness that washed over anything – or anyone – he was involved with. Grace sighed at the thought of it. It had been so long since she'd thought about him. Her lost brother.

'Your name,' she said eventually. 'Malin. Malin Head – it's the most northerly point of Ireland.'

'Yes, I know – now,' Malin said. She'd looked it up while she was alone in Grace's car – scrolled through Google's offerings, savouring each fact, photograph, map, until she'd had to stop because none of it fit together. It was like puzzle pieces in the wrong box – you thought they were part of the picture but no matter how you tried you couldn't fit them in.

'Michael worked there at one time.'

'He did?'

He did. Grace could recall the conversation with her ma. The worry in her voice when she found out Michael was trawling off the top of Ireland. *He knows what he's doing, Ma*, she'd said – or something equally trite.

'So . . .'

Grace heard the edge of hope in the girl's voice.

'So . . . do you think it could be him – in the photograph? Do you think . . .'

'It certainly looks like him, but . . .' Grace was choosing her words carefully because it was, beyond a doubt, Michael in the photograph.

'So what do you think happened?'

'I don't know,' Grace said. 'I don't know.' The scene from *The Perfect Storm* came back into her head. She pushed it away.

'But . . . but do you think it could be possible? That he . . . survived?'

Grace considered Malin's eyes. Green, like Michael's. 'Irish green' her mother had called it, citing some past connection that was likely a fancy because, as far as she knew, the only thing they had ever shared with Ireland was a wide stretch of sea. She thought of the photograph, the postcard, the newspaper clipping, the girl's name – the light feeling in her chest when she imagined him back in their lives, then opened her lips and let the words drift out.

'It could be possible – I guess, although if it was . . .' She could feel the words swelling in her chest, pushing at her heart. '. . . it would be . . . a miracle.'

She sat back in the chair almost dizzy with the saying of it. Malin leaned towards her, eyes glittering with tears, nodding. 'So what do you think we should do?'

Grace looked at the girl. If it were true that Michael had survived, then here was her niece, her da's granddaughter.

'I think there's only one thing we can do,' Grace said, because surviving a sunken boat in a stormy sea would be miraculous enough, but Michael returning home, coming back to the farm to help her with her da, the money, the relentless work – that would be worthy of a letter to the Pope. *He's risen from the sea to save me*, she could say, and lay down all her worries, sleep in her own bed, find some time to start thinking, to start living again. 'We should go and look for him.'

CHAPTER 16

Grace knew the minute she closed her eyes she wouldn't be able to sleep. *We should go and look for him.* What on earth had she been thinking? She'd opened her mouth to take the words back, but the look on Malin's face had stopped her. Beaming like the sun was shining out of her. So she'd busied herself getting her da to bed, bustling from the bathroom to the bedroom to the yard until she had him settled, then gone back to the kitchen to say she was turning in early.

'It's 382 miles,' Malin said, glancing up from her mobile phone. She was still smiling. 'Or . . . six hours, forty-one minutes.'

'What?'

'To Whitby. That's how far it is to Whitby.'

'Oh. Right. Well then, we'll . . . we'll talk about it in the morning . . .' Grace had turned tail before the girl caught the look on her face – alarm, pure alarm – and went back up the stairs, taking the envelope with her.

Her da was already half asleep – snoring by the time they'd got to Dogger and Fisher – so she'd clicked off the cassette, settled herself under the duvet and waited for sleep to come. After twenty minutes she hauled herself upright, switched on the night light and took the envelope off the bedside table. She examined the address on the front, then tipped its contents onto the bed. *The evidence*, she thought, as her eyes drifted over the photographs, the postcard, the newspaper cutting.

But evidence of what? That Michael had survived, moved to Whitby, fathered a child? That they could travel up there and simply present themselves: long-lost sister, father and – wait for it – *a daughter*, and he would welcome them with open arms? It was more likely evidence that Michael had survived and the burden of it had been too much – the shame had taken him off and out of their lives as good as if he had drowned. And as much as she wanted to think that would not be possible – that he would never have abandoned them, leaving them empty-handed and wondering – she knew it was.

She had been sixteen when Michael left home, her life still governed by the rhythms of the farm and school, Greg and Harry still part of an unseen future. There'd been some sort of row between him and her da (which wasn't unusual), then Joseph had come to visit (which was unusual) and before they knew it Michael had packed a small case, his camera and farm waterproofs into Joseph's truck and, without a backward glance or wave to the three of them lined up at the gate, bounced away down the track. His leaving had caused some kind of rift between her ma and da, a chilliness that was eventually thawed by the necessity of working side by side. Apart from occasional postcards and phone calls that put the fear of God into her mother – Michael's voice straining above the lashing wind and rain in some far-flung fishing port – he didn't come back for years. Not properly. There was a single flying visit that left them all bewildered: the height of him, the strength, his appetite; the unspoken worry that he was nothing but a stranger.

Then, out of the blue, everything changed. Her mother had called late one evening with the news.

'What is it?' she'd said. There was a note of excitement in her mother's voice that had her worried. 'What's happened?'

'It's Michael,' her mother said. 'He's coming home.'

It turned out to be not strictly true – in her excitement her mother had not given her the full story, which was that Joseph had fixed up a contract in Milford Haven and the two of them were moving there.

'At least now we'll always know where he is,' her mother had said.

Another premonition, of sorts.

* * *

Grace re-packed the envelope, slid it under her pillow and turned off the lamp. *We should go and look for him.* She lay in the dark, listening, and every sound she heard – the steady purr of her da's breathing, the wind at the loose panel on the barn roof, the creak of a gate that hadn't been properly shut – told her she couldn't do it: she had neither the courage nor the energy to leave the familiarity – the safety – of the farm. The idea had been nothing but a fantasy, a moment of spontaneity, which paid no heed to the routine of things – her job, the dogs, Shirley, her da, the cost . . .

On and on she went, shoring up her case, until she had it settled in her mind: she would explain to Malin first thing in the morning that she'd have to make the journey alone, because trailing her poor da to Whitby was an impossibility.

CHAPTER 17

'Room service.'

Grace woke with a start. 'Da?'

She raised herself up onto her elbows and peered around. The room was light. Too light. She swung her legs off the bed, and stopped as he appeared at the top of the landing – carrying a tray.

'What's . . .' She reached for her dressing gown.

'No, no,' he said. 'You stay put, hinny. Now then . . .' He teetered towards her and set the tray down on the bed. 'No papers this morning I'm afraid, Madam,' he said, with a grin. 'Kippers neither. Just can't get the staff.'

'What time is it, Da?'

'Time to get going.' He was rifling through the chest of drawers.

'Going? Going where?'

But he wasn't listening; he was pulling out clothes and flinging them onto his bed. She ignored the breakfast tray and went over to him.

'Are you all right, Da?' It was plain he wasn't. 'What are you doing?' She put a calming hand on his arm.

'Packing, of course,' he said, shrugging her off.

'Packing . . .'

He didn't answer – he was counting out a heap of socks onto his unmade bed. 'How many, do you think? Six or seven . . . ?'

But Grace was already halfway down the stairs.

The kitchen looked like it had been commandeered by some military operation. The road atlas was propped up against the bread bin and Malin – wearing her da's reading glasses – was peering at it. The table was layered with Ordnance Survey maps.

'Grace. You're up.'

'Yes . . . my da came up with a tray. Is . . .' She stopped herself. *Is he all right?* she wanted to ask, but it was a silly question because she knew he wasn't. She could hear him in the spare bedroom now, rummaging through the cupboards. 'I think I might need to take him back to the hospital,' Grace said. 'Get him checked over. He seems a bit . . .' She hesitated. '. . . a bit worked up.'

'Oh. He seemed all right earlier.'

Earlier? Grace turned and checked the clock. It was almost ten.

'He had some more ideas, actually,' Malin said. 'About, you know – our trip.'

Grace slid herself onto a chair, not sure what to say. She'd slept in – something she'd not done for years. She should have been feeling rested, but here she was, already edging towards guilt.

'Our trip?' she said. 'I thought I said we were going to talk about that . . .'

'I know,' Malin said. 'But I was up early and thought I'd do a bit of, you know, research, and then Jack came down and, well . . . I think between us we've got ourselves the beginnings of a plan.'

The words unleashed a tug of panic in Grace's chest – the feeling of something set in motion that was going to pull her along with it. She dug her heels in against it.

'Hang on a minute. What exactly have you said to him?'

Malin's face was etched with alarm. 'I just said we were thinking of a short trip. The three of us, I thought . . .'

'You *thought*?' She masked her fear with indignation. 'Well, *I* thought I'd made myself clear last night. We were going to talk about it, isn't that what I said? I'm not sure if you understand our situation here, Malin. We can't just up and off at the drop of a flaming hat.'

She was being unfair and she knew it because, in the heat of the moment, she'd led the girl to believe that was exactly what they were going to do.

'So did you tell him why? Why we were going on this *trip*?'

'Well, no . . .'

'And Michael, did you mention Michael? Is that why he's so . . . so bloody het up?'

'No. But . . .' Grace could see Malin was floundering, but then again, so was she.

'Well, we can't go. *I* gave it some thought before I went to sleep last night and . . .' She got no further. Her da was on the move. She listened to the footsteps as he crossed the landing, then the huff and puff of him as he came down the stairs. He had his binoculars slung round his neck. He gave her a toothy grin, then stepped up to the kitchen table and considered the maps like some wartime general.

'Has the girlie explained the plan, then?' he said.

'Not exactly,' Grace said, ignoring the look on Malin's face.

'In that case,' he said, 'time to listen and learn. Gather round, girl. Gather round.'

Like some chivvied ewe she fell in beside him at the kitchen table and watched as he held his specs on with one hand and let the other hover – mainly over the Irish Sea – calling out various place names: New Quay, Aberaeron, Aberystwyth, Aberdovey, Barmouth, Abersoch. He straightened himself up and swiped a drip off the end of his nose.

'That's right, isn't it, Gracie. Them's the places the boy worked,' he said, and smiled at her like a child who'd just got all his spellings right.

He wasn't right, but she said nothing. He was simply naming the places that he and her mother had visited after the accident. Michael and Joseph had never worked close to home – not until Milford. They'd favoured places you couldn't find on the map; seas that ran off the edges of the atlas.

'I need to take the dogs out for a run,' she said and stomped out into the hall. She unlatched the front door while she was pulling on her wellies and let the air come swiping in. There was a commotion in her head that she couldn't quell. A trip to Whitby? She shook her head at the absurdity; a trip to the supermarket was as much as they'd managed in months and that required enough planning to get a whole bloody platoon on the road. She dragged her coat off the hook and stuffed her arms into it. She needed some time on her own; some time to think, to get her head straight. She was almost out through the door when Malin appeared.

'I'll come with you, Grace . . . if that's OK?'

Grace couldn't trust herself to speak. She grunted a reply and stomped out into the yard.

CHAPTER 18

They walked in silence at first: a shared pretence of quietly admiring the scenery. The slope in front of them was a thrill of colour; a glowing patchwork of late gorse and heather lit up by the slant of the sun like some jewel. Grace led the way, making an unnecessary fuss of the dogs. She could hear Malin trudging behind her but she didn't stop. She kept on, trying to piece together what it was she wanted to say, until she'd reached the top of the slope and the boulder that marked her usual turning point. She pulled to a halt and looked out over Cardigan Bay. It took her breath every time, whatever the state of the weather – or her thoughts: the knowledge that the place was part of her fabric and she was part of it: they were joined together by some invisible stitching. There had been a time she'd have scoffed at the idea: keen to move on, move away, but now – older and wiser, or maybe more fragile – she cherished it.

'Oh, wow,' Malin said. 'That's . . . that's just . . .'

Grace nodded. If her da had been with them, he'd have been full on with the tale of Cantre'r Gwaelod. Instead she folded her arms across her chest and concentrated on the sea. It was flat today – a sheet of dulled metal – a lid of sorts, she thought, that hid the things that lay beneath: layers of life she would never observe, threading and weaving their way above an ocean floor littered with lost ships, lost kingdoms – and lost people.

'We've lived a long time knowing Michael was dead,' Grace said eventually, and the words surprised her, slipping out of their own accord. 'So now, I'm afraid . . .'

Malin looked at her, waiting for more, but Grace couldn't go on. She imagined trying to explain herself to the girl. Telling her how the objections she'd constructed in bed the night before were nothing but a distraction – a careful skirting around the real crux of the matter, because her reluctance to make the journey was not fuelled by her love of routine – work, the farm, her da – but her need for it. Without it she had to face the invisible axis around which she now revolved – the fear that the lid she'd fixed over her own life, fastened down in the name of self-preservation – would give way. She knew if a search for Michael delivered only disappointment, it might not hold; she might not hold, but would be swamped by the things, the people, she kept hidden beneath it. The very thought had her in a sweat. She didn't know what to do and there was the truth of it – so her only option was to stick to her guns and do nothing.

'I'm afraid . . .' Grace said, keeping her eyes fixed on the sea. 'I can't take the chance of . . .' she paused to step over the lie, 'of disturbing my da's routine. We both know what happened when you did that, so if you want to go looking for Michael, you'll have to go on your own.'

'But surely . . .' Malin stepped forward and took hold of Grace's arm.

Grace shook herself free. 'No. You don't understand,' she said. 'You don't understand what you're asking me to do. I can't just take him off, there's too much to think about, there's . . . there's . . .' The pitch of her voice – the wild note of panic – brought the dogs milling round her feet. She yipped them forward and strode off after them before Malin had the chance to say anything else.

She could have left it there – should have left it there – but no, she pulled to a halt and shouted back at Malin.

'Give me one good reason,' she yelled. 'One good reason why I should leave all this,' – she gave a dramatic sweep of her arm – 'on the strength of an ancient postcard and a newspaper clipping.'

She regretted it the moment the words left her lips. She marched on, trying to shake her mother's image from her mind: the pursed lips; the solemn shake of the head; the words she was so fond of delivering ringing in her ears. *Tempting Fate there, my girl.* She stumbled down the hillside alarmed by her foolishness, praying that Fate wasn't listening.

Fate, it turned out, was not only listening, but was in a generous mood. She'd asked for one good reason – it gave her two.

The first was served up immediately: the soft ping of her mobile and a message to say the social worker was calling round 'for a chat' later that afternoon. The prospect chinked her armour, but not enough to change her mind.

Until the birds arrived.

She wasn't sure if she saw them first, or heard them, but she was at the gate, her agitation making a fumble of the latch, when the sky suddenly darkened and the dogs started barking. She looked up as a great flock of birds passed over her head. Hundreds of them, wheeling and crying out, black wings thrumming against the blue of the sky – they circled the farm once, twice, then, following some invisible signal, dropped, onto the roof of the barn. She gazed up at them, then hurried across the yard towards the house.

Her da was already at the porch door. 'They turned up just after you left,' he said. 'I've been keeping an eye on them till you came back. Starlings. Unusual. Don't usually stop here . . .'

'Yes, I know.' She squeezed past him into the hall, and made a meal of taking off her boots, trying to buy herself a bit of time because she knew what was coming next.

'I reckon your mother would have had something to say about them.'

'I know.'

She'd known as soon as she'd seen them, that her mother, without a doubt, would have given thanks and declared the birds a sign. More than a sign, because there'd been a deeper layer to her mother's beliefs, some vein laid down by chapel, no doubt, that allowed her to recognise – or request – the hand of divine intervention. It could magically transform an ordinary blackbird on the kitchen windowsill into the message she was waiting for, or a feather found in a certain spot (despite the fact they kept chickens) into the answer to some private question. This Grace had never been inclined to mock because, even at a young age, she'd found the notion somehow comforting: a God who not only cared but was willing to send signs and messages – if you were willing to see them.

Greg and his family 'didn't do God', so she'd buried that part of herself away – until Harry died when, to her amazement and relief, it resurfaced. She'd spend hours at the window, in the early days, watching for signs and learned that the jaunty stare of a robin at the bird table would grant her more peace than the tablets the doctor had prescribed; more closure than the murmured words of a bereavement counsellor.

'Have we still got Mum's books, Da?'

'Well, I should think so, hinny. I've not moved them – as far as I can remember. She had them on the bookshelf, didn't she?'

Grace left him in the hall, pushed open the sitting room door and went in. It was a space they never used: clamped onto the back of the house, its outside wall dug into the bank and bedrock, lending it a damp chilliness that defied any stove.

Grace shivered as she scanned the bookshelf then, before her da was tempted to join her, grabbed what she thought was the right book. *Birds in Mythology.*

She was at the kitchen table, studying the index when Malin walked back in.

'Have you seen the birds?'

'Gracie's just looking it up,' her da chirped. 'Like her mother used to do, isn't it, pet?'

Grace ignored them and turned to the page she was looking for. She read in silence for a few minutes, then sat back in her chair.

'Well, what does it say?'

'It says . . .' She pushed the book away and got up from the table. 'You read it,' she said, then went outside and sat down on the short bench beside the porch. The birds were still there.

She remembered the story because they'd done it at school. *The Mabinogion*: a communal groan in the classroom every time they had to get the book out. She'd not seen the relevance at the time and her attempts with it had been half-hearted. If she'd been more engaged, she might have already known the story of the princess Branwen – how she was imprisoned in Ireland and trained her pet starling to go and find her brother. And how that brother waded across the Irish Sea to rescue her. The details were tangled, she knew that, but there would have been no doubt in her mother's mind. She would have been up the stairs and packing their bags. She would have been down the road in a flash and wouldn't have settled until she'd rescued him.

Grace squinted up at the birds and thought of Michael. Her brother. Lost in the Irish Sea.

Branwen had sent one starling. She'd been sent a whole bloody flock.

CHAPTER 19

Half an hour later they were in the camper van and ready to leave.

Grace had made sandwiches, cobbled together a short message to the social worker, then presented her plan to Malin: a plan, she knew, that was something of a compromise – and not entirely honourable. *A weekend trip to search the places Da's indicated on the map*, she'd said, knowing, that in terms of finding Michael, the trip could yield nothing. It was a deception but it served them all well: it put the smile back on Malin's face, it gave them a short reprieve from the farm – and the social worker's visit – and it had her da scouring the under-stairs cupboard for his sun hat.

'It's November, Da,' she'd said, as she squeezed past his bony backside. She caught a glimpse of her own face in the hall mirror. There was no denying it – the thrill of excitement she'd felt when she phoned Shirley to explain they were going away for the weekend – that it was just the dogs that needed feeding – had put a smile on her face she couldn't quite wipe off. She'd gone upstairs for the cassette and cassette player and found herself gazing out of the bedroom window, conjuring up images of harbour-side cafés, the three of them polishing off tea and scones, fish and chips, enjoying the sea breeze, the whipping of rope against mast poles. She'd had to reel herself in because her mind had started painting pictures of its own – Michael smiling up at them from his boat, his eyes wet with relief, Michael walking towards them, his arms outstretched, Michael back at Velindre Farm chopping wood out in the yard . . .

'Ready, Da?' She'd settled him in the back seat of the van: lodged him between a pile of pillows on one side and a rolled-up duvet on the other. He stuck his two thumbs up at her. She smiled back and slid the door shut.

'Will he be all right?' Malin said.

'I think so. It might be good for him. The fresh air, the change of scenery, you know.' She wasn't as sure as she was trying to sound – the bruising on his face was a shock every time she looked at him and the stay in hospital had shaved flesh off him that he didn't have in the first place. On top of that he already had his afternoon face on: the tell-tale look in his eyes that said he was losing track. She lowered her voice. 'But we'll say nothing about Michael, yes? Like we agreed?' This had been part of the compromise: somewhere between the packing, the maps, the talking, her da had mislaid the reason for the trip and Grace had reasoned that the best way forward – the least confusing way – was to keep quiet about it.

'So . . . what's our first stop?' Malin asked.

Grace considered the road atlas on her lap. 'New Quay.'

'Should I put it into the satnav?'

'What? No. No need for that. Take a right when we get to the road, and then we turn left onto the A487.'

'What? Turn left and just keep driving?'

'Yes,' Grace said, and felt the thrill of excitement again. *Just keep driving.* 'Like Thelma and Louise,' she said and smiled. A road trip. No farm, no work – just miles of open road.

Malin put the van in gear. 'You're sure you're OK with this, Grace?'

'Yes, I'm sure . . .' Grace unwrapped the sandwiches, handed them round, then wound down the window and lifted her face to the breeze. She breathed in the salt tang of the air, considered the sea to her left, spangled under the autumn sun like a carpet of diamonds, and turned to look at Malin. 'I can't remember the last time I did anything like this. I feel so . . .' She stopped, struggling to find the right word. Excited? It was more than excited – and more than happy. She glanced at the envelope, propped like some small figurehead on the dashboard: a postcard, a newspaper clipping and a photograph. Not much to build your hopes on, she knew that, but the feeling in her belly was undeniable. 'Hopeful,' she said, and the word sent a wave of warmth from her stomach to her chest and loosened the crease in Malin's forehead. *Hopeful.* When had she last felt that? She found herself imagining they were going away for a week, a month – forever. She might have pushed it away but instead she wondered, as she glanced back at the farm, whether this is what Michael had felt the day he left home. Whether this sense of freedom and release was what took hold of him, what kept his gaze on the road ahead rather than looking back at the three of them, lined up and waving from the gate.

CHAPTER 20

Michael

The row with my da had been running a week or more and looked like it would never stop running: the two of us had hunkered down in separate corners and neither of us were willing to give an inch. Ma and Grace were sick of it and, truth be told, so was I, but I didn't know how to let the thing go. This was mainly down to having forgotten what the argument was in the first place, which didn't really matter because it was down, no doubt, to some fault or failing on my side. The real problem – the one neither of us could face – was that things had gone further than they'd gone before: Da and I had argued ourselves past the sarcasm and shouting and strayed into the uncharted territory of pushing and shoving.

Da pushed first, an exasperated lunge at my shoulder as he hurried me out of the way of whatever task was taking too long. Without thinking I delivered a sharp blow to his back as he stormed past. He spun on his heels and shoved his face up to mine.

'You sure you want to do this?' he said.

It was the smirk on his face that fired me up. 'Sure *you* want to, you mean?' My grin was pure show, but the adrenaline I felt coursing down my arms and into my fists was real enough. I waited to see what would happen next, alarmed by the realisation that what I wanted – really wanted – was to fight him; to give him a pasting. The look on my face must have warned him because he muttered something I didn't hear and took several steps back.

I don't know if Joseph's arrival at the farm a couple of weeks later was a happy coincidence – or something Da had quietly organised – but his sudden turning up was nothing but a relief: not only did he lighten the atmosphere (and Da's beer supply), but he set me thinking. It would be fair to say that I decided he was everything my father was not. They shared the same degree of strength, that was clear, but somehow Joseph carried his better: he was taller, more upright, walked with a longer stride . . . and he laughed more. In short, my head was turned, and several nights into his visit, I realised what I needed to do. We were all at the kitchen table, full of Ma's food, Da's drink and Joseph's tales of high seas and wild fishing ports, when Grace got up and started in on her poetry. I don't remember the words as much as the feeling that suddenly flooded over me. The feeling that my life on the farm was at an end and my real life – one at Joseph's side – was about to begin. At that point I didn't give a damn about leaving the farm or my da or, to a large extent, Grace. But my mother – I didn't know how I was going to break the news to her. It transpired, of course, that I didn't need to.

* * *

'Are you awake, son?'

It was a Sunday morning. Too early to be up, too early to be awake, but awake I was, and not ready to leave my thoughts behind. Thoughts that had kept me up most of the night. I'd tucked my camera beneath my pillow and, heady with romance and the prospect of the pictures it would capture, had lain with my bedroom window open, keening my ears for the sound of the sea. I imagined myself under a bright moon, my face tilted to the stars as Joseph and I charted some calm and watery course into a world of boundless opportunity and beauty. I imagined myself on deck, wind-whipped and tanned – Wales' answer to Jacques Cousteau or David Attenborough – angling my lens to take an award-winning seascape.

She sat down on the edge of my bed and put her hand on my shoulder.

'Tell me, son,' she said. 'Tell me what you're thinking.'

I rolled onto my back and stared up at her through the gloom of early morning. I knew the look on her face well enough – her knowing look – and I also knew what she was talking about.

'I'm thinking . . . I'm thinking of going, Ma . . .'

My ma was not one for crying, but she cried then.

'I knew it,' she said, wiping her eyes on the edge of my duvet. 'Knew it the moment I heard him.'

I nodded, because I'd heard the owl too and understood what my mother would make of it: a departure; a death or a leave-taking.

'I'm sorry, Ma. I can't . . . you know . . . me and Da, we're just . . .'

Then I said all the right things. I would keep in touch, I'd not be gone long, I'd be safe. And she said all the right things and put her arms around me.

And then she let me go.

CHAPTER 21

'We're nearly there, Da.' Grace swivelled in her seat and beamed at Jack. The journey had been nothing but marvellous: a journey she'd made countless times before, of course, but the fact that they would be travelling on, rather than simply returning to the farm, had put a new polish on it. It was like everything she saw had more of a shine. Even the traffic in New Quay.

'It's the dolphins,' she explained to Malin, as they crawled through the town for the second time, stopping every few seconds to avoid pedestrians. 'Aha, hang on, here we go . . .'

Malin pulled the van to a halt, put on her indicator and waited as the SUV backed out, then manoeuvred into the empty space. They climbed out into a wind that snatched the air from their lungs.

'Look, Jack, there's the harbour.' Malin spoke casually but Grace could see the hope on the girl's face as he scanned the small clutch of boats lined up at the quayside.

'Mmh, so it is. And there . . .' – he stretched his arm out and pointed over her shoulder – 'if I'm not mistaken, is the queuing spot.'

Grace felt her heart drop, she'd recognised her mistake as soon as she'd mentioned dolphins. 'No, Da, not today, we . . . I was thinking we could get a cup of tea and a scone. I don't know about you, but I'm parched.'

'A cup of tea? Nah! We've travelled all this way girl . . . ' – like they'd journeyed across the seven seas – 'we've got to go and see them.'

'It's not as simple as that, Da . . .' He wasn't listening. No, he was off, latched onto Malin's arm, the pair of them heading down the slipway to read the blackboard propped up on the small landing jetty. 'Dolphin Trips every hour on the hour.' She checked her watch. It was 2.45 p.m.

'Well, hinny?'

'It won't be here for fifteen minutes, Da. That's too long in this wind . . .'

'Fifteen minutes, you say? Righty-ho. Just enough time, I'd say, to visit the young chap over there.'

Grace followed the direction of his outstretched arm. 'You must be joking, Da. In this weather . . .'

He wasn't. Five minutes later the three of them were huddled on a bench shielding 99 ice-cream cones from marauding seagulls. Five minutes after that, he was back on his feet.

'Aha, here it comes.'

'Da, it will be freezing.'

'Nonsense,' he said, stepping closer to the jetty. 'It's got a roof, look.'

Sure enough the jaunty red boat puttering towards them had a small canopy roof covering some of the seats.

'Three tickets, is it, lovey?' The woman had suddenly appeared at Grace's side. Before she knew it, Jack was pulling money out of a wallet she didn't know he had and they were being helped down into the boat.

'I'm not so sure about this,' she said to Malin, as she tugged the life jacket over her da's overcoat. Pneumonia, she was thinking. Flu. *Social Services*. She took off her own scarf and draped it over his cap, then tied the ends under his chin.

He pulled a face at her and she laughed in spite of herself. Malin got out her phone and took a picture of the pair of them, and then they were off.

'Oh my goodness.'

It wasn't the speed that took Grace by surprise, but the sudden exhilaration she felt at being on the move. It was the same feeling she'd had at the start of their journey: a feeling of action, of possibility. The thrum of the engine set up a vibration in her chest as the boat bounced out across the waves and, as the land behind them disappeared, her reservations about the boat trip melted away too. By the time they'd rounded the point her face was numb and her eyes were streaming but there was a thrill in her blood she could barely contain, and when the pilot slowed the engine a notch or two and pointed ahead, she was up and on her feet, craning her neck to get a better view.

'Seagulls,' the pilot said, indicating a flock hovering in the near distance. 'They follow the dolphins, see? Pick up the scraps they leave.'

The boat rocked as a number of other people got to their feet to look. Jack grabbed Grace's arm.

'What's happening, girl?'

'It's the dolphins, Da,' she said, grinning, as the young man shifted gears and the boat sped off towards the hovering seagulls. 'We're going to see the dolphins.'

She looked down at him and the smile dropped off her face. The switch – whatever it was, wherever it was, had been thrown. His eyes were grey and lifeless. He pulled his arm away from her and swivelled in his seat and peered over the side of the boat.

'You'll not see them yet, Da.' Cajoling, like she might be able to reignite him.

'See what?'

'The dolphins . . .'

Jack gripped the edge of the boat and scanned the water.

'Dolphins?' he said, wiping his face with the back of his hand. 'It's not the dolphins I was looking for, Gracie . . . it was . . .'

Jack twisted back in his seat and studied the floor of the boat. He'd nearly said the wrong damn thing. He'd felt it as soon as they'd got on the boat. Felt it but couldn't catch hold of it. And then suddenly – not so much a door opening, but a feeling coming up from the water – it was there. *It was Michael, I was looking for Michael.* He'd stopped himself, but no matter – on it went – her school-teacher face. It wrong-footed him every time.

'You all right, Da?'

'Oh, yes.'

He put a bit of zip behind the words to throw her off scent, but *Michael* – his boy's name drifted loose from its moorings somewhere deep in his belly and lodged itself under his ribs. He pulled his coat more tightly closed and wrapped his arms across his chest.

'The dolphins,' he said suddenly. 'It was on one of his postcards.' The words popped out and took him by surprise. He didn't know whether he'd said the right thing or the wrong thing.

'Postcards? What postcards?'

Jack turned in his seat again, looked down into the water and tried to calm the uneasy swell rising in his chest.

'Da?'

'The postcards our Michael sent to your Ma.'

CHAPTER 22

Michael

Neither leaving home nor life at sea was the thing I thought it would be. Within weeks the sense of freedom that put the smug grin on my face when I quit the farm had disappeared. Acres of sea, I discovered, did not offer the same degree of security as acres of land. Instead of the familiar feel of earth beneath my feet or between my fingers I was at the mercy of a constantly shifting foundation. It left me with a sense of rootlessness, a quiet undertow of anxiety that rendered me clumsy and self-conscious. Joseph and the crew dined out on it; they celebrated my every mistake and ridiculed my every question. I took my camera out once – an error that earned me so much grief I immediately hid it. I packed it away in my case, wound it in layers of clothing and, together with my hopes for a new life, pushed it down as far as I could.

It would be fair to say I kept my word to my ma for long enough. Phone calls, at first: five-minute snatches in some quayside kiosk or noisy pub, the pair of us straining to maintain a connection despite the distance between us. Eventually though, I started to dread the calls. Not because I didn't want to speak to her, but because I couldn't bear it when the call ended. I couldn't bear the thought that I had taken myself so far from her.

Ah, the poor dab's homesick, Joseph sneered after catching me close to tears one evening. He thumped me on the back, told me to buck my ideas up and took me into a pub. *A double whisky will fix you, lad*, he said.

I wanted to tell him to fuck off, tell him I'd made a mistake and that all I wanted to do was jump in the truck and drive back to the farm. But the truth was, I was scared of losing face. And there was no truck, just the harbour, the boat, the endless sea. The realisation that I was trapped.

It turned out that Joseph knew what he was talking about that night because as the first whisky went down I felt a loosening in my head and in my guts: a gradual softening that, as the night went on, put a shine on the dismal pub, the tinny music scraping through blown speakers – and, for the first time since I'd quit the farm, a smile on my face. In short, it provided me with the escape I needed.

It became a joke: the speed at which I could get myself from the boat to our digs and to the pub, a joke I was happy enough to join in with because the thought of the first pint was what got me through each mind- and body-numbing day. I was becoming a real man at last, according to Joseph. High praise indeed because, in Joseph's books, a real man was the only thing to be.

The drawback, of course, was that real men don't phone their mammies every night. So I stopped. Instead I wrote letters: rambling, beer-fuelled accounts that steered clear of how I was feeling and concentrated on lavish, often fictional, descriptions of my days at sea. But as time went on that too started to dwindle and I switched to sending postcards: short, chirpy messages that told my ma nothing other than the fact I was still alive.

CHAPTER 23

A sudden commotion on the boat drew Grace's attention away from Jack. Several people were on their feet, holding cameras, mobile phones, smiling and pointing.

'OK, folks.' The young pilot grinned back at them and cut the boat's engine to a slow idle. 'The moment you've been waiting for.'

'Oh, Grace, look . . .' Malin was on her feet, her phone in front of her face. 'Oh my goodness . . .'

But Grace couldn't bring herself to stand up again. She fancied the boat was rocking too wildly from all the activity, the hilarity. Her da had all but disappeared into his life jacket. She held onto his arm, unsure if she was protecting him or he was protecting her.

'I'm cold,' he said. She slipped her arm around his back. 'And . . .' – he put a hand to his mouth – 'I feel a bit . . .' He could feel it rising – the uneasy swell in his belly and chest rising into his throat.

He gave a small hiccup followed by the sandwiches, the ice cream, the lot of it, down his front, his shoes, her shoes, the floor of the boat.

'Malin . . .' Grace shouted, but the wind snatched her voice away. 'Da, wait . . .' But he was on his feet now, and his shoes were already sliding in the pool of vomit. She grabbed for his arm and missed, managing instead to knock him sideways towards the edge of the boat. She grabbed again and caught hold of his coat sleeve but her scarf had slipped loose and the wind was whipping his hair across his face, into his eyes. He batted her away with his free hand until she could feel her hold on his sleeve slipping.

'Da.' But her voice was too small, her feet were sliding, she couldn't hold him any longer . . .

'Grace. Oh my God.' Malin suddenly darted forward and launched herself at Jack. She caught hold of the straps on his life jacket and yanked him towards her.

'Be careful . . .' Grace shouted, but it was too late: Malin stepped in the pool of vomit and teetered – Jack clenched in her arms like some unwilling dance partner – towards the boat's low rail.

Grace watched as if it were a dream: she saw her da's head snapping back, his dentures dropping loose, his arms flailing at his sides and Malin struggling to stay upright. She dived forward, aiming herself at the rail, landed, almost belly down on the wooden bench that ran around the edge of the boat, then swivelled herself round so that she was half sitting and wedged herself between her da and the boat rail. He crashed onto her lap.

'Oof,' he said.

She flung both arms around him.

'It's all right, Da . . . it's all right . . .'

'No,' he shouted, and tried to twist away. 'It's not all right. It was my fault. My fault the lad went away . . .' And, to her horror, he started to cry.

* * *

They'd had no choice – the mess of him – but to book into a B & B. Malin had volunteered to find a launderette and opted to sleep in the camper van, which made things cheaper, thank goodness, so Grace had booked a twin room overlooking the sea, which, she reasoned, as she listened to the soft humming coming from the bathroom, ought to have been something to celebrate. Instead it was taking all her resolve to keep from bundling him up and taking a taxi, a bus – anything – and fleeing back to the farm. Fleeing back to the safety of the place, the familiarity. Like she'd done years earlier.

'You all right in there, Da?'

He was, but she couldn't shake the memory of him almost pitching over in the boat, the look on his face, his tears; the thought that she could have lost him.

'Wouldn't mind a few more bubbles, hinny. Oh, hang on a minute . . .' He ripped off a loud fart. 'That's done the trick.'

'Father!'

'Sorry, vicar,' he chortled. 'I do beg your parsnips.'

She hauled herself off the bed and looked out of the window. He was back on form and that would have to be enough.

'Are you hungry, Da?'

'Wouldn't mind a bit of ham,' he warbled. 'If we've got time, mind. The clock must be ticking. Have you fed the dogs, girl?'

'Thought I'd go do it now,' she said. 'While you're having a soak. Is that all right?'

It was the wrong thing to say because before she knew it he was at the bathroom door, dripping and naked.

'Better get to my watching post, then.'

He streaked past, wiggled his bare backside at her, then plonked himself on the chair by the window. She grabbed a towel and wrapped it round him, wondering what he would say when he looked out and saw the sea and not the farmyard. He said nothing, merely looked at her over his shoulder.

'Go on then, girl. Get them done and then we can turn in and tune in.'

'Okey-doke,' she said, wondering how far to play along. She could chance slipping out into the street and waving up at the window. Maybe finding an open shop and some supper for them both? Or she could play it safe and simply wait outside the bedroom door for a minute or two. She did neither, because, while she was deliberating, her phone rang.

CHAPTER 24

'Hello?' She didn't recognise the number that flashed onto the screen. 'Malin?'

'Erm, Grace. It's Dan here.'

'Dan?'

'Halliday. Dan Halliday.'

'Oh. What's . . .' She put her hand to her throat. 'What's wrong?'

She didn't hear his answer because her mind had set off at a gallop down the path towards social services. What if someone had witnessed the sorry events on the dolphin boat and decided to report her? Or what if the landlady – who was visibly horrified at the state of Jack – had raised some kind of alarm?

'Grace?'

'Oh. Sorry, Dan. I . . . I didn't quite catch what you said. A bad connection . . .' She lowered herself onto the hard chair by the door.

'Ah, right. Yes. So. There's nothing wrong – well, not that I know of . . .' He trailed off with a small laugh and Grace heard the discomfort in his voice. 'I'm not at work, no . . . erm, I was just calling to, you know, catch up. After all that business with your father and all?'

'Oh. Well, thank you. That's very kind of you.' She waited for him to say something else but he didn't.

'So, how is he?' he said eventually. There was an awkwardness to the conversation that made her recall how he'd been at school – well-liked, but shy.

She looked across at her da, huddled up by the window, swaddled in the bath towel. 'Well, his face is a bit worse for wear, you know. A lot of bruising, but . . .'

'Who are you talking to, girl? I thought you were going to see to those animals. I've been sat here ages waiting . . .'

'Da. Wait a minute, I . . .'

But a minute was too long. He was up off the chair, the towel in a heap round his feet. She flung the phone onto the bed and charged towards him. 'Da, be careful, you'll—'

But she was too late. Down he went, bare backside in the air, his hands like two flailing starfish.

'Ouch.'

She didn't know what to do first – pick him up, cover him up, end the phone call. She pulled back the covers of one of the beds, scooped him up and slotted him in.

'Oh, no jamas?' he said, and pulled the duvet up to his chin. He was already fishing in his mouth for his dentures.

He plopped them on her hand, then hooked his specs off and passed them to her.

'They're warming by the stove,' she said. 'I'll go get them now. Stay in bed, yes?'

Her heart was going bareback. She grabbed the phone off the bed and let herself out of the bedroom and onto the small landing.

'Dan?' she said. 'Are you still there?'

'What happened?' he asked.

'My Da,' she said. 'He tripped up over the towel. He's fine. It's . . . it's nothing. It happens all . . .' She stopped herself from saying any more. *He's the police for God's sake*, she thought. *The police.*

'I'd better go,' she said. 'I have to get him to bed now.'

She winced at how desperate that made her sound. Sad and desperate. 'But thanks for ringing, it was really . . .' She paused, hunting for the right word. 'Really considerate.'

She hung up, counted to twenty to steady the shakiness of her legs, and went back into the room. He was waiting for her, his hair fluffed out against the pillow, his hands resting on the top of the duvet in anticipation.

'Is it time?'

'Nearly, Da. Ten minutes to go.'

Ten minutes. She reckoned that would be enough time to have a quick bath, brush her teeth . . .

'No cocoa?'

Cocoa. Pyjamas. Dentures. Specs. *The old routine.* It was never-ending, even now, away from the farm, from work. She shook her head: only hours earlier she'd been telling herself it was what held them together. She threaded herself beneath the damp sheets, turned off the bedside lamp and clicked the cassette player on. The hiss of the tape filled the room. She could hear him waiting for his cue; the intake of breath as he readied himself.

'Attention all shipping.' She heard the smile in his voice, the relief. She turned on her side and waited for sleep to come.

An hour later, unable to switch off despite her weariness, she was still waiting. It ought to have been the day's drama that kept her awake, but it was Dan Halliday. She had a pale memory of sitting next to him in History – or was it English? He'd had one of those faces that blazed red every time he had to speak up in class: two hand-sized patches that suddenly swamped his cheeks and made you feel embarrassed on his behalf. His phone call had puzzled her. She'd replayed it over and over, trying to catch hold of the reason behind it. She'd managed to boil it down to two options: it was either official and he was fishing for information on behalf of social services, or – and this was the option that unsettled her – it was unofficial and he simply wanted to talk to her. The thought had her out of bed and at the window.

She pulled the curtain aside and looked out. The tide was in: an inky wash that she could hear through the thin glass. What would she do, she wondered, if that were the case: if Dan Halliday simply wanted to talk to her, or ask her out, maybe? A quick coffee, a meal at the pub; what would she say? *I could, maybe, if...*

She watched as a car pulled up and parked by the sea wall. There was a short burst of radio as a man got out and went round to unlatch the boot. He looked up towards her window as if he could see her. She stepped back and let the curtain drop back in place.

I could, maybe, if... She would get no further than that and she knew it. It was the 'ifs' that did it: if she didn't have her da to consider, or the farm, or money, or work. The real 'if' was something entirely different, of course: starting over with another man would require confidence and courage, and she no longer had either. She went into the bathroom and studied herself in the mirror: the new sag of skin at her jaw, the lines that streaked out from the corners of her eyes towards her greying temples. She opened her pyjama top and studied the stretch marks that striped her belly. They were an ugly disfigurement according to Greg – and her own fault. But she loved the way Harry had left his mark on her. A signature of sorts.

She'd been about four or five months pregnant when Greg followed her into the bathroom one morning and suggested she needed to start charting her weight gain – or more accurately, that he was going to start charting her weight gain. She'd laughed. 'Hey, I'm not on the team,' she'd said, then realised her mistake because, at that point, he was spending more time on the bench than the pitch. He'd scowled at her, pulled out a small notebook and nudged the bathroom scales towards her with his foot.

'You're not serious, Greg,' she'd said. But he was. He treated her pregnancy like a project: accompanied her to every class, appointment, scan; monitored her diet, weight, sleep – but despite all his best efforts, she still managed to disappoint him.

'Are you still eating chips on the way home?' he'd asked one evening as she got in from a late shift. She'd known it was coming: she'd managed to gain half a stone in just over a week. The following evening he was waiting for her outside the hospital when she finished. *So sweet*, her colleague said, and she'd smiled and nodded, then realised he'd not brought the car. They'd half marched the two miles home, Greg in the lead and Grace trying her best to keep up.

It had turned out to be the story of her life, really.

CHAPTER 25

Michael

I'd been working with Joseph and the boys for several months and every bit of me was raw: my hands, my feet, my nerves. I was a slow learner, a fucking retard according to Joseph, but I'd learned one thing quickly enough: there was no pleasing him. My drinking seemed to be the only thing he approved of, which was ironic, because he had no idea where drink had once led me or where, I knew, it might lead me again.

* * *

I'd been fifteen, almost sixteen. Our annual family visit to the Royal Welsh Show. My da had been in a foul mood all day because Ma had messed up our hotel booking and we were reduced to borrowing a tent and setting up camp, something we'd never done before or, according to him, would never bloody do again. I'd taken myself off for a walk and, drawn by the steady beat of music drifting over from the nearby bars, crossed the bridge and wandered into town.

The high street was jammed: people and music spilling out of every pub and bar. I pushed my way into the first place I came to and, reasoning it somehow looked more legitimate, ordered myself a couple of pints, then threaded my way back out onto the street. I'd been there maybe five minutes when a group of girls shouted over to me. I downed my first pint and wandered across, smiling the smile that girls always seemed to like and, for the first time that day, felt myself relax. It was halfway through my second pint that I suddenly got the feeling I was being watched. I lowered my glass, turned round and saw a bloke leaning against the pub wall. He took a drag on his cigarette and nodded at me. He was tall, older than me and on his own. I nodded back and turned to resume my conversation. Try as I might, though, I couldn't concentrate. I couldn't shake the feeling that he was still watching me. I casually repositioned myself and glanced over. His eyes met mine instantly, a slight lift in his eyebrows that sent a sudden thrill through my body: a thrill I'd never felt before. I soldiered on with the story I was relating until I could stand it no longer. I downed the rest of my pint and turned to face him.

He smiled, pushed away from the wall and said he was going to get a bit of fresh air. And just like that, as if some final puzzle piece had slipped into place, I knew what I wanted to do. I watched for a minute or so as he pushed his way through the crowd. And then I followed. I followed as he crossed the road and cut through the large car park that sat on the edge of the town. The broad path that ran alongside the river was lined with trees but in the light that filtered over from the street I saw him look back at me. He walked a little further, then stepped off the path into the gloomy edges of the riverbank.

It was glorious. For five minutes it was glorious: a feeling I had no words for as he reached for my hand and guided me towards an iron bench that overlooked the rushing water. Without saying a word he pushed me gently down and knelt in front of me. I took a deep breath as he unbuckled my belt, then, as his fingers grazed the bare skin of my belly, leaned my head back and gazed up at a night sky that had never looked so clear. All I knew, as the stars swirled above me, was that this was the thing I'd been waiting for: this feeling of electricity, like every cell in my body had suddenly been switched on. Then, just as suddenly, it was switched off.

'Sshh.' In one quiet move the bloke got up off his knees and slid onto the bench beside me. I listened, but other than the sound of the river and my own thumping heart, I could hear nothing. And then, out of the darkness, a rough shout.

'Matt?'

The bloke beside me put his finger to his lips.

'Oi, Mattie . . . what you doing down there?' A different voice – some laughter.

'Get ready to run,' the bloke whispered.

'What?'

'Come on, Matt. Put her down. Taxi's coming in ten.' More laughter.

The bloke beside me stood up, 'Keep quiet,' he whispered, and started walking towards the path. I slowly re-buckled my belt.

'Oh. Who the fuck are you, then?' I couldn't hear the low, rumbling discussion that followed, but the rising aggression was unmistakeable. 'So who's that down there with you? Oi . . . you down there . . .'

I should have taken my bloke's advice and made a run for it, and this is what I thought afterwards, when I was lying back in my sleeping bag, jittery with adrenaline and humiliation. But beer and naivety had got the better of me and before I knew it, I was off the bench and on the path. There was a moment's silence, I remember it hanging heavily, then some kind of throaty laugh followed by a swift punch to the mouth that had me floored and staring at the stars again. The next thing I knew I was on my feet, yelling at the top of my voice, swinging blind punches, raging like a madman for what had been stolen from me. The more I fought, the more I wanted to fight: there was a fire blazing in me that I couldn't seem to extinguish. It fizzled out quickly enough, however, when the police suddenly turned up and hauled me back to the campsite.

I counted myself lucky that my da had sunk several pints because the police officer's explanation – that I'd got into some trouble over a boy – went straight past him. He simply scowled at me and sent me to my sleeping bag, which was a win on all fronts for me because that was exactly where I wanted to be. I lay in the dark, fingering the sharp edges of a broken front tooth, tentatively working the crack out of my bruised jaw and thinking hot thoughts of what might have been.

CHAPTER 26

'Shirleeee? Are you there, girl?'

Grace pushed the bathroom door open and peered out.

'No, Da. It's me. Grace.'

'Oh. Right. Well, what time is it, girl? I'm parched.' He clambered out of bed and padded towards her. The bruising on his face had spread overnight into a sickening swatch of yellow that trailed the side of his face almost to the jawline. Getting him to shave would be a total non-starter.

'Any tea in that pot?' he asked, oblivious to the fact they were in a strange room.

She could have made tea there – boiled the travel-size kettle, used the measly provisions on the formica tray – but the room felt suddenly claustrophobic.

'Why don't you get your togs on and we'll go down and look.'

She was poring over the OS map when he trotted back out.

'Plotting your escape, hinny?'

She looked over her shoulder at him. He'd put his shirt on over his jumper and tucked the lot into his trousers.

'You'd better not go putting ideas in my head if you want that cup of tea,' she said, then re-folded the map and slid off the bed. 'I think it's Aberystwyth today, Da. Do you remember it?' She waited to see what he'd come up with. There'd been no further mention of Michael but if anything was going to bring him back, it would be Aberystwyth.

ATTENTION ALL SHIPPING

* * *

Michael's phone call had come out of the blue. He was in Aberystwyth, and he had a surprise for them, he said, as if his call wasn't surprise enough. It had been over five years since he had left and she was alarmed at how nervous the thought of seeing him again made her feel. One reason was because she knew her memories of him had been rose-tinted by his long absence. They'd got on well enough, but farm life didn't allow for a lot of free time or small talk and, if she was honest, apart from occasionally seeking her out at school, Michael had largely ignored her. The other reason was more complicated; although she and Greg weren't married or even engaged then, she was aware (and at that point, proud) of the new shine their relationship had put on her and was half-hoping, half-dreading Michael would recognise it too. Her ma, of course, giddy with the thought of him being so close to home, had loaded the Land Rover with half the food in the pantry and off they'd gone.

The surprise, it turned out, was twofold: half good, half bad. The good part was that he and Joseph had decided to set themselves up as independents – he was back to take collection of their new boat. They followed him to the marina, her mother marvelling at the size of him, and gazed down at the new purchase. Grace knew nothing about boats but fancied it had something of a jaunty look about it. *Red?* her da said, like there was something amiss about it. Michael ignored him. He clambered down onto the shining deck and took hold of the tarpaulin that was draped across the prow. *Ready?* he shouted, squinting into the sun. *Ready*, her ma had shouted, and he'd tugged the tarpaulin away – and revealed the boat's name. *The Laughing Girl*, her da had muttered, *why the hell do you want to call it that?*

He found out soon enough.

Michael leapt back onto the quayside. He had a bottle of champagne in one hand and a photograph in the other. Her mother's eyes filled with tears when she saw it. *Remember it, Ma? Remember that night?* Her mother had simply nodded her head, then passed the photograph over.

'Oh . . . it's me.'

'It's you, Sis. Do you recognise it?'

She'd recognised it straight away: Michael had snapped it during Joseph's visit to the farm. He'd leapt up from the table and captured the four of them: Joseph's hands scribing the air as he related some wild tale; her da's elbows on the table, his face like thunder; her ma gazing lovingly into the camera and herself, face shining with tears, in tucks of helpless laughter.

'It was the night you did your poem. Do you remember?'

Grace remembered, because, for a short while, she had blamed that poem for Michael's departure. Joseph's visit to the farm – as unexpected as it was – had seemed nothing but a tonic. He'd stayed a small handful of nights and, as far as she'd been concerned, lit the place up like it had never been lit before: One evening, the five of them still creased and wiping their eyes after some tale he'd been telling, her da had suddenly called on her to take the floor. *Do your eisteddfod poem, pet,* he'd said and, instead of shaking her head, she'd agreed.

'Sea Fever' by John Masefield, she'd announced, like she was on the stage at the village hall, then launched in.

I must go down to the seas again, to the lonely sea and the sky,
And all I ask is a tall ship and a star to steer her by . . .

Her eyes scanned the small audience as she worked her way through the verses – but came to rest on Michael. He was staring at her with a look on his face she'd never seen before. She'd taken it for admiration, but next day, when he'd suddenly upped and offed, she'd feared that he'd taken the words as inspiration or, worse still, that they'd furnished him with some kind of message or answer. It had been a relief to hear her ma and da arguing over the circumstances of Joseph's visit a couple of days later.

It was while they downed the champagne – passing the bottle round (like bloody heathens, according to her da, who declined on account of being in charge of the driving) that Michael slipped in the second half of the surprise – the half that had her mother subdued and tight-lipped for days after: he wasn't staying in Aberystwyth, he was putting to sea at high tide and meeting Joseph in some Scottish place they'd never heard of. They'd waited with him, marking the slow rise of the water as it climbed the sides of the harbour, then watched as he navigated the boat out of her mooring. She'd thought he was waving at them, until the glint of the sun caught his camera lens. *Wave*, her mother had shouted. *Wave*. And they did: hands in the air, stiff-legged and awkward, they waved back – not knowing they would never see him again.

* * *

'So, Da. Do you remember Aberystwyth?'

Jack gave his head an exaggerated scratch and pulled his Stan Laurel face.

'Nice statues,' he said. 'On the seafront.'

She nodded and raised a quizzical eyebrow.

'Pebbles, not sand and . . .'

She waited, a smile hanging on her lips like some kind of encouragement.

'And . . .' His face had clouded over. 'Starlings . . .'

'Starlings?'

'Yes,' he said, and his eyes lit up again. 'Under the pier.'

He thrust his hands into his trouser pockets and went to the window. 'Are they there now?'

'No, not now. But they'll likely turn up later.'

The thought sparked some excitement in her. Would they, she wondered, be the same starlings that had set her off on this journey? Might they even – and, despite its foolishness, she didn't dismiss the idea – be waiting for her: looking down from giddying sky to make sure she'd not turned back.

'Come on then, Da,' she said, holding out her elbow. 'Let's go find that tea. Malin will be here in a minute or two . . .'

* * *

Malin was still sitting on the sea wall gazing down at the beach. The cold damp of the stones was seeping through her jeans but she made no move to shift herself. She was stalling – rehearsing what she was going to say to Grace; preparing herself for what Grace was no doubt going to say to her.

The day before had been a disaster and she'd spent half the night re-living it. Jack had been moments, inches, away from toppling into the sea and that was her fault. Her responsibility. She'd been so caught up in the excitement of it all: the dolphins, the whipping wind, the laughter – the journey that might lead her to her father. They'd saved Jack, yes, but it was afterwards – after the hasty return to shore, the young skipper scooping Jack out of his seat and setting him down on the quay – that the horror of it had really hit her. She'd watched as Grace peeled Jack's life jacket off, her voice a soft murmur over his low moaning. And Jack, shivering like a wet dog, his teeth chattering, gazing around like he'd just woken up.

It's all right, Grace kept saying. *It's all right.* But all she'd had been able to think of was how close they'd been to falling in:

how, for a second, she had closed her eyes, pulled Jack more tightly to her chest, and waited for the shock of cold water.

She looked at her watch: late already yet she still didn't move. *Meet us in the dining room for breakfast*, Grace had said, but eating was the last thing on her mind. Her stomach was still at sea. All she could think of was apologising to Grace for disrupting her life, then offering to drive back to the farm. After that . . .

She didn't know what came after that.

* * *

But the morning did not unfold as Malin had imagined: she walked into the dining room of the B & B with a long face and her rehearsed lines, to find Grace and Jack laughing and joking with the young waitress.

'Aha, here she is,' Jack said, as she approached the table. 'Our own Grace Darling. Sit down, sit down.'

Malin took a seat and looked at Grace, hoping for some clue as to what Jack was talking about, but Grace simply rolled her eyes, then, as Jack cleared his throat, said with a smile and a raised eyebrow, 'Brace yourself.'

'Right then,' Jack said, with a dramatic lick of his lips. 'Sit down, girlie. Sit down and pin back your ears because have I got a tale for you.'

With that he straightened the collar of his shirt and, in the manner of some TV host, took the floor. 'Now then . . . Grace Darling was the bravest lass you could ever meet, which is why, of course . . .' – he paused and gave a theatrical sweep of his arms – 'I named my own daughter after her.'

Then, after another eye-roll from Grace, he folded a serviette in half, lined it up with the edge of the table and picked up a butter knife.

'Right then,' he said, tapping the serviette with the knife. 'Here we have the Northumberland coast, and here' – he made a group of the salt and pepper shakers, a couple of sugar sachets – 'we have the Farne Islands. This one,' he dinged the pepper, 'being Brownsman Island, and this one,' he tapped the salt, 'being Longstone Rock, which . . .' he leaned over and twirled the salt shaker, 'in 1838 – the year of this tale – had a lighthouse. Still has, in fact . . . erm . . .' He glanced over at Grace.

'And the lighthouse keepers . . .'

'Oh yes, that's it.' Jack licked his lips. 'The lighthouse keepers were William Darling – and his daughter, Grace.'

Malin sat back in her seat at that point, let go of her rehearsed speech and tuned in to what Jack was saying.

'So . . .' He picked up a piece of dry toast, and placed it on the table in front of her. 'The SS *Forfarshire* . . .' he put his finger on the piece of toast and steered it past the salt and pepper, 'with sixty passengers and crew.'

Malin nodded.

'Unfortunately,' he said, bringing the toast to a halt, 'at some point during the night a storm struck up and they got into difficulties – so the captain decided to turn back . . .' he steered the toast towards the pepper, 'to seek shelter at the Farne Islands.'

On and on he'd gone. Malin hadn't wanted him to stop. It was his voice, the look on his face – it had picked her up and before she knew it she was with Grace Darling: she was pulling on the oars as towering waves broke over the small boat, bending her back against the gale-force wind and rowing the mile of hellish water that separated her from the survivors who were stranded on the perilous Harcar Rock.

'But how . . . ?' she'd whispered, after he finished.

'Courage, girl,' he said, patting her hand. 'Good old-fashioned courage. Like you on the boat yesterday. Thought I was a goner. Would have been if it wasn't for you two.'

She glanced over at Grace, who was dabbing at her eyes with a serviette.

'Anyway,' he said, taking a bite out of the SS *Forfarshire*. 'Isn't it time we got cracking? Those starlings won't wait.'

'Starlings?'

'Aberystwyth,' Grace said. 'He means the starlings at Aberystwyth.'

CHAPTER 27

The Grace Darling rendition knocked the stuffing out of Jack – like Grace knew it would. They stopped briefly at Aberaeron, Grace doing her best to ignore the anticipation on Malin's face as they trudged past the shops. Grace loved the place: the contrast between the square neatness of its harbours and the belligerence of a surf capable of tossing rugby ball-sized rocks against any car brave enough to use the car park. It did nothing for Jack, of course – some distracted nodding as Malin took him by the arm and walked him along the quayside – and then the slow walk back to the van. Grace climbed onto the back seat with him and tried to perk him up with a crossword, but he was asleep before they'd got back onto the A487.

'That was an amazing story, wasn't it?'

'Mmh?'

'Jack's story. About Grace Darling.'

'Oh. Yes. One of his party pieces.' Grace stretched out her legs and dabbled her feet in a patch of sunlight. She looked out of the window – the passing scenery was a blur of sea and sky, a skim of bare hedges and faded grass – quietly acknowledging that it was a bloody well-timed party piece considering she'd been up half the night bemoaning her own lack of courage.

'Have you always lived at the farm, Grace?'

The question came out of nowhere. Grace sat up. 'Pardon?'

'The farm,' Malin said. 'Have you always lived there – you know – with Jack?'

'No, I . . .' *Always lived at the farm?* Grace folded her arms across her chest. She didn't know whether to laugh or cry. Is that how she came across these days? Like some spinster daughter. 'I came back a few years ago.'

'Oh, right. Of course.'

Of course. Like she understood. It was an easy enough fix, Grace knew that: she could tell Malin her story, spill the beans, get it all out in the open. But she'd lost the knack of conversation and there was nothing easy about her story. Nothing at all. Where to begin for one thing – at the point where everything started going wrong, or the point when her whole world tipped and she'd slid off?

'I came back because . . . because my marriage broke up . . .' There. She'd said it. Said enough. She didn't need to say anything about Harry.

Grace sat back and considered the passing scenery again – the glittering expanse of Cardigan Bay, a couple of big tankers on their way to Milford, a small fishing boat trailing some distance behind them. She traced its path for a minute or two, then set the road atlas aside, made a great show of yawning and closed her eyes

It had already been dark, the day she left Greg; too dark to make such an impulsive journey. She'd left him in the kitchen – smirking at her attempt to take in what he'd told her about his affair – and gone up the stairs. When she came back down, ten minutes later, trailing two suitcases, he'd burst into laughter. *Don't be so ridiculous, Grace.* He'd followed her out into the drive, his hands on his hips as she loaded up the car, shaking his head like they were in some sitcom scene; *you don't even know how to use the bloody satnav.* Those were his parting words as she pulled out of the drive and drove off like a woman who knew where she was going. She'd driven for hours, following some internal map that had delivered her, eventually, to the farm. Her da was at the kitchen table, catching the late *Shipping Forecast*, when she'd stumbled in through the porch door, her face wrecked with tears. *My little homing pigeon*, that's what he called her.

Next morning she'd remembered nothing of the journey: she'd woken up and found herself there. A mixture of grief and shock, the GP said, when she'd tried to explain herself, but the words had slid off her like she'd been coated with glass. She'd taken to her bed – her old bed – and stayed there, lulled by the sounds of her da downstairs or out in the yard; the television; the radio – the *Shipping Forecast*.

She'd stayed there for weeks trying to piece herself back together. She'd had to give up in the end and accept that too much of her was missing.

But now – she ignored the voice that told her she was clutching at straws and concentrated on finding the thing that would keep hope afloat in her – she had the chance to replace some of what she'd lost: Michael, maybe, and if not, this quiet young woman. Harry's age, more or less. Not a replacement – never that: but compensation, perhaps. Family.

CHAPTER 28

Michael

It's hard to say whether the experience at the Royal Welsh Show changed my course, or if it simply revealed it, but it became increasingly obvious to me that it wouldn't be a course I could steer at home. I started to feel hemmed in. Not just by the farm, but by everything that came with it: my family, Young Farmers Club, sheep sales, the *Farming Times*. It was a bubble I no longer fit in and it was suffocating me. My ma's solution to my increasing moodiness was to get myself 'a nice girlfriend'; easy enough to arrange because girls liked me. So I spent a full year playing the part: stringing along one poor girl after the other, trying to ignore the tug of a different path. And then Joseph arrived: a chance not only to escape *where* I was, but to explore *who* I was.

Within months, though, I learned that the company of hard men and the steel hull of a trawler were a damn sight more confining than green fields and sheep; that being on the sea was not the same as being bordered by it. Joseph ran a tough crew: there was some leader-of-the-gang swagger to him that the men seemed to admire, but put the fear of God in me. There was no escape from him: his voice, whether was booming out across wild water, a rowdy bar or our shared digs, was the constant backdrop to my every waking and sleeping hour. It stole from me any hopes of following a different path until, one night, my luck suddenly changed.

We were in some forlorn quayside bar. *It's a tough place*, Joseph had said, as we were going in. *So keep your fucking mouth shut.*

I managed well enough, until some bloke, who looked as out of place as I felt, edged up to the bar and struck up a conversation with me. He was explaining how life at sea was ninety per cent boredom and ten per cent terror when Joseph suddenly appeared. He slapped his hand down on the bar and said, 'What's going on here, then?'

'I . . .' I didn't know what to say. Joseph looked like he was ready to take the bloke by the scruff of the neck and throw him outside.

'I don't know what you mean,' the bloke said, but he was down off his stool and walking backwards. He shot me a quick look as he grabbed his coat. 'Nothing's going on.'

'In that case,' Joseph stood up and put his hands on his hips, 'why don't you just fuck off out of here.' He looked around at the rest of the crew. There was nothing kind about the smile on his face. 'Fuck off to your poncy boat and leave us *men*' – he spat the word out – 'to our drink.'

The man did as he was told, and quickly, barely out of the door before the place erupted into laughter. Joseph turned to me, his face full of glee. 'You need to watch out for blokes like that, Micky. Poncy wee shites, the lot of them.'

I raised my glass, as if I agreed, took a long swig of beer and joined in the laughter. But for the rest of the evening my mind was elsewhere, and try as I might I couldn't keep it away from thoughts of the bloke sitting on his boat, alone. I fought against it for an hour or more, but eventually the pull was too much. I sank the rest of my pint, told Joseph I was heading off, then, looking back over my shoulder the whole way, set off to the marina.

I walked quickly, keeping to the edges and the shadows, telling myself I was just curious, just going to take a look, to offer an apology, maybe, for Joseph's behaviour – all the while knowing it wasn't true.

Afterwards I left quickly. I walked back to the small guest house we were holed up in and let myself into the room I shared with Joseph. Our digs were the same as always: devoid of any trace of comfort or homeliness, thin duvets and thinner curtains, cold and tepid running water, a storage heater that would have found a home in a museum. I peeled off my clothes as quickly as I could, got into the narrow bed and then lay, willing sleep to come. Somewhere in the distance a clock was chiming. It was a lonely sound on that dark night and brought with it thoughts of home and family: the Rayburn ticking in the corner, the dogs settling down in the barn, my ma squaring the place up before turning in for the night. It was loneliness that had taken me to him, that's what I told myself. Loneliness and the need to feel something other than the constant sting of salt water, the burn of wet rope, the tilt of the sea. But I'd known as the bloke had gently peeled off my clothes, as he'd lain down on the bunk beside me and put his hands on me, known that what I was really there for went beyond sex: what I craved was the human contact, the warmth and the reassurance that I was not lost.

CHAPTER 29

Jack was not asleep. He was thinking, or, more accurately, he was trying to net a thought. It was the slippery bugger kind of thought, the kind that slid quite happily from the back of his throat to the end of his tongue and then, the moment he opened his mouth, disappeared into thin bloody air. He'd tried all his usual tactics but it wasn't interested. Grace Darling had sparked it off, there was no doubt about that, but she wasn't helping him now. He'd retraced the story in his mind, hovering over each part, but none of it was helping.

He pictured the painting they had at home: Grace steering the half-submerged boat with one oar while her father sits behind, straining to pull them through the roiling waves. The boat is tilting, half submerged even, but her face, turned to look over her shoulder, is calm. She's wearing a thin cotton dress, a small waistcoat and neckerchief. She's merely a girl. He searched it for clues. It gave him nothing. His mind was an empty sheet of paper.

The emptiness had been the start of it: blank spots that suddenly appeared, like someone had been at his head with an eraser. A senior moment, ha ha, he'd joked and knuckled down, determined to beat it, quietly devising ways to put himself in the winning seat – like sneaking up on a question from behind, snatching the answer before it dropped from sight, or pretending he'd not asked a question at all, then waiting patiently and scooping up the answer when it drifted to the surface. It had served him well for a time until, one morning, things took on a whole new turn: he'd woken to find himself out in the yard in his pyjamas and, try as he might, he had no idea when or how he'd got there. That would have been bad enough, and he would have got away with it if Huw hadn't suddenly appeared with the milk.

'All right, Jack?'

He'd braved it out, spun some tale about a sick ewe, then remembered as Huw's pick-up pulled away, that there were no ewes. They'd gone to the sheep sale long back. Well, there was a bit of humour to be had out of the situation so he set his mind to dwell on that rather than the feeling in his head. Empty, he might have said, but there grew to be more to it than that. The doors in his head might have been the worst of it: the tantalising way they suddenly opened, then slammed shut before he was halfway through, but no – the worst part was the constant feeling that he was lost.

Jack opened his eyes a crack and tried to get his bearings. Grace was sitting beside him, he knew that much, the familiar scent of her. Like a ewe with a lamb he was. He let his head droop slightly to one side so he could look at her. The dim light of the farm kitchen was a damn sight kinder than the sun coming through the van window, that was for sure: at home he told himself she was coping – they were coping – but here, the tired greyness of her was less easy to ignore.

'All right, Da?'

This is how she was: tuned into him like he was a radio channel; like she knew what he was thinking before he'd bloody thought it.

He yawned and rubbed his eyes but said nothing.

'Are we here?' It was out of his mouth before he had a chance to stop it. He looked out of the window for a clue as to where *here* might be, and slumped back against the seat and waited – hoped – for some inspiration.

'We certainly are.'

Grace slid the van door open as soon as they came to a stop. A blast of sea air hit Jack in the face. He gulped it down, eased himself off the seat and clambered out into the cold.

'Aha,' he said, mostly to himself, because there, staring down at him, was the only clue he needed. He angled his head back and shaded his eyes and *whoosh,* the door in his head flew open.

'Aberystwyth,' he said with a nod, and watched as Malin climbed out of the driver's seat.

'What do you think, girlie . . . ?' He pointed his bony finger at the topmost statue – an angel, her feet barely touching the plinth beneath her, as though she had just landed or was just about to leave.

'She's lovely, Jack, lovely . . .'

'Victory. That's what she's called. And . . .' He stood back and smiled at the statue at the foot of the plinth. 'That one there, the one with the . . .' he gave a theatrical cough, 'with the bosoms . . . is Humanity. As you can imagine, she caused quite a stir back in the day.'

He'd always thought there was something of a ship's figurehead about her – the wild and windswept hair – but Wenna had disapproved and favoured the angel. That was chapel for you.

'We used to eat our sandwiches over there,' he said, turning away from the statues. But neither Grace nor Malin were listening: they had wandered off from him and were leaning against the rail, staring out at to sea, so, buoyed up by the cleverness of himself, Jack left them to it.

* * *

Malin's eyes were fixed on the horizon. Grace had barely spoken to her since her poor attempt at making conversation, even though there was surely so much they could be talking about, should be talking about. She considered phoning Vee to let her know she'd taken the camper van – but at best that would pique Vee's curiosity and take her down the road of trying to explain why. At worst it would prompt the apron-string lecture and leave her feeling more at sea than she already did.

She'd made the mistake once of asking her mother what she'd been like as a small child. She'd been hoping for a couple of anecdotes – something rose-tinted and homely, maybe – but Vee had laughed. *A complete pain in the backside*, she said. *Always round my feet, clutching onto my bloody apron strings. I was forever trying to shake you off.* Malin had been horrified. She'd lain in bed that night conjuring up pictures of Vee striding away as she clung on, bobbing behind like a small balloon. She'd woken in a sweat halfway through a dream in which Vee was rifling through the kitchen drawer, looking for the scissors.

After that the apron strings became a regular part of her life, as if Vee, suddenly reminded of her child's weakness, doubled her efforts when it came to instilling the need for independence. University, of course, had been part of it.

'Go on, shoo,' Vee had said, laughing, when she'd dropped her outside the halls of residence two months earlier. No words of comfort; no last-minute advice; definitely no tears. So Malin had lugged her stuff up to the room that her mother hadn't even bothered to look at, nodding at the clumps of other new students, parents, brothers and sisters.

'Welcome to your next big adventure,' Vee had shouted, as she drove off and Malin had smiled, waved even, trying to ignore the sudden tug and snap of something inside her. The realisation that she was not just alone – she was adrift.

'I think I'll have a bit of a walk along the beach. Stretch my legs, you know . . .' She let the words trail off: Grace had either not heard her, or she wasn't interested. *Have you always lived at the farm with Jack?* She cringed at the thought of having said it: how the words had implied some sort of dependence, some lack. She could have tried to explain herself – told Grace about the string of shoddy places she and Vee had lived and how she'd always longed for a proper home. She could have said that although things had gone wrong with her marriage, at least Grace had had a home to return to. And a father.

CHAPTER 30

Grace watched Malin picking her way across the beach. She might have told her that the pebbles were murder to walk on and the sea at this end was hopeless for swimming: the tide didn't so much come in as throw itself at the shoreline; a daunting wall of roiling water, waist high and impenetrable, that spun everything in its path, then dragged it back out to sea. She might have told her a lot more than that, of course – given the girl a bit of reassurance rather than serving up short answers and long silences. *You need to start letting people back in, Grace.* That's what a counsellor had once said. She'd smiled back, tight-lipped, and said nothing, and somehow the habit had stuck.

She glanced back at Jack. He'd waylaid some poor woman walking her dog. Her first thought was to hurry over and intervene but she stopped herself: his face was all action like it had been at the breakfast table, full of enjoyment and tale-telling. The woman too, by the looks of it: she was gazing up at the statues, nodding and smiling. There was no denying that, despite the bang on the head and the close call on the dolphin boat, he was better than he had been for weeks. This store of information flooding out of him: Grace Darling; Victory; Humanity – postcards. It was as if the change of scenery and the company had dislodged something in him. Was it possible, she wondered, as she watched him – his one hand holding his cap steady against the wind, the other aloft, indicating some sculptural detail – that he might yet hold information about Michael; that the right word from her could loosen some deep pocket of memory and bring something meaningful, *useful*, bobbing to the surface?

* * *

'Well, I do believe Mr West might approve of this.'

Jack was stretched out on the pull-out bed, his arms arranged on top of the sleeping bag, his elbows pointing east and west.

Grace shuffled herself away from the sharp points of him and into the hard edge of the cupboard.

'Three little sardines, that's what we are,' he said, turning his face to her. He reached out his hand and tapped the underside of the bunk above them. 'Ahoy there, Jim lad. All right up there?'

'I'm fine, Jack,' Malin replied. 'Tired, though.'

'Tired? A girl your age, tired? Well, let me tell you . . .'

Grace tuned out. He'd been at it all day, apparently. She lay, in the half dark, waiting for a chance to steer his thoughts towards Michael. Eventually he shut up and she, worried that he'd drop straight off, jumped in.

'Do you remember that time we went camping, Da?' she said, aiming at nonchalance.

'Pardon?'

'Camping,' she said. 'You and Mum and me . . . and Michael?'

He shuffled onto his side, and peered at her.

'Camping?'

'Yes, you know . . .' She trailed off. It wasn't going to work. She'd racked her brains for something to say, some shared memory that involved Michael and might turn a key in the right door, and the realisation that there were so few to choose from had left her unsettled and, if she was honest, bewildered. Her early life on the farm had always felt so busy, so full, but on closer examination it had been nothing but a rolling calendar marked by the seasons or the weather. Family outings, celebrations, holidays – that was something that other people did.

'In a tent, you mean? That kind of camping?'

She wasn't sure what other kind of camping there was.

'Yes, in a tent. On the showground, remember?'

He wasn't going to fall for it. She could hear it now, as she posed the question: some artificial, rehearsed quality to her voice. He didn't say anything, and she wasn't sure if he was thinking, or if he'd dropped off to sleep.

It had been 1987. Her mother had messed up the booking for their usual Royal Welsh Hotel and the four of them had ended up braving the campsite. It had started badly and ended even worse.

We look like a troupe of bloody travelling gypsies, her da had announced, before taking himself off to the sheep pens, leaving the three of them gazing forlornly at several bags of canvas, an assortment of enamelware and billowing rain clouds. God knows what he was expecting on his return – her mother rustling up sausages on some prairie campfire, maybe, or the three of them strumming tunes and toasting marshmallows. As it was, he came back – half-cut from the members' tent, thankfully – to find them waterlogged and cross-legged in the porch, sipping cold soup and staring out into the rain. After ten minutes of her ma's tight-lipped silence – a sure sign a row was brewing – Michael had announced he was going for a walk and she had slipped quietly to bed. Next thing she knew, all hell broke loose.

'Do you remember, Da?'

'Nah.'

'Michael got into trouble . . .' She left it open-ended, an invitation – but nothing. 'The police brought him back, remember . . . ?' Silence.

Michael – they found out later, had taken off into the town. There he downed several pints of Carlsberg and got into a fight. He was fifteen.

'He was always getting into bloody trouble, was Michael.' She pricked her ears up and waited. And waited.

'Yes, he was,' she said eventually.

'What?'

'Trouble,' she said. 'Our Michael – always getting into trouble . . .'

'Yes,' he said, then creaked over in the bed to look at her. 'Do you know what I've just remembered though?'

She lifted her head off the pillow and readied herself. 'What, Da? What do you remember?'

'Those bloomin' green sleeping bags. Four peas in a pod, your mother said. Hah. Do you remember that?' Then he wriggled onto his back and tucked his arms tight by his side. 'But now we're three little sardines, that's what we are. Three little sardines . . .' And off he went again.

* * *

Malin was trying her best to tune Jack out but every time she drifted towards sleep she was snatched back by his endless chatter. She was more than tired; she was exhausted. It was the sea air, of course, and the fact that Grace had asked her to watch Jack while she'd gone to do a bit of shopping. She had agreed, picturing a slow amble around the harbour followed by a nice long sit in a café where she could ask him more about Michael. Instead, as soon as Grace disappeared, he'd taken her by the arm and, with all the enthusiasm of a tour guide, marched her the full length of the promenade.

He was still at it now: Grace humouring him, but obviously as worn out as she was, and Jack chatting away like a teenager on a sleepover. Eventually – thankfully – she heard Grace butt in.

'Hang on, Da,' she said, 'I think it might be time.'

Malin raised her head off the pillow and peered over the edge of the bunk. *Is it time?* That's what Jack had asked her when she'd taken him off in the camper van, and she hadn't had a clue what he was talking about.

But Jack barely broke stride. 'What?' he said. 'Time already? Nah! We're still on our adventures. You need to start enjoying yourself, Gracie.' Then he took a quick breath and set off talking again.

Malin watched as Grace sat up and leaned over the front seat. There was a soft click followed by whirring static, and then the van filled with the sound of music. It was a lilting, waltzing tune that shut Jack straight up until, as it ended, he announced, in a voice deeper than his own, 'Attention All Shipping.'

Malin lay with her eyes closed, listening. She knew about the *Shipping Forecast* like she knew about *Gardeners' Question Time* or *The Archers*: it was on Radio 4 and therefore not really her thing. Their thing: Vee denounced anything to do with the BBC as propaganda. But this, this recital, this – she could barely find the words to describe it – was like poetry. It brought to mind boats out on a dark sea, dim bulbs lighting cramped cabins, men hunched over, hoping only for good news. *Michael.* Had he, she wondered, heard the words that heralded his own fate; staring out at rising waves hoping for his own Grace Darling? Or had he survived? Despite what Jack and Grace and Vee knew – or thought they knew – was he out there now, listening in and, just as she was, hoping for good news?

'Now then, are you ready, girl?' Jack's voice cut through the lulling recital. 'Here you come. Shannon, Rockall, Malin . . .'

Her heart caught at the sound of her own name on the lips of the announcer. *North westerly five to seven, occasionally eight, backing south westerly, wintry showers, moderate becoming good . . .*

'Oh yes, good news indeed,' Jack said, as the announcer finished. 'Good news indeed.' There was a loud click as the machine turned off. Then silence. Malin lay still, waiting for Jack to chime up again, but no – after a couple of minutes the sound of his soft snoring drifted up towards her. She turned on her side and let it lull her to sleep.

CHAPTER 31

Michael

It was a Saturday night. We were in a Stornoway bar; our pockets full of payday cash, bellies full of beer and our mood somewhere between elation and euphoria.

'Your first proper wetting, boy,' Joseph had said, as we filed through the low doorway, steaming like a band of gladiators fresh from the fight. I sank my first beer still standing at the bar and felt the relief as it washed the salt brine out of my mouth and poured its magic into my agitated blood, thinking if that had been my first wetting, I wanted no part in a second.

The day had started no different to any other: we were away as the reluctant November sun was just showing itself, our course set towards the scratch of pink that tipped the horizon. A couple of hours later we were fixing to shoot the nets, all four of us silent and intent on our individual parts, when Joseph suddenly ducked out of the wheelhouse. He had the radio in his hand. His mouth was a grim line. We knew his news before he delivered it, because behind him the sky was already darkening: a sepia tint that put a sick wash over the sun, and over me.

'Severe gale nine coming at us, boys,' he hollered. 'Look sharp. Let's get her ready.'

I watched as the rest of the crew slid into a routine I neither knew nor recognised – or had any part in – and braced myself for what was coming. The storm arrived within minutes. It hurled itself down on us like some wild and furious berserker, shrieking and howling, a torrent of rain that swamped the air until all there was left to breathe was water. Down it came, a thundering flood that set the deck drumming and rendered me half blind and half drowned. I stood firm as I could and tried not to show my alarm as the sea rose up like some dark and formidable foe and rammed the boat with such thudding blows surely she would break in two. The engine, a thing of pure folly, I realised, as I clipped myself onto the rail, was our only ally. I shrank back into the safety of my hood, closed my eyes and concentrated on its soft puttering heartbeat.

* * *

'Quiet up now, boys.' The barman was looking over. He had the TV remote in his hand. 'Time for the news . . .'

'Oh Christ,' Joseph whispered. 'Not the *Antares*.'

A hush descended as the newsreader shuffled the papers on the desk in front of him and started in on the story. We didn't really need to listen, because it was all there in his tone of voice; the injection of BBC gravity; the way his lips shaped themselves round the words. He sat in his warm and comfortable London studio and – with an expression he surely perfected in the mirror – told us that the missing fishing trawler, the *Antares*, had been found and raised, that three bodies had been recovered, one was still missing. And then he introduced the weather.

I got up from the table and went outside. Three bodies had been recovered, one was still missing. I lit a cigarette and thought about that missing man. I imagined him alone in the water, shouting for his crewmates, or swimming, maybe, striking out for land he could not see. I gazed up at the stars and wondered if he might be doing the same: straining his ears for the sound of rescue; the drone of a ship's engine; the whirring approach of a helicopter.

'Y'alright there, mate?'

I turned to see where the voice had come from and saw a bloke leaning against the wall just a few yards from me. He was tucked well back and almost obscured by a thicket of ivy that clung to the pub wall, as if he was sheltering from the weather – or hiding. I rubbed the back of my hand across my eyes and took a drag on my cigarette.

'Fine, mate, yeah.'

'Don't think I've seen you round here before.'

'No.' I couldn't place his accent, but he wasn't Scottish. I tossed the cigarette and stubbed it out under my boot, thinking I'd dodge back inside and tell Joseph I'd had enough of the day, that I was getting away to my bed, but the bloke pushed himself away from the wall and came a bit closer.

'You in the business then?'

'What business is that?'

The bloke put his head on one side and smiled at me. I could have feigned ignorance: wished him a good night, turned my back on him and gone in to Joseph, but instead – my *wetting*, the *Antares*, the missing man – I smiled back.

'Thought so,' he said. 'Come on . . .'

I followed him to a small car park at the back of the pub. He had a van. He wanted it straight away, outside, leaning against the cold metal, but I shook my head. As desperate as I was for the feel of him, of anyone, I knew Joseph and the boys were only feet away.

'Inside,' I whispered, as his hands fumbled with the buttons on my fly, then waited while he shook a bunch of keys loose from his pocket and opened the back doors. He swiped a pile of tackle to one side with his arm and cleared a space big enough for us to climb into. It didn't take long, or I didn't take long. There was a short tussle with the buttons on my jeans, and then I was moaning into his ear, urging him on as my head emptied of everything except the feel of his cold hand round my warm dick. He pulled me close afterwards, a moment's tender embrace that brought sudden tears to my eyes, then guided my head down. I closed my eyes and savoured the salty taste of him, the feel of his hands in my hair. Afterwards we leaned awkwardly against each other for a few moments, the yearning I'd felt for him only minutes before already dissolved. I climbed out of the van and hurried away without looking back and was still fumbling with my fly as I rounded the corner of the building, and walked straight into Joseph.

'What the hell are you doing out here?'

I turned my face away from him so he wouldn't see the colour burning my cheeks.

'Same as you, I suppose. Getting some air, having a piss . . .' I stopped and held my breath as the bloke from the van walked past. He acted like I wasn't there; turned his collar up and nodded at Joseph, then disappeared through the pub door.

'Who was that?'

'What? I don't know who the fuck he was, do I? Some random bloke.' I tried to keep my voice even, but I could hear it rising. 'Anyway, I was just coming in to find you. I'm off back to the digs. I'll see you in the morning, yeah?' I pulled my hat down over my ears and walked away feeling a tremble in my legs. How reckless I'd been, how close I'd come to being caught.

CHAPTER 32

Grace lay as still as possible bearing in mind her knees were braced against the wall and Jack's elbow was wedged in her back. Her head was too full to sleep: there was much to think about, and it wasn't all about her da – or Michael.

Her shopping trip had gone better than she'd expected. She'd left her da with Malin and set off with half a plan: to pick something up for their supper, to stock up on TENA pads, then to get a newspaper and find a sunny spot in a café. That's where she was when Dan Halliday phoned again.

'Oh, Dan. Hello.' She'd pushed the crossword to one side and tried to compose herself. He was obviously driving because the signal, and his voice, kept fading in and out. Eventually he'd rung off, saying he'd try again later, leaving her staring down at the newspaper, her heart racing, because, despite the bad connection, she'd managed to get the gist of things: he was hoping they might meet up at some point. She'd picked up her bags, gone back out into the street and into the first clothes shop she saw.

'You look like a different woman,' the shop assistant said, as Grace stepped over her pile of discarded clothes – the sweatshirt and saggy jeans – and emerged from the changing rooms. She looked in the mirror and saw it was true. She'd taken the girl's advice and opted for a pair of wide-leg trousers the colour of a slate roof. She'd teamed them with a boxy clean-cut white T-shirt. Grace tucked her hair behind her ears and looked in the mirror. 'Gosh, I look so . . .'

There were many things she might have said: so different, so elegant . . .

'I look almost like I used to look,' she said and it was true. The work on the farm, looking after her da – she was probably in better shape now than she'd ever been. There was some satisfaction in the thought.

'So . . . what about these?' The girl held out a pair of short, black leather boots. Grace slipped them on and considered her reflection.

'I'll take it all,' she said, giddy with recklessness, and swung out of the shop like a woman in a TV advert. As she walked back towards the seafront, she tilted her face to catch the last of the day's sunlight and considered the conversation she'd had with Dan Halliday. He wanted to meet up. She caught a glimpse of her reflection in a shop window and, to her amazement, thought – well, why not?

She'd spotted Jack as she approached the promenade. He was leaning on the railings, chatting to a couple of young women. Malin was sitting on a nearby bench – something of a droop about her.

'He's still full of beans, then?'

'Oh, Grace. I hardly recognised you. You look . . . lovely. But yes.' Malin hauled herself straighter and nodded. 'He's been like this all day.'

'Sorry,' Grace said, except she didn't exactly feel sorry – even though the girl was clearly worn out – and she'd just blown half her salary on a single outfit.

The two young women moved off from the railings and Jack came trotting over.

'These starlings,' he said, craning his neck back and squinting at the sky. 'I reckon they're a bit late.'

Grace shuffled some space on the bench and sat him down between her and Malin. He lasted for a minute or so then sprang to his feet. 'Do you think they've gone somewhere else?'

'Sit down, Da. It's not quite dark enough yet, is it? Dusk is when they come . . .'

But he was up again, heading for the railings. He shaded his eyes with one hand and studied the struts of the pier.

'Maybe they're already under there, maybe . . . ah, watch out. Here we go.'

Grace followed his gaze. She gave Malin a gentle nudge and got to her feet. She'd written a poem once about the Aberystwyth starlings. *Staccato dots against the tired sky, the memory of Africa fluting your wings . . .* 'Very thought-provoking', the teacher had written in the margin of her English book, and given her an A minus. She'd been disappointed because the poem hadn't been intended to provoke thought – but feeling. She considered the look on Malin's face as the birds gathered and guessed that the girl would have understood this.

'I wonder . . .' Malin started. 'Do you think they might be . . . ?'

'Our starlings?' Grace said, and tipped her head back to watch the show. 'I'd wondered the same thing too.' The words hung in the air between them.

'They're glorious,' Malin said. An old fashioned word for such a child, Grace thought. The kind of word her mother would have approved of. And she was right – there was something undeniably glorious about the starlings, about a performance whose only function seems to be the expression of joy and community.

Grace adjusted her position carefully and closed her eyes. She had lots to think about: the starlings, Dan Halliday, herself for a change. Her da was right; they were on their adventures. She decided to take a leaf out of his book and start enjoying herself.

CHAPTER 33

Michael

The sinking of the *Antares* dealt Joseph a heavy blow – one that he struggled to right himself from. Although he masked it at first with bad temper and drinking, it was apparent to me that he'd lost something. Over the next couple of years he developed a reluctance to take on certain work, throwing out half-baked excuses about the condition of a boat, a member of a crew, a weather report. No work meant no pay, of course, and one by one the rest of the crew left us behind. Joseph was unperturbed: he had a good cache of money banked and was happy to sign up for one-man jobs that kept him close to shore. There was something of a silver lining in this because it gave me the opportunity to sign up for trips that took me away from land, and him, for weeks at a time. I became obsessed with pushing the boundaries – on the atlas and within myself – and it would be fair to say my youth and strength and growing expertise earned me a reputation on both counts.

I was happy. For the next three years this is what I told myself. I was seeing the world, my bank balance was tipping towards six figures and, when we docked at some far-flung port, I was free to do whatever the hell I wanted with whomever I wanted. The problem was I *wasn't* happy. I'd gone past the quest for warmth and human contact and become addicted to the thrill of the initial encounter, but each liaison – and there were several, both with men and women – left me scooped out and hollow, circling the dark empty place inside me, wondering if I would ever find the thing – or person – to fill it.

I was on the way back from a long tramp in Norwegian waters, weary of travelling and weary of myself, when the idea came to me. If I'm honest, it wasn't so much an idea as a feeling, a feeling that instead of pushing forwards all the time, I needed to stop. At night, when the day's gutting and freezing was done, I lay in my bunk trying to visualise a different life – one which allowed the freedom I required, but offered the sense of purpose and meaning I seemed to have lost. I don't know if it was the throb and drone of the engine that worked something loose in me, because my thoughts drifted unexpectedly towards home, to Cardigan Bay, and the farm – the place I'd so willingly quit five years earlier – suddenly acquired a new and magnetic pull. By the time we docked in Scotland I had the bare bones of a plan that seemed, at the time, to offer the solution I was searching for. I would find work closer to home, something that would allow me to see my ma and to maybe patch things up with my da. To my surprise, it was Joseph who added the finishing touches.

'A proposition,' he said, when he tracked me down in the bar. He'd found a boat. We could buy it between us and set ourselves up as independents. I listened with one ear only, ready to decline, until he mentioned the fact that the boat was docked in Aberystwyth.

CHAPTER 34

By the following afternoon Grace's new leaf was already fraying at the edges. Despite her best intentions the trip was feeling less like an adventure and more like an endurance test. Although Aberystwyth had started well – the starlings, the three of them tucked up in the camper van, Jack so full of beans – it had ended badly.

Grace had woken suddenly in the night, alerted by a noise she couldn't make any sense of. It wasn't until her da suddenly swung his legs off the bed that she understood it was the sound of him unzipping his sleeping bag.

'Hang on, Da.'

It was too late. As soon as his legs were free he got to his feet – and hit his head on the metal rail of the bunk above them. He let out a yelp and sank back onto the bed. Grace scrabbled round for the light switch, praying that he wouldn't strike up. But strike up he did – a thin wail that had Malin peering down at them.

'What's the matter?'

'It's nothing,' Grace said, running her hand over Jack's head.

Go back to sleep, she might have said, but the unmistakeable tang of fresh urine told her there was going to be no chance of that. It took them over an hour to get him settled again, if settled was the right word, because he sank into a sleep so deep that she spent the rest of the night worrying that the bang on the head had been more serious than she realised. It didn't help when he woke next morning with a lump the size of a small egg on his forehead, looked out of the van window and asked where the farm had gone.

Nonetheless they'd soldiered on – left Aberystwyth to the students and the starlings and headed up the coast, neither of them acknowledging the half-hearted feel to the day. Grace told herself it was the lack of sleep that was getting to her – or the self-inflicted hole in her budget – but it was more than that. It was the look on Malin's face as they strolled the harbours and quays of Aberdovey, then Barmouth – the hopeful expectation that Grace knew could be met with nothing but disappointment. The secret futility of their quest weighed heavy on her: heavier still the feeling of shame at having devised it. She allayed the urge to confess her duplicity with the knowledge that their trip was almost over: Abersoch was their last port of call, and then they could turn the van round and head home.

* * *

Grace didn't hear the police siren straight away. She'd been asleep, or half asleep, lulled by the road, the sun and the fact that Jack was snoozing. It was the soft *whoop* and the awareness that they were stopping that brought her round.

'Wha . . . ?'

'I don't know.' Malin was angling the van into a lay-by. 'They suddenly came out of nowhere. I'm just pulling in to let them pass. Oh, bugger . . .'

Grace turned in her seat and watched as the police car pulled up behind them. Its light was still flashing.

'Did you . . . ?'

'No, I didn't do anything, I . . . oh, God. They're getting out.'

'What if . . . ?' Grace couldn't finish – the words stuck like an unchewable lump at the back of her throat. *What if social services have reported me?* It was illogical; she'd left a message, she'd told them what she was doing. *But what if they hadn't got the message? What if they declared her unfit? What if they took him away?* An image rose unbidden – her alone at the farm, her da distraught, not knowing where she was. She'd no sooner dismissed it than the next thought landed hot on its heels: *What if it's Dan?* As implausible as this was, the thought had her straightening her top and checking her hair in the passenger mirror. She glanced at Jack, who was still asleep, clicked open her door and stepped out to watch as the two officers approached. Neither of them was Dan Halliday.

'What's wrong?' Malin asked. 'Have I done something wrong?'

'Well, that's what we want to find out, Miss, so – if we can just ask you a couple of questions . . .' The officers led Malin away from the van and left Grace hovering gratefully by the passenger door. She had been seen, obviously, but seemed to be of no particular interest to them – at least not at that point. One of them started walking back to the squad car, talking into her radio, then, a couple of minutes later, Malin – accompanied by the other officer – reached into the van and got her phone off the dashboard. Grace edged closer but it was impossible to hear what was being said. It was evident, however, that Malin was in tears.

'Excuse me.'

Grace spun round. 'Oh. Yes. Hello. Is everything all right?' She raised her hand to her face as if she were shielding it from the sun and wiped the sweat from her forehead.

The policewoman was barely a metre away – notebook and pen at the ready. 'If I could just take your details, Madam . . .'

'My details?'

'Yes. Name. Address. That kind of thing.'

Grace attempted a smile. Her top lip stuck to her teeth. The policewoman narrowed her eyes, took a step back and considered the van. 'Is everything all right here?'

'Yes,' Grace said. Too fast. 'Sorry, but I was asleep when you pulled us over. I've just woken up, I'm a bit . . .'

'Have you been drinking, Madam?'

'No. Of course not. I was asleep, I . . .'

'Any . . . ahem . . . any medication?' The officer made a great show of breathing in deeply.

Cannabis, Grace thought. That's what the bloody woman was insinuating. *Cannabis*. 'Absolutely not,' Grace said. 'I'm a farmer, for goodness' sake, and a . . .' *And a carer*, she was about to add, but stopped because there was no need to add further complications. Which was ironic because that was the moment Jack suddenly woke up and started shouting.

The policewoman's eyebrows shot up. 'Sarge,' she said – in a louder voice than necessary, Grace thought. 'Need you over here, Sarge. Got a bit of a situation . . .'

'A situation?' Grace spurted. 'It's just my father. Here . . .'

She slid open the side door and there he was, trousers round his ankles, urine streaming down the insides of his thighs. He looked at her – then at the policewoman – and burst into tears. She knew what he was going to say before the words were out of his mouth.

'Please . . .' his two hands were clasping the front of his sodden underpants, 'please can we go home now.'

Grace glanced at the policewoman and realised there was no way it was going to be that easy. She opened her mouth, then – unable to identify any point of the story that might be the best place to start – shut it again.

'I need the toilet, Gracie,' her da piped, shuffling from one foot to the other.

'I'm sorry,' Grace said, but I'm going to have to deal with this – so if you can just give us a minute . . .' Then, without waiting for a reply, she climbed into the van and shut the door behind her. She was just easing him into fresh clothes, still racking her brains for some acceptable explanation, when she heard a car start up – and drive away. She peered out and watched as the police car pulled back onto the main road. A few seconds later, Malin – white as a sheet – slid open the door.

'Grace. I'm so sorry. I . . . my mother . . . they thought. Oh God, what a mess . . .'

She plonked herself down in the doorway and started to cry. To Grace's amazement her da levered himself down beside her and took hold of her hand.

'There, there, girlie,' he said, stroking it like it was one of the farm cats. 'It'll be all right, you'll see. You're home now and I'm here. Everything will be all right . . .'

Grace took a step backwards. Ten steps backwards. To the night she turned up at the farm alone – her at the kitchen table blind and choked with tears, unable to say why she'd come – her da quietly stroking her hand, telling her he'd make everything all right. And he had. He'd rescued her, set her back on her feet and – as hard as it was now – she knew she never wanted to be without him. They were a team. Neither of them would survive on their own.

CHAPTER 35

Michael

Aberystwyth. It was the closest I'd been to home for years. My ma had wept when I called to say I was coming. She left the phone dangling in the hall while she shouted outside for my da. The excitement in her voice creased me in two. I imagined him looking up from his work and ambling across the yard. *What's all the fuss, girl?* I heard his gruff, *oh*, and then the clatter as she picked the handset up.

'Ten o'clock, Sunday – we'll be there, son.'

'By the statues,' I said.

'By the statues.'

* * *

I looked at my watch. Just gone nine. I'd arrived the day before – dropped the hire car, done the business with the boat, then booked into a seafront hotel. I slept with the windows open, breathing deep as the air blew in from Cardigan Bay: breathing deep as I pulled off the covers and let it play over my bare skin. I closed my eyes and imagined it washing me clean: wiping away any evidence that might alert my ma and da to the sorry reality of my life.

I wasn't prepared, that's what I told myself afterwards. Not ready for the moment they arrived, the three of them lined up on the bench seat of the Land Rover, necks craning this way and that as they crawled past, searching out a parking space.

They didn't see me, which was just as well because the mud on the wheels was the undoing of me. Mud from the farm. The tears were there before I knew they were coming. Followed by a shout. My ma's voice. Christ. It was the hardest thing I'd ever done, getting myself off the bench and walking towards them, drying my eyes on my sleeve as I took in the difference the years had made: my ma thinner and older, her arms stretched wide as she fair galloped up to me; Grace laughing and smiling, less . . . farmerish; my da, trailing behind, his face hidden as he tugged his flat cap down against the wind.

'Now then, lad . . .' I untangled myself from my ma and Grace and smiled at him.

'All right, Da?' I gave him a cautious smile. We'd barely spoken a word since I'd left home. Always too busy to come to the phone, or out on the farm. I wondered, as I took in the lines on his face, whether, like me, he felt the need to mend the rift that had lain so long between us. I had my answer soon enough.

'Where is he, then?'

I thought he meant the boat. 'She's over there. In the harbour.'

'I don't mean the bloody boat, boy, I mean Joseph.'

Boy. I wanted to tell him I was no boy but a man; to tear off my jacket and show him the muscle and sinew the sea had wrought in me. But the thought that he might see right through me stopped me.

'Oh. He didn't come . . . he . . .' The truth was that when Joseph had presented his plan to me, he'd held certain aspects of it back: he didn't tell me about the woman he'd met, nor about the contract he'd got lined up. Both of which would tie us firmly to Scotland. 'He's working,' I said. 'Anyway . . . follow me . . .'

The boat was a show all of its own. The gleam of the sun set off her colour and shine just right. I'd got everything ready: the tarp draped across the prow, the champagne cooling in a bucket, the photograph in my pocket. 'Wait there,' I said, and climbed down onto the deck. I'd planned a few words but decided against them. I whipped off the tarpaulin and revealed the lettering that ran along the prow.

'The *Laughing Girl*,' my da said. 'What kind of nancy-boy name is that?'

His words took the smile straight off my face.

'Jack! For goodness' sake, man. Ignore him, son . . . honestly . . .'

'Does Joseph know?'

Does Joseph know? The question had me grabbing at the handrail. I studied his face for some evidence of knowledge. A sly upturn at the corners of his mouth, maybe, that told me he wasn't referring to the name of the boat, but to the secret part of me I thought I'd kept hidden.

'Jack!' My ma nudged him in the ribs.

My da folded his arms across his chest and glared at me, waiting for my reply.

'Well . . .' Joseph didn't know about the name. I'd figured that seeing as I was paying the lion's share of the boat, the naming of her would be down to me. 'Here . . .' I slid the dog-eared photograph out of my pocket and handed it to my ma. 'Here's how she got her name.'

My ma pulled her glasses to the end of her nose and peered across the top of them. 'Well, I never! Oh, son . . . that's marvellous. Grace, my girl – you're famous!'

It was the only photo I had of them. I'd taken it the night before I left home – the sudden realisation of what I was going to do had me up and out of my chair, snapping the four of them as they sat at the kitchen table: Joseph's hands outlining some tale; my ma gazing into the camera; my da looking less than amused; and Grace – my quiet, unassuming sister – with her head tipped back, face damp with tears, laughing fit to bust.

'So . . . how long are you staying, son?' my ma asked.

I waited until I had the cork out of the champagne bottle before I told her I was leaving at high tide.

CHAPTER 36

Jack was expounding his theory of silver linings. He'd started well but now he was completely in the woods. Grace didn't mind because, other than an occasional nod of agreement, she was free to ponder the events of the afternoon. He was right, of course; being stopped by the police might have seemed like a stormy cloud at the time, but it had brought with it the most unexpected of silver of linings: Vee.

Malin's mother, it seemed, had returned from Calais early, found her camper van missing and – Bristol being Bristol – jumped to the obvious conclusion and reported it stolen. It had been spotted in Pembrokeshire, followed up the west coast of Wales and apprehended just outside Pwllheli. That was the stormy side. The brighter side came several cups of tea and a couple of phone calls later.

* * *

'My mum would like to talk to you . . .'
'Oh. Well, I . . . erm . . .'
It was the last thing Grace had wanted, but Malin handed the phone over and promptly walked away. 'Hello?' she'd said, with no clue as to what she was going to say next, then realised with some relief that she didn't need to worry – because Vee was fixed to do all the talking. And talk she did: she started with a tart, *I don't know who the hell you are but*

what's all this nonsense about Michael? followed with a deluge of information that had Grace scrabbling in her bag for a pen and paper, and ended with a brisk, *Right, put Malin back on.*

'Sorry,' Malin said, as she put the phone down. 'What did she say to you?'

Grace ignored the question. She was still trying to make sense of what she had just been told. She smoothed out the notes she'd managed to scribble down and looked them over.

'You told your mother what you were doing?'

Malin nodded.

'And?'

'She wasn't impressed. "Total fucking folly", to be precise.'

'And what did she say? About Michael?'

Malin hesitated. Her mother had started off with a 'water under the bridge/let sleeping dogs lie' sort of angle and ended with a rousing 'on your own head be it', which had left her afraid to probe any further – she'd simply handed the phone over to Grace and walked away so she wouldn't see her crying.

'She said what she's always said. It was an arrangement . . .' the word put a hitch in her voice, 'it was an arrangement between "two mutually consenting adults" . . . and he's dead.'

'And the photograph?'

'She . . . she kind of floundered . . .'

Grace nodded because, underneath Vee's indignation, she'd detected a fair degree of floundering too: some loose-edged feel to what the woman was telling her; a vagueness around dates and places; a rehearsed quality to the way she reeled them off – like she was reading out a piece of fiction.

'Did she tell you anything useful?' Malin asked.

'She said she met him in Ireland – in the late nineties.'

'At Malin Head?'

'She didn't say. She veered off a bit . . .' Grace looked down at the notes she'd made and realised that Vee hadn't veered off as much as simply changed the subject. 'I asked her if she'd seen him after that and then . . .'

Then Vee had exploded into a theatrical performance.

'Of course I saw him after that. Isn't that what this . . . this charade is all about. Finding a daddy?' She'd spat the words out. 'Christ. She's so fucking needy.'

'But . . .' Grace found herself speaking up for Malin. 'Needy?' she said. 'What's so needy about wanting a father?'

But Vee wasn't for stopping or listening.

Grace had held the phone away from her ear and waited for the woman to wind herself down. 'So what about the photograph, Vee?'

'Oh, for God's sake. The bloody photograph. It was a one-off. I . . . I took her to see him – *once*.'

'Took her where?'

'Christ almighty, does it matter? The man is dead.'

'It seems to matter to her.'

'I can't remember . . . some seaside place in Yorkshire . . . anyway, I can't imagine why this is all so bloody important to you. Who the fuck are you?'

'I'm Grace James. Michael was my brother,' Grace said. 'And as far as I know, he died in 1999. That's two years before Malin was born.'

CHAPTER 37

Michael

I knew, as I manoeuvred the *Laughing Girl* out of the harbour, that buying her had been the right thing to do: from the thrum of her engine beneath my feet, to the light and supple path she steered through the water, there was a solid steadiness about her that told me I'd made the right decision. This was more than I could say for myself.

Although she did her best to mask it with a cheery and detailed inventory of everything she'd brought from home – pies, cakes, cheese, eggs from the yard, socks, a sweater, a hat, a stash of writing paper and envelopes – my leave-taking near tore the heart out of my mother. The sight of her sobbing from the quayside almost had me forsaking the agreement I had with Joseph and turning back. It would be no lie to say that, in the years that followed, there were many times I wished I had. Instead, as if I were merely off on some short jaunt, I pulled out my camera and, with one hand on the wheel, leaned out and took a photograph of the three of them. *My family*, I thought, then rounded the harbour wall and steered away from them.

It was clear from the get-go that, when it came to our new venture, our partnership was not going to work. There were flies in the ointment. One was Joseph, but the more problematic one was me. Our time apart had increased our differences rather than ironed them out. He, I thought, with my deep-trawling swagger, was too cautious, too quick to turn us home. Whereas he regarded me as reckless and greedy, always chasing a bigger catch. While he remedied his discontent with booze and bad temper, I started thinking about ways of escaping. I devised a private plan; an exit strategy. It involved saving as much money as I could as quickly as I could, buying out his share of the boat and setting up on my own. I dreamed of sailing back to Cardigan Bay single-handed and free; a smile and a wave as I passed Bardsey Island and steered into the glorious waters of home. With this in mind I found us a contract that took us north of Scotland and her islands. The pay was enough to convince Joseph to ignore the objections (and ultimatum) of his new woman and we signed up.

Within a day or two of setting off I knew I had made a mistake. It wasn't the rough height of the seas that wore me down but the perpetual cold. As soon as we were north of Shetland we were assailed by a slicing wind that flung itself down on us like a sworn enemy. It smashed our faces with ice, knifed its way into our very bones. Its effect was only compounded by the cold distance between Joseph and me, and before long I found myself revising my dreams: as we bent to our work of hauling, gutting, freezing, packing, I found myself dreaming not of Cardigan Bay but of warmer waters; warmer people.

Be careful what you wish for. It had been one of my ma's sayings. Always delivered with a wry smile and, generally speaking, spot on. It's not that she was against the *wanting*, more she was uncannily aware that it often came with consequences you hadn't allowed for. Oh how I wish she'd been there to caution me then.

We were in Stornoway for two reasons: we needed to get the boat overhauled in a yard we knew and trusted, and we needed to find an extra crewman. The first part had gone smoothly enough and the *Laughing Girl* was oiled, serviced, greased and ready for action, but the second part was proving more difficult. Our timing was off: a couple of big outfits had been in before us and taken every spare crewman with them. It was unusual for Joseph and me to spend any time together off the boat but that particular evening we'd agreed to meet up and have a last try at finding someone. Failing that, we needed to discuss the possibility of altering our trip.

The weather was a complete arse and I'd lain too long on my bed, putting off the moment I'd have to take myself out into it. I was in a foul mood when I arrived, not only because the short journey had me soaked through, but because I was late, and that would wind up Joseph.

I saw Patrick as soon as I walked in. He smiled from behind the bar and the pulse of electricity, a bright current that sparked the air between us, almost had me off my feet. I shucked off my wet coat, dried my face with my sleeve and walked, as calmly as I could, towards him.

'What you having, mate?'

Australian, I thought as I watched him reach up for a glass. I saw the flat plane of his belly beneath his T-shirt, the clench of muscle in his tanned arm, the soft curling smile that played at the corners of his mouth; I could barely bring myself to speak.

'Guinness,' I muttered, nodding at the nearest pump. 'And . . .' I turned away from him and scanned the room. Joseph had already seen me and was waiting – with his empty glass aloft – to catch my eye. 'One for my uncle.'

'Aha – so you're the mystery man.'

'What's that?'

'Joseph. I was talking to him just now. He said I might be just the man you're looking for.'

I could make no sense of what he was saying.

'Patrick Tierney,' he said, holding out his hand. 'I reckon we might be seeing more of each other – if you're willing, that is.'

I don't know what I might have told him if Joseph hadn't suddenly appeared at my side.

'What do you think, then?' Joseph said, raising his glass in Patrick's direction. 'Think we've found our man?'

CHAPTER 38

'What then, Grace?'
'Mmh?'
'What did my mother say then?'
Grace waited. She felt the weight and shape of the words in her mouth – words that might change everything: for her, for Malin, for Jack. There was an unfurling in her chest – like something coming back to life.

'It was when I told her Michael was my brother. She . . . she sort of . . .'

Vee had let out a small sigh. Like she'd suddenly run out of air. *Your brother? Fuck . . .*

'So . . .' Grace paused. 'It seems that what she told you wasn't entirely true. Michael didn't die before you were born, it was just something she told you to make things . . . easier.'

She hadn't wanted the inconvenience, that's what Grace had picked up between the lines of Vee's explanation: he was an unnecessary complication so she'd simply erased him from her own life – and Malin's.

'OK. So the photograph . . . ?'
'She took you to see him – once.'
'Took me where? To . . .'
'To "some coastal town in Yorkshire".'
'Whitby, you mean? Like the postcard?'
Grace nodded. She smoothed out the piece of paper in her

hand and turned it over to show Malin what she'd written on the back.

Henrietta Street, Whitby.

Malin took hold of the page.

'It's a long time ago, of course,' Grace said. 'Your mother said it was an old address . . .'

'But what if . . .' Malin was still staring at the piece of paper. 'What if he's still there? What if . . . my God . . . what if he's still there? Still alive?'

'I don't know. Vee didn't know – or said she didn't.'

'But what if she was lying again, what if she *does* know. There could be a chance . . . a real chance . . .'

'I know . . .' Grace had to look away. 'Could you . . . just . . . can you give me a minute . . . ?'

Grace walked to the far end of the lay-by and followed a short, flattened path that took her to a field gate. She leaned against it and tried to breath away the banging in her chest. A chance. *A real chance* – not the meaningless charade she'd staged. She pictured the empty farm waiting for her; social services prowling at the door; the never-ending tug between work and home. The constant guilt. She tapped the office number into her phone before thinking got the better of her. And waited for the answer machine to pick up.

'Hello, Thackley and Co.'

'Oh. Mr Thackley . . .' She gulped. 'You're in the office . . . on a Sunday?'

'I am indeed. Just a bit of catching up, you know.'

She wasn't prepared for a conversation – she'd got no further than devising a short message, but now . . . She pulled in as much breath as she could and launched into her explanation and excuses. A couple of minutes later she pushed away from the gate and threaded her way back along the path. Malin was waiting for her by the van, leaning back against its side, like her legs wouldn't hold her up.

'Did she say anything else, Grace?'

'What?' The conversation with Thackley was still buzzing in her head. She'd readied herself for disapproval – dismissal even – but instead he was sympathetic and that had almost reduced her to tears.

'My mum. Vee.'

'Oh. Right. Well . . . her parting shot was "tell Malin that if she wants to pursue this lunacy, then she'll have to deal with the consequences". How about you? What did she say when I handed the phone over?'

'She wants the van back by Friday – "back in the drive where it bloody well belongs".'

'That doesn't give us much time then, does it? Right . . .' Grace glanced at her watch. 'How far is it?'

'To Bristol?'

'No, not Bristol. Whitby.'

Malin's hand flew to her mouth. 'You mean . . . oh my God, Grace, are you sure?'

Grace was more than sure. Thackley's understanding had been the final nudge she needed. 'Well, my boss has just given me the week off so it seems to be the only thing to do, now, doesn't it?' She looked at Jack – he was dozing again; his bottom dentures askew. 'Let's book somewhere tonight, get a good night's sleep, then set off early in the morning.'

Malin stepped forward and wrapped her in a quiet embrace. Grace closed her eyes and lost herself in the warm teenage scent of the girl; the loose-limbed length of her; the soft beating of a young heart against her own.

CHAPTER 39

Michael

I would say that the following couple of months were the best I'd known. Patrick was indeed our man: there was an easiness about him that lightened every aspect of our work, even my relationship with Joseph. The downside was that we didn't have him for long: the bar work, it turned out, had been something to keep him occupied while his own boat the *Free Runner* was in dry dock. He said he'd had it with the fishing business. There'd been too many close calls, and he had enough money in the bank, so his plan, once she was back in the water, was to point her towards her new home. Spain. He was going to buy a patch of land, one that was already planted with grapes if he got enough money for the *Runner*, and join the wine-making business. The thought of it had me dizzy: the more he talked about his plans, the more I convinced myself I could be part of them. I was stupid enough to think that he was the answer to my prayers, and a beautiful answer at that.

In short, I think I fell in love with him.

Love, of course, is a blind thing. It sees only what it can touch or feel. Both were out of the question, but I read his every glance and smile, every casual brush of his hand against mine as a sign that he felt the same way. I slept badly, my hand resting on the thin partition that separated our bunks, my head dancing with the possibilities that life had served up for me. I was aching for time on my own with him and for the first time in my life it wasn't a single night of quick and unsatisfying passion I was envisaging, but the opportunity to talk, to start planning a future together. The chance came unexpectedly and knowing we were only days away from his planned departure, I grabbed it with both hands.

We were drinking at The Sail, an end-of-trip session that had started as soon as we'd got the *Laughing Girl* turned round and tidy. The place was rowdy, big men throwing their money around, a heavy feel in the air that they'd be throwing punches before the night was out.

'I'm going down to check the boat, mate.'

It was the way he said it, a soft whisper, close enough to my ear for me to feel the warmth of his breath.

'You want to come?'

I nodded, drank down the rest of my pint and followed him outside.

It should have been relief that I felt as we walked towards the quay, our breath pluming and mingling as we strode along, relief that at last we had the chance to talk, really talk. But no, the thought that he'd asked me to go with him to his boat, and that we would be alone there, had lit a fire in my belly and in my groin and flooded me with a desire that drowned out all reason. I sauntered beside him barely able to hold it back. He slowed as we neared the quayside.

'There's something I want to show you,' he said, and the sudden touch of his hand on my shoulder took the strength from my legs. He led the way down the quayside ladder onto the deck of the *Runner*. I waited as he slid back the hatch that led down to his living quarters, breathing in the scent of him, imagining the feel of him, then, with a last look at the moon that hung low and yellow above us, stumbled into my future like the lovestruck fool I was.

I feigned a misstep as I descended into the dark cabin, a casual clumsiness that had nothing to do with the amount of beer I'd drunk, and everything to do with getting my hands on him.

'Whoa, steady on there, Micky!'

I should have heeded his warning, leapt away with some half-assed apology, but I persevered, my hands cupping his face, my lips hungry for the taste of his own.

His fist came out of nowhere, a sharp crack that near swivelled my head on my neck. And then the light.

'What the fuck, mate!'

He glowered down at me where I lay sprawled across a low bench seat.

'I'm sorry, Pat . . . I thought . . .'

'You thought what, for Christ's sake? You thought I was a *queer*? Ha! Christ Almighty. Get up.'

I couldn't move. *Queer.* He spat the word down at me.

'Come on, get the fuck up – and get the fuck out before I . . .'

He stepped away as I got to my feet. 'Look, Pat, I'm . . .' I put my hand out to steady myself.

'Don't you touch me, mate. Don't you fucking touch me. Just get the fuck out of here. I don't want anything to do with this or with you. You can tell Joseph . . . no, fuck it, I'll tell him myself . . .'

With that, he was gone, up the ladder and through the hatch, leaving me slumped and weeping, listening to the drumbeat of his feet as he crossed the deck.

Reason should have had me off the boat and running after him, calming him with explanations and pleading for his silence. But reason had deserted me. I sat back on the low bench and, keening my ears against the wild knock of my heart, waited. I sat like a condemned man hoping for some last-minute reprieve, some divine intervention that would pick me up and carry me away from there, wash me up in a place where no one knew me, a place I could get my head straight and start again.

I don't know which I noticed first, the whisky bottle or the envelope propped against the two glasses lined up beside it. There was something of a display about the grouping, some still-life poise that brought back Patrick's words. *There's something I want to show you.* I forced myself past the memory of my own foolish interpretation, reached over and picked them up. I pulled the stopper from the bottle, took a heavy slug and opened the envelope.

A postcard; a photograph; a newspaper cutting.

I considered each one in turn. The cutting and the postcard were both in Spanish and although I could translate a word of neither, the pictures told their own story. There was no surprise in the story because it was the one Patrick had already told me. A mountain vineyard, a farm for sale. The photograph, though, was a different matter. It was soft and crumpled, from a pocket or frequent handling, I decided, as I considered the pretty, dark-haired woman smiling back at me. She was holding a baby in her arms, tilting its small face towards the camera. I took another slug of whisky and packed them all away. A photograph, a newspaper cutting, a postcard: not much for a man to build a dream on, I thought – but enough. Then I blundered out into the dark night knowing my own dreams were in tatters.

CHAPTER 40

A destination can be at once freeing and finite. This is what Grace was thinking as Malin eased the van onto the A55. They had decided, given Vee's ultimatum – and information – to quit the sightseeing and head, as quickly as they could, for Whitby. The decision, Grace could see, was sitting well with Malin: despite the roasting from Vee the day before, the girl had more or less woken up smiling. Pale in the face, but smiling. She, on the other hand, was trying to shake the doubts – and the dream – that had descended on her as she'd fallen asleep the previous night.

* * *

The three of them were lined up in the narrow chilly divans of a family room: damp sheets, matching candlewicks and lumpy pillows. They'd had the cassette twice through before Jack dozed off, and Grace was on the edge of sleep herself when Malin's voice trailed through the dark.

'What if Michael is there, Grace? What if we find him?'

There'd been some thrill in the girl's voice that she couldn't match, so she'd feigned sleep and stayed quiet, and then considered the question long into the night. *What if they found Michael?* She'd tried to conjure up the rosy reunion: smiles and tears all round for what had been found – a lost father; a lost brother; a lost son – but doubt had crept in and clouded it over. Would they be disappointed? Would he simply shrug them off, like he'd done twenty years ago? And if he did – how would she cope? How would her da cope?

She rolled onto her side, a small attempt to turn her back on the questions; to switch off the endless circling of her mind. It worked for a minute or two – a lull of peace inside her head until another thought rose to the surface. It wasn't the thought of finding her brother but of how much she'd give to find her own lost son: to travel to some far-off place and discover him waiting for her. Eventually, balanced somewhere between hopefulness and dread, she willed herself to sleep.

It was an old dream, familiar. The kind you recognise straight away, some known quality to it that draws you along, your hands tracing the walls as you walk, maybe, quietly distracting you until suddenly, round some corner there it is. The thing you don't want to see, the thing you thought was safely tucked away – out of sight, out of mind – looming towards you. Harry. On his swing in their old back garden perhaps, or running towards her at the school gate, or maybe on the sofa watching the Saturday cartoons or at the kitchen table eating cornflakes. But sometimes, like tonight, Harry – still in his football strip – being pulled from the back of the ambulance, the paramedics moving fast, shouting his name, and running, running, running towards the bright lights of the hospital and her not able to catch up for fear of what she knew – what she already knew because there it was on the faces of the paramedics, ashen with the effort of trying to save him. He was dead. Her son was already dead.

She woke to a morning that seemed to have nothing on offer but grey; from the light making its way through the washed out curtains, to the colour of her face in the bathroom mirror. Jack was still sleeping, so she sent Malin down for breakfast and stayed behind waiting for him to wake. Eventually, unsettled by the sight of him – his face slack and blue-tinged by the light coming through the thin curtains – she gently shook him.

'Ahoy there,' he quipped, then promptly nodded off again. She was debating what to do – wake him or leave him be – when Malin returned.

'Oh, he's still sleeping.' She glanced at Jack curled up and snoring in his bed, and sat down on the armchair by the window. 'I was wondering last night, Grace . . .'

But the dream had left Grace in no mood for talking. She had her handbag on her shoulder and her fingers on the doorknob before Malin could go any further.

'Yes. I . . . I'll give him another half hour,' she said, from the open doorway. 'It'll give me time to pop down and get some breakfast – ring me if you need me, yes?'

Then she was out of the room, down the stairs and wedged in behind a small table tucked into a draughty bay window. She ordered tea and toast from a young girl who looked like she'd just got out of bed herself and considered the 'sea view' through a window that was thick with salt grime outside and condensation inside. She was jawing her way through a plate of cold toast when some unseen clock struck nine – and her thoughts suddenly turned to work. She should, she realised, be celebrating the fact that she wasn't there; that Thackley had been so understanding. *Let me handle Joy*, he'd said, and in the relief of the moment she'd believed he would – or could. Instead, weighed down by the dream and the weather – and the misgivings that had assailed her in the night – she was suddenly worried that Joy would talk him round, that there would be a brief phone conversation, maybe some formal letter, and then . . . then . . . She choked the thought down with a mouthful of tepid tea, fled the damp dining room and hauled herself back up the stairs to their room.

Jack was up and dressed and, in his own words, ready for action. He had his perky face on – voice to match – but Grace wasn't entirely convinced. She studied his eyes, gauged the depth of light in them.

'So, what's on the agenda today, hinny?'

'The agenda, Da? Well . . .' She picked the road map up and folded it to the right page. 'This is where we are now . . .'

'Oh, yes,' he said, waggling his specs like Eric Morecambe.

'And this is where we're aiming for.' She snaked her finger along the thick green line. 'Flint.'

'Ah, Flint. Do we know it?'

'Nope. It just seems a good watering spot before we . . .' She watched his face for a reaction. 'Before we head for Whitby?'

Nothing – and by the time they were packed and in the van he was yawning, then – within a few miles – dozing.

* * *

Grace tried to work off her growing anxiety about what she was doing – risking her job, her da's home at the farm, their security – by concentrating on the passing scenery. But the shape of the place gave her no comfort: Conwy Bay, Colwyn Bay – a different part of the same sea, she knew that, but she was cast adrift by unfamiliarity of their headlands and coastline. She turned to small talk, but her meaningless observations about the landscape, the weather, the breakfast felt as flat as she did, so she gave up. Jack was on the back seat, wedged in between the duvets and pillows, oblivious. Or so she thought.

'I was thinking,' he said suddenly.

Grace, released from the discomfort of trying to make conversation, swivelled her attention to him.

'Oh yes?'

'Yes. About what you said last night.'

'What did I say last night, Da?'

'No. Not you, Grace – the young lassie. What she said about Michael. When we were in bed. She said what would we do if we found him?'

Malin leapt in before Grace could close the conversation down. 'I thought you were asleep, Jack. I thought you were both asleep.'

'Oh, no,' he said. 'Not at all. I had my thinking cap on.'

'Right.' Malin allowed a small pause. There was a note of expectation in it. 'So what did you think?'

'I was thinking . . .' he said. 'I was thinking . . . that if we find him, I could tell him that I'm sorry.'

CHAPTER 41

Michael

All I had coming at me were consequences. In a panic I lurched along the cobbled harbour side, knowing that the worst of those consequences was Joseph. I imagined Patrick, bristling with macho indignation, exploding into the Sail and laying out the whole humiliating story. I imagined the smile it would put on Joseph's face, the one that had nothing to do with humour and everything to do with the opportunity to ridicule, belittle – torment.

The plan seemed to start in my feet rather than my head – some casual change of direction that took me around the other side of the harbour towards the *Laughing Girl*. The moon had climbed and brightened and she was shining like some kind of beacon. I could simply take her, I thought, as I stumbled along. Simply take her a short way down the coast, drop anchor and sleep. I don't know if it was the whisky or the sudden prospect of escape that served up the next part of the plan. *The obvious part*, I thought, as I greeted it with a drunken and desperate grin. I would sleep and then, in the morning, I would take off. I would take off and somehow disappear; get myself a dream of my own. A life of my own.

I climbed carefully down the quayside ladder and, in a half crouch, crept across the wet deck. The cabin was unlocked, as I knew it would be, so I slid open the hatch, lowered myself in and clumsily groped my way towards the small galley. I pulled open the drawer beside the sink and felt for the engine keys.

They weren't there.

I sat on the edge of the bunk and tried to remember where I'd put the spares. It was a mistake: the whisky in my blood and the soft give of the mattress beneath me was a powerful seducer, too difficult to fight. I stretched myself out and felt the relief of it, the small pleasure of closing my eyes, just for a moment, a minute . . .

* * *

When I awoke it was to daylight, the drone of the engine, the rise and fall of waves beneath the hull, and the low mumble of Joseph's radio. The first thought that came to me, as I lay there trying to work out what to do, was both ridiculous and attractive. I would escape. I would climb quietly up onto the deck, and then slip overboard. Rather than face whatever Joseph was aiming to say or do, I would simply swim for it. It was, I reasoned, a braver option than running away. I was cured of the idea the moment I hauled myself upright: my head was nothing but pain, a molten throb cut through with a sword-sharp ache that ran from one side of my jaw to the other. I half closed my eyes against it and staggered to the galley sink. I had my hands cupped beneath the tap when the sudden dimming of sunlight in the cabin told me Joseph was at the hatch. I straightened up and turned to look at him. His face told me everything I needed to know. He knew all about me – what I was, what I'd done – and he despised me for it.

'I reckon you and me are finished, boy. I'm taking you back home,' he said, and strode away.

I splashed the water over my face, into my mouth, through my hair, to the sound of his boots hammering across the deck.

CHAPTER 42

Grace let Jack's words settle. They landed in a loose bunch somewhere in her chest.

'What do you mean, Da?' She'd not meant to say it out loud, but there it was, hanging in the air between them.

'For him leaving, you know.'

'What . . . leaving the farm you mean? Going off with Joseph?'

He mumbled some small reply but she was too caught up in her own thoughts to catch it. By the time she'd spun in her seat to ask him again, he was asleep.

'Do you know what he meant, Grace?' Malin's voice was a whisper.

'No . . . well, yes. Probably. I thought Joseph's visit was random, you know. That he was passing by and called in? But it wasn't.'

'It had been arranged?'

Grace nodded.

'By Jack?'

Grace glanced over her shoulder to make sure he was still asleep. 'Yes. I guess so.'

'But why?'

'Michael was . . . difficult. Eighteen, and full of himself, you know? They were always at loggerheads. Maybe he thought a few weeks away from the farm would straighten him out.'

'But what about your mother?'

'That's a good question. She went along with it – she let him go but . . .' Grace swallowed down the catch in her throat. 'I don't think she ever forgave herself for it. She died . . . she died without ever knowing . . . God, without knowing any of this.'

'Was it a long time ago, Grace?'

'2006. She was sixty-six.'

'That seems young.'

'Yes.'

There'd been a great irony to her ma's early death – her so fit and so healthy – but later there'd been some comfort in it too. Comfort that she'd not had to suffer the loss of her grand son as well as her own son.

The first sign had been tiredness – a bone-deep exhaustion that had stopped her in her tracks; that, for the first time in her sixty-six years, kept her in bed. The shock of it when they'd arrived at the farm that Easter – no roast on the table, no tins of cakes and scones lined up in the pantry – instead her da at the stove, heating up Heinz tomato soup, and her mother on the sofa, dozing. He'd waved them off from the porch, pale and vulnerable in his vest.

Grace wound down the window to blow the memory away.

'Ah, is that your phone, Grace?'

'Erm . . . hang on . . .' Grace leaned down, fished the pinging phone out of her bag and frowned at the screen. There was a string of messages and missed calls – from Shirley. She tapped on the number trying to imagine what was so urgent – the dogs got loose maybe? A burst pipe?

'Shirley, it's—' That was as far as she got.

'Grace. At last. I've been trying to get you all day, I—'

'I've not been in signal. What's the matter?'

'It's social services. They've been looking for you – for Jack?'

'Oh. Why?' There was a silence on the other end of the line. 'Shirley? Why are social services looking for my da?'

'Well, it's something to do . . . something to do with the hospital, I think. Something about . . . erm . . .'

'Come on, Shirley, spit it out for goodness' sake.'

'Safeguarding . . .'

Grace almost dropped the phone. 'Safeguarding?' Her voice was shrill.

'The ward weren't entirely happy about Jack.'

'What do you mean? They were happy enough discharging him. Couldn't get shot of us fast enough. What weren't they happy about?'

'Grace – I don't know. That's as much as I could get out of them. They want to speak to you. You need to give them a ring. I think . . . well, I got the impression . . . that the police might have contacted them . . .'

'Oh Christ.'

The memory of the two officers from the day before suddenly resurfaced.

'Right. Thanks. I'll ring them. I'll ring them now. Safeguarding, for God's sake,' she said, and hung up. Abrupt, she knew – she'd not asked about the dogs or the farm but she'd needed to get off the phone, needed to sit somewhere quiet – maybe stick her head in a bucket of cold water.

She found the number for social services in her phone and tried to settle herself for the long wait. The Verve's 'Bitter Sweet Symphony' chimed into her ear. Somebody had got that right.

'Is everything OK, Grace?' Malin swivelled slightly in her seat. The only bit of colour in her face was her eyes.

'No. I don't know. We might have to . . . oh, hang on.'

The music stopped and someone answered the phone.

'It's Grace James here,' Grace said, rooting in her pockets for a pen with her free hand. 'I believe you want to talk to me?'

'Grace James?'

She could hear the woman tapping on the computer keys. 'Erm, no. Nothing coming up. How are you spelling that?'

'J-A-M-E-S,' Grace said, fighting the urge to say something sarcastic. 'Try Jack,' she said. 'That's my father. Jack James.'

More tapping. 'Ah. Velindre Farm? Oh. Yes. Just hold the line a minute.'

The violins resurfaced. She imagined the woman bolting out of her chair, running down the corridor, arms flapping. *All systems go – I've got her.*

'Just putting you through now.'

The line hissed and crackled across the miles.

'Ah, Grace. Thanks for calling . . .'

It was the 'look after yourself' woman – Grace recognised her voice.

'I was just wanting to catch up with Dad after his little accident. I've popped round to the farm a couple of times – just to check in, you know, but I gather from erm . . .' There was a rustle of papers.

'Shirley.'

'Ah, yes. Shirley. I gather you've taken Dad away?'

Taken him away. Like she'd stolen him. 'Yes. Just for a few days.'

'Oh, lovely. So . . . anywhere nice?'

'Pwllheli.'

'Ooh, lovely. Any particular reason?'

Christ. 'A bit of a break, you know. A family holiday.'

A silence. 'So – how is he. Dad?'

'He's fine. Why?' The edge in her voice was doing her no favours but she couldn't stop herself.

'Well, nothing to worry about but we were hoping to catch up with you both . . . just give me a second, will you?'

Grace tried to catch the whispered discussion taking place on the other end of the line.

'I ought to know this, really' – the woman gave a small titter – 'but do you have power of attorney for your father, Grace?'

She didn't. It cost a fortune.

'Why?'

'Well . . .'

Grace jumped back in before the woman started on the 'best interest' lecture or set to on plans for a mental capacity assessment. 'We'll be back in a day or two . . .'

'Mmh. A day or two? Well, actually we were hoping to see you – to see Jack – before then, Grace. A few concerns have been raised and we need to check them out. We were thinking of tomorrow? Look, give me a minute. I'll ring you back.'

'No, I'll . . .' But it was too late. The line was dead.

'What's . . . what's happening?' Malin had pulled the van into a lay-by.

'Those two police officers yesterday.' Grace wound down her window and let the breeze take some heat out of her face. 'Seems they got in touch with social services.'

It was all she could do to stop herself getting out of the van, laying herself down on the ground and saying, *I quit.*

'What did they say, Grace?'

Grace took a deep breath. 'They think I'm not looking after him properly, not coping, you know. The bang on the head, the fiasco yesterday . . . they want me to take him home.'

It was only half the truth and she knew it – what they really wanted was to find a reason to take him away from her.

CHAPTER 43

Michael

Home. It was suddenly the very place I wanted to be and every raw inch of me keened towards it. I steadied myself against the galley stove and let myself imagine it: the creak of the farm gate as I pushed it open, the riot of chickens and dogs as I crossed the yard, my mother's face at the window as she saw me approaching. Christ. To be at the kitchen table with her now. Or to be lying in my old bed listening to the sound of her rattling the Rayburn to life. I would stay a month or two maybe, put my back into a bit of farm work, tease some of the sea out of my blood, try to forget the past and think about the future . . .

It could never happen and I knew it, because my future had been written clearly enough on Joseph's face, in the sneering curl of his lip and the jut of his chin. The bastard couldn't wait to tell them what had happened, what I'd done. I drank down a glass of stale water, then climbed up onto the deck.

The day was a good one. Thin ribbons of high cloud in a sky that was too bright for my sore eyes. I surveyed the surrounding waters for some familiar feature that might tell me where we were, but my bearings were shot: the coastline that lay to our left and the low stretch of land to our right were impossible to read.

Joseph was a different matter. As soon as he saw me on deck

he stepped out of the wheelhouse and took what appeared to be a readying stance, like he was preparing to deliver his lines to some absent audience – or fixing for a fight. Hands on hips, legs spread wide – it was somewhere between a pantomime pirate and some old Western gunslinger.

'Oh, here she comes. Our little sleeping beauty.'

He grinned at the sheer wit of himself.

I stared at him – this man who had the key to the rest of my life and couldn't wait to use it.

'Fuck off, Joseph,' I muttered, and pushed past him.

His arm snaked out and grabbed my own.

'What's that you say, boy?'

I smacked his hand away and spun round to face him. 'Where the fuck are we?'

'Where are we? Oh . . .' He lifted his two hands, palms up, playing to some invisible front row. 'The boy wants to know where we are. Well, I'll tell you where I am, sonny. I'm up shit creek with a fucking pervert and . . . with no fucking woman to go home to. That's right, you poncy wee shite. While we've been chasing the money, and you've been chasing arse, she's found herself some other bugger. But that's me. You on the other hand . . .' He leaned in and prodded me in the chest. His breath was hot and beery. 'You are finished, my boy. A fucking laughing stock, an embarrassment. Oh, you had us all fooled . . .'

I had him fooled? How the fuck did he think I'd ended up with him in the first place? Because I was completely fucking fooled by him, that's why. He'd sold me the promise of escape, and I, young idiot that I'd been, had bought it. I may still have been an idiot, but I was no longer so young – and neither, I thought, as he ranted on, was he. I watched him carefully as he built up the head of steam I recognised; the hot bubbling simmer that would suddenly erupt into violence. I'd seen him fight often enough – he favoured the surprise attack; an iron-fisted, hammering blow that could put a man on the floor before he knew he'd been hit. I took a step away from him and readied myself. It was the cue he'd been waiting for.

'Oh, that's it, back away why don't you. Not man enough to stand up for yourself now, eh?'

It was the grin on his face that did it – the swaggering smirk of it. I lunged forward and smacked him, hard. He staggered back, but he didn't go down – and the smile didn't leave his face.

'That's it?' he yelled. 'That's all you've got, laddie?' And then, drooling blood and spit, he launched himself at me.

It was like being hit by a train. Holy Christ – the man was the wrong side of sixty but he still had some steel in him. He clamped his arms around my chest in an unnatural embrace that pinned my arms to my sides and took my feet from under me. He tightened his grip on me as we stumbled backwards across the wheelhouse floor.

'This is what you like eh, laddie?' he whispered, as he whirled me round like some wild and demented dance partner. I turned my face from the sour, bloody stink of him and tried to wrestle myself free. I felt the captain's chair at my back – a brief steadying support that allowed me a moment's respite, the chance to almost right myself, before it spun away and landed me – us – flat on the *Laughing Girl's* control panel. I heard the change in her engine straight away.

'Joseph!' I yelled. 'The engine . . .' I tried to twist us away from the throttle – I could feel it against my back . . . 'Joseph!' I screamed. 'The fucking engine . . .'

She was at a shriek now, a screw-loosening, bolt-shearing shriek: a cry for mercy, a last-ditch appeal for help that did nothing because, moments later, she simply gave up: a small hiccup, a short high-pitched whistle, and then silence.

I felt Joseph's grip on me loosen. 'What happened? What have you done?'

'What have *I* done, you fucking moron?' I shoved him off me and twisted round to the control panel. I pushed the throttle into the off position, then slid it back and forth a couple of times to check for damage. Joseph was staring at me. He looked like a man who'd just woken from a dream.

'What . . . what happened?'

'What happened? You happened, you animal.' I pushed past him and stamped off across the deck. I levered the cover off the engine hatch and sat back on my heels. The smell was enough – that hot oil-spitting smell that said she'd split a seal or – worse – thrown a piston. Joseph came up behind me and peered down into the cavity.

'Can you fix it?'

Good question, I thought, because from where I was looking, there was no chance of fixing anything.

CHAPTER 44

'They want me to take him back home.'

It wasn't so much a statement as an experiment: Grace needed to hear how the words sounded, and how they felt. Nothing but defeat on both accounts.

'What? Now?'

Grace shrugged. 'I don't know. I . . . Christ.'

She couldn't find a clear space in her head to formulate an answer – let alone a solution. She shuddered at the old familiarity of the feeling.

I wish you'd stop with all this dithering, her mother once said. She'd been at the farm with Harry when Greg had phoned. He'd invited people for supper – *new contacts* – and he needed her at home. She spent the last day in the farm kitchen worrying about what to cook, what to wear, how to dress the dining table – no room in her head, no space in her chest to explain to her mother how easy it was to make the wrong decision, to get things wrong – to endure an evening of Greg's quiet disapproval with a smile, knowing what was going to happen when everyone had left. A debriefing, he called it, like she'd just done ninety minutes on the football pitch rather than at the dining table. It paralysed her – that's what she might have told her mother. Living with Greg simply sapped the strength from her, left her spineless, unable – or unwilling – to stand up for herself.

'But we're so close, Grace, we're . . .'

'I know. I know that.' She could hear the fraying edge in her voice. 'But they want to see him. Tomorrow.'

'But why?'

'Because . . . they're worried about him. About me. They think I can't cope.'

'But that's not true, is it? Just tell them, Grace. Tell them you can cope, that everything's fine. Oh . . . Grace . . .'

The tears came without warning. They sprang from Grace's eyes and coursed down her cheeks before she had time to stop them.

'But it is true,' she sobbed. 'Look at what's happened this week – the hospital, the boat, the police. And now all this . . . this . . .'

'Upheaval,' Malin said.

'Yes . . . no. No. I didn't mean it like that. I didn't mean to include you in it all, I just . . .'

'But Grace . . .' Malin reached over and put her hand on Grace's wrist. 'I am included in it all . . . I want to be . . .'

'Hah. I don't think you know what that means.' She might have gone on – elaborated on the exhausting details of her life – except Jack, alerted no doubt by the sound of her sobbing, suddenly struck up.

'What's the matter, Gracie?'

'What's that, Da?' She swiped the tears away with her sleeve because he was off his seat now, his small head poked between the gap in the two front seats.

'Why are you crying, hinny?'

'I'm not.' She was. The concern on his face had started her off again.

'Is it Harry?'

Harry. 'No,' she gulped. 'No, Da, it's not Harry, it's . . .'

'It's the authorities, Jack,' Malin said. 'They want Grace to take you back to the farm.'

'The authorities? What's that when it's at home?'

'The social worker, Da. You know that woman who comes to see us at the farm.'

He didn't know. Social workers, occupational therapists, district nurses – they were all the same to him: visiting strangers he forgot the minute they were out of the door.

'Well, I hope you put them straight, hinny. Told them what we're doing.'

'Hah!' That was the last thing she could do. *Oh yes, we're just on our way to find my dead brother.* Community mental health would be out like a shot – and not for her da.

Malin reached across and touched Grace's wrist. 'What did you tell her, Grace?'

'I said we were having a holiday. A family holiday.'

'And what did she say?'

'She said . . . oh shit.' She grabbed her phone off the dash. 'I meant to turn it off – they're going to ring back.' She was fumbling with the password when the screen lit up and the call came through. 'Oh hellfire – yes, sorry, hello?'

That was as far as she got because Jack snaked his arm through the gap in the seats and grabbed the phone off her.

'Da!'

She spun round as he darted back to his perch on the back seat – too far away for her to snatch the phone back. She had two choices and neither would serve them well: she could cause a rumpus or simply let him get on with it. Either way they were snookered.

'Hello . . .' he trilled. Grace stayed put, praying that the call had dropped out; that he had inadvertently switched it off. But no—

'Oh, yes. This is he.' *It's the snooty one*, he mouthed, then lifted the end of his nose with one finger and sent a smile in her direction. 'Oh, yes indeed,' he said, and tipped her a wink.

Then silence – his head cocked to one side as he listened. 'Ah, well, I'm not sure about that. Just give me a moment while I confer.'

Confer? Grace looked at Malin.

'She wants to know when we're coming back.'

Grace stretched her hand out for the phone but Jack shook his head.

'Ahem. Well, I'm afraid we don't have a specific day in mind. Rather enjoying the break, don't you know . . . ah yes, glorious weather for . . . for this time of the year.' There were a couple more minutes of listening and nodding, and then, after a chirpy 'toodle-oo', he prised himself off the seat and handed the phone back to Grace.

'Well, I think I fixed that.' He was beaming with the sheer cleverness of himself.

'What did she say?'

'Mmh, well, let me think . . .' He took hold of his chin and arched an eyebrow: enjoying his moment; building a bit of drama. 'Ah, yes. She said she'll call back next week.'

CHAPTER 45

Michael

Engines were the one thing I had over Joseph. Although he could beat me hands down on navigation and map-reading, when it came to engines my experience with farm machinery left him standing. This meant the consequences of our spat were not what they might have been. Joseph knew, and he hated it.

'So what's the plan,' I asked as I reached out for a spanner.

'I already told you that,' he said, slapping the thing into my hand.

I put the spanner down and hauled myself out of the hatch. I knew what was wrong with the engine. It was a ten-minute fix, tops, but I wasn't going to tell him that, at least not until he'd told me what I needed to know: where we were, where we were headed and what, if anything, he'd said to my da.

I sauntered towards the galley, conscious of his following gaze. I paused at the cabin hatch and looked up, as if to admire the sky. It was already darkening, a gauzy grey wash that took the colour from everything and predicted rain before the hour was up. We'd dropped anchor, but there was a heavy tug to the drift that said we'd be likely getting more than rain.

'How long's it going to take?'

I answered his gruffness with an exaggerated calm.

'Not sure,' I said, enjoying the discomfort in his face. 'It all depends . . .'

The bastard gave in eventually, but not until we'd had the first gale warning. 'Time to stop fucking about, boy,' he growled. 'Time to get that fucking engine fixed and get us out of here.'

'Well, I'm ready when you are,' I said, taking a slow sip of my coffee.

'Milford Haven,' he said. 'We're heading for Milford Haven – and we're still fucking miles from there.'

'And my da – have you told him?'

'Which part?'

'Fair enough.' I took another sip of coffee as the first peal of thunder rumbled overhead.

'For fuck's sake. No. I haven't told him anything.'

'Thank you,' I said, and put my cup down. The '*yet*' hung in the air between us, the winning piece he dare not chance. I felt him flinch as I squeezed past.

We were away within twenty minutes, my ears oblivious to the rising pitch of the wind and tuned only to the pitch of the engine. I stayed on deck, gauging her steady throb through the soles of my feet, listening for some tell-tale hesitation in her rhythm. Joseph had hunkered in the wheelhouse; shut himself away with the maps and the radio. He emerged a while later – his face pale and grey in the stark beam of the deck lights.

'I'm taking her in.'

I scanned the dark outline of the distant coastline for the glow of the oil refinery. 'Not Milford?'

'No.'

That was it. No clue as to where we were until I saw the lights of the ferry terminal. Fishguard. It was the closest I'd been to home since I'd steered the *Laughing Girl* out of Aberystwyth harbour.

CHAPTER 46

By the time they'd stopped for a quick cup of tea and a sandwich in a service station the day was tipping towards afternoon. Malin spent a long time contemplating the satnav and eventually suggested a route that missed out the M62. Grace peered at the road atlas – at the complex knot around Manchester – and agreed. They would pick up the M56 near Ellesmere Port, then join the M6 near Lymm. After that it was a straight line north.

Grace might have been sitting back and savouring the unexpected reprieve from social services – and would have been if it hadn't been for the dangling end that Jack's words had left floating in the air. *Is it Harry?* There was some strained silence in the van that told her Malin was biding her time – waiting for the right moment to pose the obvious question – so she took a deep breath and jumped in before the girl had a chance.

'Harry was my son,' she said, keeping her eyes on the road ahead. 'He . . . he died five years ago . . .'

'Oh, Grace . . .'

Grace braced herself for more questions but Malin lapsed into an uneasy silence which, after a few uncomfortable minutes, Grace set about filling with conversation and questions of her own. It was tougher going than she'd expected. Malin's answers were short and distracted: she'd just started her first year at Swansea University – History and Politics; she was living in student accommodation with four other girls; it was . . . OK.

It was a relief when Jack suddenly piped up. Grace abandoned the struggling conversation and turned all her attention to him. An hour later, though, he was still rattling on and by the time they were on the M6 he was firing in all directions. Not quite agitated, but heading that way. Teeming with facts and figures like he had been in Aberystwyth. He'd started with a history of Whitby, then somehow navigated himself further north and set to on his childhood days. She'd kept quiet as he launched into the story she'd heard many times: his move from Newcastle to Pembrokeshire.

'Evacuated,' he'd said – and the word had sparked a sudden worry about his bowels, had her counting back to when he'd last been and wondering if his agitation was simply constipation.

'So you mean you weren't born in Wales then, Jack?' Malin asked.

'Oh, no,' he'd replied, then launched into the full tale: how he and Joseph were packed off at the age of five and seven, sent away from Newcastle to avoid the threat of bombing.

'We were sent to the farm,' he said. 'The farm!'

Which was where they had stayed because, three months after the boys arrived in Pembrokeshire, their parents were killed in an overnight raid that destroyed large areas of the city.

'I loved the place straight off,' Jack said. 'But our Joe, he was a different story. Always looking west he was . . .'

Grace knew this part of the story well enough: that it had been apparent from an early age that Joseph's interest was not in the land they farmed, but in the sea that bounded its western edge; that he was on the fishing boats before he left school and away soon after.

'So Michael took after him then, Jack?' Malin said.

There was a short silence. A small sniff. 'Yes, he must have . . .' he said, then skittered off down another path entirely. Eventually half slumped in her seat from the effort of keeping up with him, Grace gave in.

'Perhaps we should pull off a bit earlier than planned. Try to get my da . . . you know, settled. I was thinking a cup of tea might do the trick . . .'

She had to give Malin top marks for not bursting into incredulous laughter. A cup of tea, for God's sake? The state he was in now, a hefty dose of Valium would have a run for its money.

But Malin simply glanced at the satnav. 'Sedbergh,' she said. 'We could come off and head to Sedbergh.'

Half an hour later they were driving into the small town. Ten minutes after that they were in the café at Farfield Mill, drinking tea.

* * *

Jack was on the fidget, lining the salt and pepper shakers up with the little bowl of sugar cubes, snapping the sugar tongs, stacking the plates and saucers, swivelling in his seat and nodding at other customers.

'Da, do you need the bathroom?'

'No.'

He peered over his shoulder again, then, with his hand on her arm, leaned in towards her.

'Don't look now,' he whispered. 'But I think we're being watched.'

'What?' Grace turned her head in the direction he'd been looking.

'No – for goodness' sake, Grace. I said don't look.'

'You're tired, Da. There's no one watching us. Come on, do you fancy another cup of tea? A toasted teacake?'

'No,' he hissed. 'But I think she must know me, look.'

Grace looked across at the woman. She was sitting side on, reading a newspaper, taking no notice of them at all.

'Actually, I do.'

'What? A teacake? Or tea?'

'No. The bathroom.' He pushed his chair back and struggled to his feet.

'Hang on, Da, I'll come with you. I need to go myself, I could do with . . .'

But he was off, full tilt across the café, clutching at the backs of chairs as he went. She followed, her eyes on the seat of his trousers, praying she'd not left it too late.

'Wait for me, yes?' she said, as she backed out of the cubicle. 'I'll be in the Ladies' next door. I'll come and get you, yes?'

'Yes.'

'Don't go without me.'

'No.'

Grace studied her face in the mirror, the pale sag of it. The strip lighting was making a show of the grey in her hair, highlighting the stains on the front of her jeans. She looked as crumpled and worn out as her clothes. She smoothed the front of her sweatshirt down, like she could take the creases out of herself, and fished in her bag for a comb. God, she was tired. More than tired. Weary to the bone with the constant worry of him, the knife-edge feeling of their daily life.

Grace gave her clothes a final smoothing, then, in a lame attempt to ignite a bit of energy, smiled at herself in the mirror. She didn't know how much longer she could keep this up. Not just the journey they were on to find Michael, but the journey she was on with her da.

She pulled herself back from the train of thought, zipped her handbag shut and went to get him.

'Da?' Nothing. She pushed the door open a few inches and sniffed the air. 'Are you finished, Da?' She looked over her shoulder, then went in, calling his name.

The cubicle was empty.

CHAPTER 47

Grace charged back into the café, resisting the urge to shout his name. She flung open the door and spotted him straight away. He was sitting beside the woman with the newspaper, his head bobbing like a cork with the excitement of whatever tale he was telling.

'Da.'

He didn't break stride; he was gassing away like the *Encyclopedia Britannica* had suddenly upped and sprouted legs.

'I'm so sorry,' she said, smiling at the woman. But what could she say? That he was confused, tired—

The woman smiled back at her. 'You must be Grace, then?' Grace stared at the woman's outstretched hand, then took it.

'Gloria Kavanagh,' the woman said, as if the name ought to mean something.

'Swaledale Rams,' Jack said, with a grin. 'I told you she was looking at me, didn't I? I told her, Gloria, told her I recognised you, I just couldn't, you know,' – he gave the top of his head a loose slap – 'couldn't get the old noddle working . . .'

* * *

But it was working now. Hellfire. Jack didn't know what had put the penny in the slot but there it was, the door flung open and everything waiting for him: Swaledale Rams; the Royal

Welsh Showground. He'd shot out of the toilet and crossed the room before it all tumbled out and slipped through his fingers. Gloria Kavanagh, oh yes, he remembered it all now – she had a pair of winners the same year he got Best in Show, the year him and Wenna had splashed out and stayed in the Caer Beris Hotel, the two of them propped up in bed at six in the morning, spreading jam on their toast, listing everything that needed to be done before the judging. They'd all got talking after the photos, he'd had a pint of Felinfoel – maybe two – they exchanged addresses . . .

'Garsdale,' he said and off he went again. Gayle Farm, Garsdale. They'd sent Christmas cards, talked about going up – no – they'd met up again at the show the following year, or maybe the year after, maybe that was the foot and mouth year, they'd met up and Marks and Spencer's had a café on the showground and Charles and Camilla came and they'd driven off for something to eat and then the next day . . . Dammit. The next day . . .

'What was it, Grace, what did we do the next day?'

She was looking at him now – her careful look, he called it. Like she was carrying more eggs than she could rightly manage.

'Which next day, Da?'

Wrong answer. That wasn't going to open any doors for goodness' sake.

'You know, after the show, after . . .'

But it was no good. It was gone: the lot of it shut off and him standing, like an idiot, in front of the closed door, teetering with exhaustion. He was tired of it. So flaming tired of it.

Grace put her hand on his shoulder.

'It's all right, Da.'

Jack gave a small nod, then let his chin slump on his chest.

* * *

'He's right,' Gloria said. 'We knew each other from the Royal Welsh Show . . .'

Grace gave half a smile in return. There was no time for small talk. She could feel her insides revving up. He'd be asleep in minutes if she didn't get him going again. She pulled out her phone to see if Malin had been in touch. She'd gone to the supermarket to stock them up, to find a launderette, to get money from the bank, but surely she should have been back by now . . .

'Are you all right?'

She looked at the woman, suddenly self-aware. Her hand clutched at her throat, her eyes were glassy with tears.

'Yes, yes. I'm fine. It's not me, it's . . .' She nodded towards Jack who was already a couple of inches lower in his seat. Switched off. *It's like a light being switched off.* She'd said that to the GP one time. *It's in his eyes. You can see it happening.* That was in the earlier days when she imagined that if she could just find the key or the cause or the trigger or the right food – the list had been endless – she would be able to keep him alight. She'd been wrong, of course, because nothing made a difference: whatever was happening in his head was governed by rules she couldn't fathom.

'Dementia?'

Grace took a deep breath, ready to deliver the lecture she secretly thought of as 'Labels'. *Well, I prefer not to think of it like that . . . blah di blah di blah . . .*

'Yes,' she said and the relief of it set her off. 'God. I'm sorry . . .' Grace swiped at her face with a serviette but there was no stopping it. She could feel it building behind her eyes, a huge deluge pressing forward, no regard for the fact that she was in a café, in a strange town, with a complete stranger – no regard for anything other than its own release.

'Would you mind . . .' She was up on her feet now. 'Would you mind sitting with him a minute . . . I just . . . the toilet . . .'

She crossed the room in a blur and shut herself in the cubicle.

Dementia. She'd rejected the word from the get-go. *Insanity*, it said in the dictionary. *Crazy, mad, out of one's mind.* She'd turned her nose straight up at the idea because he was none of those things. He was different, yes, mixed up even – but he still had his moments. Moments like earlier when the light suddenly came back on and he was himself again. She forced herself up, flushed the toilet and parked herself by the washbasins. She ignored the mirror and set about splashing her face with cold water, silently praying that the woman – Gloria – would have had the good sense to leave while she had the chance and the three of them could get themselves back to the camper van and away.

Later, when they were sitting in Gloria's kitchen, a soft sun spreading like a pool of gold across the distant hills, she was grateful that didn't happen.

CHAPTER 48

Michael

The sea got worse, a heaving swell that elevated us to a precarious viewpoint of the coastline one minute, then snatched it away and buried us in ungodly troughs of black water the next. When we made our last turn towards land – a bold manoeuvre on Joseph's part that turned us side-on to the swell – the *Laughing Girl* tipped at an angle that almost had me off my feet. I held my breath until she'd righted herself and strained my ears above the wind for the pitch of her engine, for the reassurance that she had the mettle to get us over the last stretch and into the shelter of the harbour. I nodded into the dark at the steady hum of her.

My priority, once we'd docked, ought to have been the engine: a second check of her oil and water; an extra dose of grease; pumping out the bilge water. But no, my main thought, as I did my half of getting her tidied away for the night, was that I needed to get to a phone before Joseph did. Consequently I worked with one eye on what he was doing and, as soon as he finished, I finished too. I climbed up onto the quayside directly behind him, and measured his step stride for stride as we propelled ourselves through the pounding wind and rain towards the first pub we could find.

The Ship Inn gave us what we were looking for. We stumbled in to a near empty bar, a good fire in the grate and the smell of cooking. I went straight to the bar, then followed the barmaid's instructions to the small phone booth tucked in an alcove beside an old jukebox.

My ma answered and, despite the short distance between us, her voice sounded a million miles away. A lifetime away.

'Ma . . .' My voice cracked under the weight of the word.

'Hello. Velindre Farm . . .'

'Ma . . . it's me . . .'

'Hello?'

I pictured her out in the draughty hall, half swamped by the rack of coats and jackets, smoothing her pinny down; impatient to be on with whatever job I'd called her away from.

'Hello?'

'Ma, it's me. It's Michael.'

I imagined her in the dim light – her hand at her throat now, or maybe lowering herself onto the bottom stair.

'Michael . . .'

Although what I told her was not entirely straight – I said we'd taken work in Milford – I answered her questions truthfully enough: yes, Joseph was with me; yes, I was planning to stay a while and yes, I'd be visiting just as soon as I could.

Our conversation was short but it set us both in a whirl. I heard it in my ma's voice as she called for my da, some lilt that told me she was smiling and crying, and I felt it in my step as I walked unsteadily back into the bar, not sure whether it was the floor or my feet that were at fault.

Joseph, I was relieved to see, had set himself up on a small table by the fire. The empty glass in front of him was good news indeed, a sure sign he was fixing for a good session, something that generally led to him dropping into bed early. I ordered us two pints of Guinness and, figuring it would speed things up, added a shot of vodka to his. Our conversation was zero, a curt update on where we were spending the night (the barmaid had fixed us up with a guest house a short walk away), and then nothing except black looks and a brooding silence. The fact I'd got my phone call in ought to have afforded me some relief, but it didn't. I could feel it in the air and see it in his face: he was busy forging some plan that would be my undoing. I left him to it. I moved back across to the bar and lodged myself on a high stool. I watched him from a distance, scowling down at his food; ignored him when he arrived at my side to order more beer, then nodded as he passed me on his way out.

'Half seven,' he growled as he steamed past. 'And don't be fucking late.'

I craned my neck as he skirted the jukebox and phone booth, then, satisfied I was safe for the night and relieved to be on my own at last, I settled down to some serious drinking.

It was a mistake.

CHAPTER 49

Malin had her eyes fixed on the back of Gloria's red Land Rover. She was counting – again. She was six days late, or maybe seven, if she included the day she'd stayed at Velindre Farm, and she didn't know whether it meant anything or not. She'd read and re-read the leaflet that came with her pill and she'd scoured the internet but nothing she found gave her any peace of mind. The problem was not lack of clear information – the problem was her. Because, as the decision to go for contraception had been less about needing it and more about wanting to fit in, she'd not been entirely conscientious about taking it. Not at first. She'd considered ringing Vee – loitered in the supermarket café when she was supposed to be buying groceries, finding a bank, a launderette. She'd lingered there, phone in hand, trying to formulate some way of telling her mother what was happening – or what she thought was happening. Then, suddenly aware of how long she'd been gone, she'd half run back to the café to find Grace and Jack in the company of a strange woman.

Grace had been crying, that much was obvious, and Jack was slumped in the chair, his dentures crooked, the front of his shirt wet with saliva. It had been like a dream – the woman, Gloria, offering them a bed for the night. A safe haven.

'Yes,' she found herself saying. 'Yes, please. That would be amazing, wouldn't it, Grace?'

But Grace was beyond deciding. She'd given a small shrug,

then turned away, a serviette clutched in her hand. So on she'd gone, nodding and smiling until somehow, there they were – Jack tucked up in the back of the camper, following Gloria's red Land Rover along open roads that wound like ribbons through the sheep-dotted fields.

The farm was halfway up the shallow slope of a hill. Perched, rather than nestling, Malin thought, as she watched Gloria unlatch the gate. Like it was looking out at the weather rather than hiding from it. The hedges in front of the farmhouse were angled from bracing against the wind.

'We're here,' she said, not sure if Grace was dozing.

'What?'

'We're here. The farm.'

Grace pulled herself upright. 'The farm? Oh. Yes.' She rubbed her eyes and looked out of the window. 'Gosh,' she said. 'Isn't it lovely?'

Malin steered through the gate and Grace climbed out to close it. 'You can leave me here,' she said. 'I'll walk the rest of the way.'

Grace waited for a minute and watched the camper van heading up the short track. The air had more of a bite to it than she'd expected. She pulled in a lungful, then lifted her hair and let it play across the back of her neck. She needed to wake up. She half laughed at the thought: what she really needed was to go to sleep. To go to sleep in a warm bed, someone taking care of her da, someone making sure everything was all right. *A night or two's respite*, Gloria had said. Had she any idea, Grace wondered, what that meant?

* * *

Gloria, it turned out, had every idea of what it meant. Grace sat by the kitchen window, watching her da and

Gloria, arm in arm, stride out across a small paddock. She could see, even from this distance, the jaunty look of him. She stretched out her legs and considered the room. Plain, you might call it, but something soothing in that plainness. Something like relief, perhaps, or solace. She could hear Malin upstairs in the bathroom. *You have the first bath*, she'd said and the girl had gone straight up, leaving her to sit, sipping tea while the knots in her unravelled and slipped away to the ticking of the clock and the muffled spitting and sparking of the Aga.

* * *

Malin was trying her best to relax. She should, she knew, be enjoying it, making the most of this unexpected gift, but no – she was counting. The pharmacy bag was hanging on the back of the bathroom door. She'd rushed in at the last minute, grabbed the box and paid for it before she could change her mind. But now she was too scared to face the next step. This wasn't how she'd imagined it. Her imagination had always conjured up a husband, a dog, a nice country cottage – not lying in some stranger's bath pretending she didn't know what was happening.

She'd been telling herself it simply wasn't possible because it had only happened once and they'd used a condom. But this feeling inside her – like her heart was riding a wave, like she was hurtling forwards, propelled by some force larger than herself – told her she was wrong. She thought about Connor Allan: not even a boyfriend, but a one-off thing in fresher's week. They'd been drinking, but neither of them was drunk enough to mask the fact it had been the first time for both of them: half an hour of awkward fumbling, then a week of nodding politely to one another across the canteen. She'd hoped for more but didn't know how to ask for it. But now . . .

She knew her reasoning was nothing but foolishness, but she couldn't get past the idea that if she *was* right, then somehow – despite the timing and the circumstances – it was meant to be. She knew how Vee would respond to that particular line of logic – Vee for volcanic. And Grace? There was no way she could talk to Grace. It was not simply the fear that such news might have her and Jack on the earliest train home, but the impossibility of discussing such a thing with a woman who had lost her own child.

There was only one way to settle it. She needed to do the pregnancy test.

CHAPTER 50

Michael

I was still drunk when I set out next morning. Drunk and, truth be known, wretched. My perch at the bar had afforded me time with the barmaid, time that took me past idle chat to the warm and heady realm of flirtation. When she closed up for the night I made it no further than the small room she rented above the pub. There'd been some relief in it, I suppose: a physical distraction that took my mind off Patrick, Joseph – my sorry self – but as ever, it didn't last. I staggered out of the pub at 7.45 a.m., collecting knowing winks from every man I passed, and hurried towards the *Laughing Girl*.

I knew Joseph was watching every step of my approach but he wouldn't catch my eye when I stumbled on board. He tossed a bundle of oilskins at me – his way of telling me more bad weather was on its way – and started the engine. I propped myself up against the stack of bins and rolled a cigarette – there was nothing for me to do other than wait for the moment we docked at Milford; nothing to ready other than myself. The truth is I felt ready for nothing other than a day in bed, some time to sleep off the drink, get my head together before I saw my ma and I was contemplating going down into the cabin, stretching out on the bunk when Joseph came out of the wheelhouse.

'You checked that engine?'

'Yeah.' I hadn't.

'It's coming in rough so I'm taking her further out.'

I shrugged. I could see the struggle on his face. The desire to be rid of me, and his reluctance to tangle with bad weather.

'You want to turn back then?' I was goading him and he knew it.

'Severe gale warning, Lundy, Fastnet . . .'

I smirked at the concern in his voice. 'Irish Sea?'

'No . . .'

'There you go then. It'll miss us. We've weathered worse than that anyway, haven't we?'

He narrowed his eyes and shook his head. 'Aren't you bloody right there, boy.'

* * *

A couple of hours later it was obvious that I wasn't right, that turning back was exactly what we should have done. But I said nothing. The *Laughing Girl* soldiered on, even though above the hammering wind and water I could hear the strain in her engine, and above that, the strain in Joseph's voice as he shouted into the radio. He poked his head out of the wheelhouse and waved his arm. 'I'm changing her course,' he yelled. 'They're saying west is better.'

I gave him a slight nod that suggested I didn't care one way or the other, that the roiling water and the bruised and heavy sky didn't bother me. The truth was some part of me was enjoying the battering we were getting. Some strange part that reasoned I deserved it, even needed it. I also knew that, despite his shying away from it, Joseph was one of the most experienced skippers around, so when he wiped the wheelhouse window with his sleeve and ducked back through the door, I assumed all would be well. I left him to it. I turned my face into the worst of the wind and imagined it blowing right through me, some cleansing blast that would take all my mistakes and secrets with it.

The conditions turned from hard to nasty in seconds. Like a man roused up by drink, it quit its swaggering display and got its fists out. The first few punches hit us broadside – sharp and unexpected. The *Laughing Girl* reeled, then righted herself, but above the victory roar of the wind I detected a brief change in her rhythm; a small pause like she was trying to catch her breath. Joseph swung her around, readying her for the next onslaught. His face was grim but I saw no fear in it, so when he suddenly threw open the wheelhouse door and yelled, 'Get the jackets out,' I somehow didn't take him seriously.

'What?' I shouted. I daresay I even smiled because I'd never heard him say such a thing before.

'The life jackets for God's sake, boy – she'll not take much more of this.'

I moved like a man in a dream, holding onto the rail with hands I could no longer feel as I clawed my way to the storage locker. The life jackets? Surely it wasn't as bad as that?

It was.

'Oh Christ, here we go . . . hold on Micky, hold on . . .'

I looked up from the storage hatch as a rank of waves – white-tipped and high enough to cast a shadow on the deck – suddenly rose in front of us, and heard the wild rev of the engine as Joseph steered the *Laughing Girl* towards them. She cleared the first wave, but the second was at her before she had time to recover. I felt her determination as she staggered headfirst into it, as she bent herself to the job of getting us up and over. And then, as she crested, I heard the missed beat, the slight pause. The brief silence told me she was giving as much as she had. I held my breath as we climbed again, clenching my teeth against the scream of the engine, counting the seconds as she pitched herself at the task we had set her, upwards, onwards . . . She was almost there, near enough to feel the water flatten out beneath the hull; near enough to feel the release from the struggle; near enough for me to let go of my breath—

I couldn't say exactly when I heard Joseph's voice, his *Mayday, mayday* so firm and unshakeable it didn't quite seem real. Nor exactly when I realised the sudden stillness that descended did not herald victory, but defeat. It wasn't a lull in the storm, but in the engine. We were dead in the water, drifting broadside; the *Laughing Girl* had done all she could and we were on our own. There was nothing to do but wait for some miraculous rescue, or the killer wave. The first, I knew, was impossible, unless God himself was going to reach down and snatch us out of the Irish Sea; but the second, that was just a matter of time. I braced myself and stumbled back to the storage hatch. I was crouched down, unscrewing the fastening when I realised the deck water was ankle deep and no longer running off. I pulled myself up, pushed back the hood of my jacket and shouted across to Joseph. He had his back towards me, the radio in his hand.

'Joseph, Joseph!' I don't know if he heard me, nor exactly what it was I wanted to say to him, because the next thing I knew the deck water was past my boots, then past my knees. I stood, mesmerised and disbelieving as it kept rising, until the deck simply disappeared from under my feet and I was pitched headfirst into a cold and spiteful sea.

CHAPTER 51

Grace lowered herself into the warm water with a smile. Her mother had been a great one for appreciating the simple things in life – a digestive with her tea; half an hour on her own with a radio play; a nice piece of fish for supper – and a warm bath at the end of a long day would, she knew, have made the list.

She rubbed soap into a flannel and ran it over her arms and legs, the back of her neck, then down to her belly. She traced the silvery lines that ran either side of her navel and the fine white line above her pubic bone and thought about Harry. His entrance into the world had not been the romantic event she'd conjured up during her pregnancy. Months of yoga, deep breathing exercises and raspberry leaf tea had culminated in a trolley dash to theatre – her howling and thrashing like something demented – and a hasty caesarean. Greg had hated the scar, of course, but years later, when Harry died, she'd given thanks that the evidence of him wasn't just the boxes she'd packed up and stashed away, but in the secret marks he'd left on her body.

She'd occasionally wondered what another man might make of those marks. A joke really, because the only man in her life right now – and for the foreseeable future – was her da. Unless . . .

It should have been Michael's name that came to her, of course: *unless we find Michael, and my life is suddenly transformed* – but no – the name that popped into her mind and brought a flush of heat to her face was Dan Halliday's. Would a man like Dan consider them a disfigurement, she wondered, or might he see the beauty in them? Not just see the beauty in them but run his light fingers across them, maybe trace the soft line of them with his . . . tongue? She closed her eyes and let her imagination take her: a hotel room maybe, new underwear, low lighting – she would be nervous, apologetic maybe, but Dan would be gentle, unhurried, smiling. Would it still be there, she wondered, the part of her that knew how to respond? The soft throb in her groin told her it would. She lay back, and let her fingers find their way. She groaned quietly as the feeling expanded into her belly; her chest; her throat. She opened her mouth and whispered the word that she found there. *Yes, yes, yes.*

It was the sound of Jack's voice in the kitchen below that eventually brought her back to herself. She clambered out of the bath and, on shaky legs, went down to face the gauntlet of cajoling him into the shower.

'Oh. Where is he?'

Malin was at the Rayburn, stirring a large pan. She was pale, despite the heat coming off the stove.

'With Gloria.'

Grace sat herself at the table, trying to place the feeling that had suddenly washed over her: guilt for leaving her da with Gloria while she'd been in the bath? Or guilt because of what she'd been thinking – and doing – while she was in the bath?

'Gloria said to open the wine.'

Wine? She didn't do wine. There was something a bit renegade about wine. And risky. *What if . . . what if . . .*

'Where is it?'

Malin left the spoon in the pan and went to the fridge. She

put two glasses on the table and watched as Grace unscrewed the bottle.

'None for me, thanks,' Malin said, and turned back to her stirring.

'So have they gone back out?'

'No. He's in the shower.'

'What?'

'Gloria's set him off in the shower.' She nodded towards a door at the other end of the kitchen.

'The shower? How did she do that, sling him over her shoulder?'

'Nope. She just said it and off he went.'

Grace took a long sip of wine. Maybe the woman had hypnotised him, drugged him even.

'That smells good.'

'Mmhh.'

'What is it?'

'What? Oh.' Malin rose slightly on her toes and peered into the pan. 'Chilli, I think. Or maybe not – I'm not sure.'

Grace was wondering what to say next – she could feel it hanging in the air, something she couldn't quite put her finger on – when the door at the other end of the room opened and Jack walked in.

'Well, who have we got here?' she said.

'First Seaman James at your service, Ma'am.' He snapped off a smart salute and marched towards her, heels together, toes pointing left and right. He was wearing a pair of striped pyjamas – the top tucked into the bottoms – and no slippers.

'What do you think?'

'Smart as a carrot.'

'Aren't I just. And,' he was stroking his chin, now, 'have a feel of that.'

Grace reached up to feel the smoothness of his skin.

'Don't tell me you had a close shave and I wasn't there to save you.'

'Close shave? I tell you, girl. I thought for a minute she was going to get the sheep shears to me, I was . . .'

'What's that you're saying, Jack James?'

Gloria came through the door. Came through like she'd perhaps just got up from watching the telly and fancied a cup of tea. Not a hair out of place it seemed. None of the damp dishevelment that usually accompanied shower time.

Grace found herself lost for words, which didn't seem to matter because her da was full of them. She sat back with her wine and listened to him. All sheep talk, of course: shows, feed, shearing, market prices, lambing. He was like an episode of *The Archers*. She tried more than once to catch Gloria's eye, to let her off the hook, but she didn't notice – happy, by the look of things to be listening, putting her own oar in if he happened to take a breath. On and on he went, his face lit up, his hands flying this way and that until, all of a sudden, he ground to a halt.

'Grace,' he said. 'I . . . Is it time?'

Is it time? The question hit some panic button in the centre of her chest. It *was* time – and here she was, swigging wine, relaxing, relinquishing her duty to some woman she'd only just met. She jumped to her feet.

'Time? Yes. No. Erm no, Da. Not quite time yet. We've not had our supper. Malin?'

Malin turned from the stove. She'd been there throughout, stirring the pan, seemingly oblivious to the rest of them.

'Did you manage to get a bit of ham?' There was no way he'd entertain chilli.

'Oh, yes. It's still in the van. Shall I . . . I'll go get it.' Malin was across the kitchen and out in the yard before Grace remembered the cassette.

'Won't be a minute, Da,' she said, and dashed out after her. The light outside spoke of a day that was just finishing – a wash of grey that seemed to have dropped from the sky and onto the ground. She peered through it and walked towards the camper van. The sliding door was open but there was no light on. Malin's small face appeared in the doorway as she approached.

'Everything OK?' Grace asked. 'You find the ham?'

'Yes, it's here.' Malin held out a carrier bag.

'I forgot to ask you to bring the cassette.'

'Right. Oh, hang on . . .'

'No, it's all right, I can get it.'

Grace leaned in through the passenger door, taking her time because it was obvious that Malin was close to tears. She could make no sense of it: meeting Gloria had to be the best thing that had happened to them since they'd set off; the only positive thing, surely. A hot bath, proper food, a bed . . .

'Do you think Gloria would be offended if I slept in the van tonight?'

'In the van?'

'If she didn't mind, of course,' Malin said. 'It's just that I just fancy, you know – a bit of time on my own.'

'Well, yes. Of course.' Grace quickly dismissed the memory of her own time alone in the bath. 'You'll have some food, though?'

'I'm not hungry, really.' Malin's stomach was only just settling. It had been bunched up in her chest since she'd done the pregnancy test.

'OK then. I'll let Gloria know. You're sure, though? Sure everything's all right? You look a bit . . .'

'No, I'm fine. Everything is fine.'

* * *

Malin watched as Grace crossed the yard to Gloria's door, then tucked herself into Jack's place on the back seat. The van would be colder without Jack and Grace – quieter, of course, and roomier – but cold. She thought about putting the heater on, boiling the kettle for tea, making up the bed, checking her phone for messages – everything and anything that didn't involve thinking, which was ridiculous because there was the test – perched on the pillow – exhibit number one, telling her the only thing she needed to do right now *was* think.

Results in 60 seconds, it had said on the box, but she'd known, as she perched on the edge of the bath, counting the seconds – eleven, twelve, thirteen, fourteen – she'd known what the result was going to be. She'd felt it, just like she could feel it now. The quiet dividing of cells, the soft waft and sway of life shaping itself inside her.

CHAPTER 52

Michael

There was a moment, I think, of disbelief: some part of me waiting for the *Laughing Girl* to right herself; for my feet to suddenly find the deck; for Joseph to duck out of the wheelhouse and yell back. I had the strange impression I was looking down on myself, that what was happening was not real, but some dramatic painting or film scene. I lay back on the surface of the water to take it in. There was a feeling of calm acceptance, some notion as I lay, lulled by the waft and sway of water at my back, that what was happening was meant to be. I smiled, maybe; raised my arm and waved – and then I went under.

There might have been some relief in it: the sudden silence, the dark; the invitation to give in and drop to the ocean floor. But no, the moment the water closed over my head and filled my mouth I was fired up with an overwhelming urge to fight. To live. I kicked off my boots, struggled out of my jacket, slipped the braces from my shoulders and loosened the trousers from my waist. I worked my legs free and kicked for what I hoped was the surface.

I emerged, gasping and choking, into a world of grey. The sea and sky were fused together like some unbeatable foe. Clouds hung like a sheet of metal over my head, water as wild and untameable as mercury clawed at my legs and urged me down, an ungodly net I could not escape.

I called out for Joseph one last time. I called out for my ma and da – for Grace. For forgiveness.

CHAPTER 53

Jack looked up when Grace walked back into the kitchen. He was spooning something into his mouth, his nose an inch or two from the bowl. Gloria was nowhere to be seen.

'Are they in, girl?'

'They're in, Da.'

'You feed 'em?'

'Certainly did. Mmh, that looks nice.'

He peered down at the chilli. 'It's lovely. Tasty.'

She considered him, and tried to gauge what stage they were at. It was gone half seven but there seemed to be some air of a second wind about him.

'So shall I get the cocoa on?' she said.

'Cocoa? Well, we could – after.'

'After? After what?'

'Erm . . .'

Grace could see he was clinging on, clutching at some thread that would lead him to the right answer, when Gloria suddenly poked her head round the door. 'Five minutes, Jack.'

'Righty-ho.' He waved his spoon at her.

'You go up if you like, Grace,' Gloria said. 'It's the room at the top of the stairs. Second on the left? There's a good few books and magazines – something might take your fancy. Me and Jack have got a date, haven't we, Jack?'

He swizzled his spoon again. 'We certainly have, girl.' He paused and gave a small nod. '*Farming Today*,' he chirped and gave her one of his grins. 'Weekly roundup special.' He pushed back from his chair and, following the sound of the signature tune, tottered across the kitchen, leaving Grace, with something that felt like panic, on her own.

It was this feeling, Grace reasoned afterwards, that had made things so much worse, because when she'd let herself into the bedroom and switched on the light her guard was already down. She was unprepared for the football posters, the Leeds United scarf pinned above one of the twin beds, the montage of tickets and programmes over a small chest of drawers. She swayed back on her heels, her head suddenly adrift, then stepped in, closed the door behind her and let herself down onto the nearest divan. Buzz Lightyear beamed up at her from the duvet cover. It was a child's room – had been a child's room. She had intended to get the room ready for her da – rig up the cassette player, turn back his bed – but instead she folded back the duvet and, without taking her clothes off, crept in. She buried her face into the cool sheets, searching for some lingering scent of the child who had spent his nights here and, ignoring the feeling of being poised on the edge of something, lowered herself cautiously towards sleep.

The dream was waiting for her – a quiet ambush that dropped like a soft net and wrapped itself round her in a tight embrace she could not escape. The more she struggled, the tighter it became until she was caught fast and helpless and there was nothing to do but give in and let it take her down; down to the place it always took her – to Harry. He was sleeping, not dead, she told herself as she freed herself from the net and walked across the ocean bed towards him. *Harry*, she called, and her voice moved through the water in a soft wave; a rolling wall that washed over him. It lifted the edge of his football shirt, loosened his tidy hair and disturbed the laces of his boots – but it did not wake him. *Harry.* She bent her back against the weight of the ocean and saw, at her feet, a length of rope; a slender cord that ran from her to him. She picked it up, felt the throbbing pulse of the thing against her fingers – and gently hauled herself towards him. On and on, never making any ground until – her legs half buckled with the effort – the rope suddenly came to an end and she was left clutching the frayed filaments.

She woke next morning to a quietness she thought was still part of the dream. She lay for a few minutes, then tiptoed across to check on her da: the small curve of him hunched beneath the duvet, the top of his head just visible. He still had his cap on. Downstairs the first colours of dawn were already painting the walls of the kitchen, broad sweeps of rose and amber that lit the room like a small church. She stood at the open door, welcoming the chill of the stone flags through her thin socks. Harry would have loved Gloria's farm. Loved it. Her da had seen the farmer in him, entertained a fancy that one day, when the lad was grown and ready, they'd be a team, and a good team at that – him with his quota of knowledge and the boy limber as a young oak. Greg had been another story, of course: as far as he was concerned the only grass involved in Harry's future was the turf of a football pitch.

Sometimes she allowed herself to imagine how things might have been and the scene she conjured up was always the same: Harry in the kitchen at Velindre Farm, grinning at some story her da was telling, and her, smiling at the pair of them as she cut into some fancy cake she'd cooked up.

'Grace. Good morning.'

Gloria was crossing the yard towards her, her cheeks flushed with the cold.

'Is that kettle on?' She eased her waterproofs and wellies off and went into the kitchen and busied herself at the sink. 'How did you sleep?'

'Well. Thanks. The bed was very . . .'

'It was the wrong bedroom.' Gloria put a jug of milk and a teapot on the table.

'Pardon?'

'You were in the wrong bedroom. I didn't realise until I brought Jack up. You were meant to be in the room next door. You slept in Eddie's room. In Eddie's bed.'

Grace watched as Gloria got a pair of mugs off the drainer. 'Oh, I'm sorry,' she said. 'I . . . I . . .'

'No. It's all right.'

Grace could see from the woman's face that it wasn't.

Grace didn't know what to say next. She could feel the thin ice of the situation. 'He liked his football, then . . . Eddie.'

'That's an understatement.'

She could have said it then. Could have said, *my son too*, but the words wouldn't come. Instead she poured milk into the mugs, then tea – and waited.

Eddie, it transpired, was Gloria's younger brother. *Down's syndrome*, she said. An unexpected late surprise for her mother apparently, although not half as unexpected as the brain haemorrhage that felled her while she was digging potatoes up one late summer's evening.

'I'd just started my nursing,' Gloria said. 'Darlington Memorial. I loved it.'

But she'd had to give it up – her dad being hopeless with Eddie – hopeless with anything really unless it had a woolly fleece and four legs. He'd not lasted long without her mother, a couple of years, and then it was just her and Eddie.

Grace couldn't bring herself to look at Gloria – or ask what had happened to him. She'd known the second she'd opened the door to the bedroom. The football posters, the scarf, the duvet cover: everything laid out like he'd just left, like he'd be back. She'd not only recognised the room for the shrine it was – she'd climbed into the lad's bed, greedy for some scent of him. She choked down a mouthful of hot tea to hide her embarrassment.

'I'll be for the high jump when he finds out someone slept in his bed.'

'What?'

'Oh, yes. He's got a nose like a bloody fox hound, has our Eddie,' Gloria said. 'Can't even change the washing powder.'

Grace had it all wrong: she'd pasted her own life over someone else's and assumed the worst, because Eddie, Gloria explained, was living in a residential college that specialised in agriculture. He came back to the farm one weekend a month and would, without a doubt, throw a wobbler over the bed.

Grace laughed. 'So that's why you're so good with my da,' she said. 'The shower last night. Hah! I thought you'd hypnotised him.' She shook her head. 'I've got myself into such a routine. Sometimes it . . .'

'Sometimes it feels like it's the only thing holding you together.'

Grace nodded. She could feel something inside her working itself loose.

Gloria was up from the table now, slicing a loaf of bread. 'I went to pieces for a while when Eddie went off to college. Lost my routine, see? Didn't realise how much I loved it really, until it was gone. Daft, eh? Anyway, that's enough about me – what about you? Jack said you're running the farm now?'

Grace smiled. 'Well, yes, amongst other things . . .' She realised she might have gone on and spilled all her beans, that she might have sat for the rest of the day drinking tea and telling Gloria the whole tale – Greg, Harry, Michael – if her da's voice hadn't suddenly trilled down from the landing.

'Oh blimey.' Grace jumped to her feet. 'He's up. I'll get him sorted, then we'll get out of your hair . . .'

Gloria fiddled with the handle of her mug. 'I'm in no hurry to be on my own, Grace. Why not stay another day?'

Grace knew it wasn't just kindness speaking, but loneliness too. Some part of her, the part that knew what it was like to be afraid of being on your own, wanted to say yes, but she didn't, couldn't.

'I'm sorry, Gloria, but we can't. We have to . . .'

Grace got no further because Jack, kitted out in what looked like the entire contents of his suitcase, trotted into the kitchen.

'Are we ready for off, then?' he said – to Gloria.

Gloria looked down at the floor. 'I'm sorry, Grace, I did mention it to Jack last night. A little run out, you know . . .'

'Richmond,' Jack said. 'We might even find ourselves some sausages.'

* * *

Twenty minutes later they were in Gloria's Land Rover scudding along dangerously close to the dry-stone walls that lined either side of the narrow road. Grace had reluctantly agreed to a short morning run, on the understanding that they would have to leave at lunchtime. It had ticked Gloria and Jack's boxes – Malin's too, because the girl looked fit for nothing except more sleep – but it had left Grace on edge. The delay – that was how it suddenly seemed – had sparked some feeling of panic in her; a feeling that they needed to get moving, that time was running out.

CHAPTER 54

Michael

Dying was not the thing I expected it to be. There were no bright lights, no last second revelations and no cine-film flashbacks. Nor was there any sense that someone was waiting for me. I floated in the water as the cold closed me down inch by inch: a quiet and gradual switching off until the only living part of me was the small flame of heat beneath my heart. When a flash of red suddenly appeared some way off to my right I imagined it was some further failing on my part: a short circuit between my brain and my eyes. I screwed them tight against the slap of the waves then looked again. There it was – a small swatch of red against the grey sloping waves: a small beacon of colour – and hope, I thought – as I thrashed my way towards it. I'd been too late with the life jackets, I knew that, but maybe . . . I lifted my head as high as I could above the water and hollered his name. 'Joseph, Joseph,' I shouted, and struggled through the swamping waves. Closer and closer with each arm-wrenching stroke, closer and closer until I could see it was indeed a life jacket – but an empty one. I propelled myself towards it, then reached out and embraced it. I buckled myself in and wept tears of thanks, salt water into salt water, for the thin thread of hope I had been given.

CHAPTER 55

'So . . .' Gloria was pouring coffee from a flask she'd suddenly produced; a flask, a couple of beakers, a packet of digestives. They were parked at the side of a fast-flowing river. Grace could smell the stones in the water through the chinked open window. Jack was asleep. Grace didn't say anything. She knew what Gloria was waiting for – a problem shared, etcetera, etcetera – but she no longer felt in the mood for spilling her beans.

'How far on is she?'

'Pardon?' Grace steadied her beaker with both hands. The question made no sense.

'Your young lass. Malin. How far on is she?' Gloria rounded her hand over her belly, then, catching the look on Grace's face, shook her head. 'Ah. You didn't know?'

Grace put the beaker down on the dashboard.

'I don't know what you mean, Gloria. She's . . . she's pregnant?'

'I reckon so . . .'

'But how . . . how on earth could you know that?' Grace heard the edge in her own voice. 'Sorry,' she said. 'But . . .'

But what? she thought. She'd spent the best part of a week with the girl and noticed nothing. And – her stomach lurched at the thought – she'd just told her about Harry. What did that say about her for goodness' sake?

'How do you know? Did she . . . did she tell you?' She had to force the words out because the thought of Malin confiding in Gloria rather than her had choked her throat up.

'Oh, no. I've not spent more than five minutes alone with the child. I saw the leaflet in the bathroom. The pregnancy test leaflet?'

'Oh. Right.' Grace blew out a short breath. So it wasn't confirmed, she thought. It was just an assumption on Gloria's part.

'Is she family then?'

Right on the bloody nose, Grace thought. 'That's a good question,' she said. 'But I'm not that sure how to answer it.'

Afterwards, she reckoned it must have been the sound of the running water that lulled it out of her, or perhaps the way the sun was dodging in and out of the clouds – lighting the grey shadowed hills with bursts of gold. Whatever it was, she'd felt her mind shrugging off its usual caution and had leaned back in her seat and let the story unravel.

'She turned up at the farm a week ago.' That's how she started. Gloria listened. She nodded every now and then, but stayed quiet. Perhaps, Grace thought, she was scared of jumping in and stopping the flow. The truth was it would have taken some stopping because out it came – Michael, Malin, Vee – the words tumbling out of her mouth like someone had turned on a tap.

'You think it's true then? That Michael is alive?' Gloria said, when she'd eventually dried up.

'I don't know. We're on our way to Whitby to find out. Or we were. If . . . if you're right though, if Malin is pregnant, then I don't know what we'll do.'

'That would change things?'

'Well of course it would change things, Gloria. If she is pregnant, it'll be her mother she's needing . . .'

Gloria gave a small snort. 'From what you've told me it sounds like she needs *a* mother . . . not *her* mother.'

'I know . . . I know – but . . .'

She knew Gloria was right: she'd only spoken to Vee once but she couldn't imagine her welcoming such news – or trading her post in the Calais refugee camps for evenings by the fire knitting bootees.

'And anyway, what if it's a father she's needing . . . a family . . . ?'

It was a fair point but it was too much. Grace gulped a mouthful of air. The Land Rover suddenly seemed too small, too warm. The weight of this extra need – whether the pregnancy was a fact or an assumption – pressed the air out of her. She wanted to tell Gloria about social services, the police, the hospital; explain how close she was to falling off the fine line she was treading. How that line was stretched taut between the safety of the farm and the possibilities of Whitby.

'That's easy enough to say, Gloria. But what if he isn't there – what if we get there and find nothing? What do I do then?' She folded her arms across her chest and turned away so Gloria wouldn't see the tears in her eyes.

Gloria tilted her head on one side and raised an eyebrow. 'I used to do that.'

'Do what?'

'Go back. I'd work up a bit of courage to move forward, make a fresh start, and then . . . first sign of a problem I'd be backing off; keeping the boat steady.'

'But . . .' *But I'm not*, Grace wanted to yell. *I'm not retreating. I'm, I'm* . . .

'Used to tell myself it was self-preservation,' Gloria said. 'Then I realised – in the middle of a WI meeting for God's sake – what that means. It means putting yourself in a jar, Grace, that's what it means. Putting yourself in a bloody jar and lining it up on a shelf in a dark cupboard. You can stick any number of fancy labels on it, but that's what it boils down to.'

Grace let the image squeeze a small laugh out of her, but Gloria ignored it and fixed her with a stare. 'So Grace,' she said. 'I have a feeling there might be a few jars in your cupboard.'

Grace stared back at her. She cleared her throat as if she was about to speak – then got out of the Land Rover and walked away.

The river was very clear. It flowed past in a rush of noise, rising and falling over rocks hidden beneath the surface. The cold air coming off the water stung her face. Grace folded her arms across her chest and breathed it in: great mouthfuls that hurt her lungs but did nothing to clear the spinning in her head – or the image of the pantry at home: her store of jam and chutney. She didn't hear Gloria approach until she felt a hand on her shoulder.

'Grace, I'm so sorry . . . I . . .'

Grace didn't take her eyes off the river. 'It's OK,' she said.

'No. No . . . it's not. I went too far. I had no business saying all that . . .'

'No, you didn't,' Grace said, and then turned so she could look the woman in the face. 'But I'm glad you did. It's time I talked about it. Is there any of that coffee left?'

CHAPTER 56

Grace sank back into the seat of the Land Rover clutching her beaker.

'My marriage broke up.' A simple enough way to start, she thought. 'My marriage broke up and I went back to live with my da. I . . . I couldn't think of any other option at the time. He wasn't ill, at that point. Just needed a hand on the farm, you know . . .'

Gloria said nothing.

'Me and Greg had been together since I was at school. He'd always been . . .'

'A complete bastard,' Jack's voice suddenly trilled from the back seat.

'Da . . .' Grace spun round as he hauled himself upright.

'Don't you go defending him, Gracie,' he said, adjusting his dentures. 'The man was only interested in one thing and that was his bloody football. Tell her what happened, Gracie. Tell her about Harry . . .'

Grace felt the blood leave her head in one sudden rush. She never talked to him about Harry and yet here he was again – like Joseph – suddenly rising out of nowhere.

'He died, Gloria. The boy died. Go on, Gracie, tell her . . .'

Grace looked at Gloria and nodded. She took a deep breath.

'We had a son. Harry. He died five years ago. He was fourteen.' She stopped and looked down at her hands. 'It was sudden – unexpected, you know? I . . . I didn't cope very well . . .'

'Hmmph.' Jack was off his seat now. 'Go on, Grace. Tell her about Greg. Tell her what he did in your hour of need, the fancy bugger . . .'

She wanted to tell her da to shut up, to give a small laugh and shrug his words off as confusion, because she'd not factored this in. This remembering.

It had taken her months to realise what was happening. She'd hardly noticed Greg's absences at the time. They were a welcome break rather than a puzzle. It wasn't till afterwards – till the big announcement – she really understood.

'He had an affair,' Grace said. 'Was already having an affair, most likely. So – I left.'

'What a bastard.'

'Complete bastard,' her da quipped.

'I didn't care, Gloria. It was . . . it was a relief.'

'So what happened?'

'We got a divorce.'

'No, I mean to Harry.'

'Oh.' Grace braced herself against the saying of it – she readied herself for the taste of the words on her tongue. 'It was his heart. Sudden death syndrome. He was playing a match.'

More common than you think. That's what they'd told her, as if the words might be soothing. Instead, they'd kept her awake for weeks, images of football fields strewn with lifeless teenagers, played to a soundtrack of Greg shouting – exasperation rather than concern in his voice – as Harry pitched headlong in the slow dive he never surfaced from.

'Greg knew he couldn't blame me and there was no way he was going to blame himself . . . but I blamed him.'

'We all blamed him, Gracie. He ran that boy like he was a machine. Stopped him coming to the farm, tell her, Gracie . . .'

He was right. There was no point in denying it, so Grace told her: she took the lid off and emptied the lot out.

* * *

In 2003 Greg was working as a coach in France. Just across the channel, he was fond of saying, as if she needed the reassurance of his proximity, when the truth was his absence was a relief. It gave her the chance to rekindle something of herself. She had a home to run, Harry to keep her company and the freedom to visit her mother and da whenever she wanted. They were her best years, if only she'd known it, because the following year everything changed.

It was 2004. Harry was four years old. He still had his baby teeth, his little round belly. He was still her boy. She'd got back from the farm one evening, Harry in his red wellies, and she was in her farm clothes; the pair of them were ripe with the smell of dog, wool and manure. Her only thought, as she drove, was to get Harry in the bath and the clothes in the washing machine. Instead, as she indicated into the drive, she found her way blocked by Greg's car. She turned off the ignition, waited for her stomach to settle back into place, swung Harry up onto her hip and fixed on a smile. It slipped back off again when she walked into the kitchen.

'You're home!' she said, aiming at chirpiness but sounding slightly unhinged.

'Obviously.'

He'd quit his job in France. His decision, not theirs, of course.

It was a long night after that – and a long week that followed. By the end of the month she realised her life as she knew it was over.

'I just need to get my teeth into a project,' he'd said, after their first row. Nothing major, but she'd felt the change – in herself, Harry, the house. Some low current of electricity that had them stepping too carefully, quietly waiting for what might come next.

They didn't have to wait long.

It was a Saturday morning – early. She'd woken to an empty bed and noises from the kitchen. Voices – Greg's fast-talking monotone interspersed with occasional high-pitched replies from Harry. She pulled her dressing gown on and went quietly down the stairs. It was a lecture of some sort, she thought. She waited at the closed door a moment, then went in.

'Oh, you're up.'

Greg was leaning against the kitchen counter, drinking a glass of water. He had his running gear on.

'You too,' she said, glancing at the clock. 'It's early.'

'Well, thought we'd get an early start,' Greg said.

'What . . . ?'

She glanced at Harry, who was at the kitchen table. He was wearing his school sports kit. His trainers. His face was still pale and puffy from sleep.

'What are you doing?'

'First day of training,' Greg said. He turned his back on her and put his glass in the sink. 'Come on, Harry.'

Harry shot her a look. More of a plea, really.

'Hang on, Greg . . .'

It had got her nowhere. From that day on Harry became the new project.

There were times, in the early days, when she felt she could have stopped it: Harry was still her boy then, Greg the intruder. But by the time he was six she'd lost him. Greg had become the centre of his universe and she was relegated to the sidelines. There'd been no let up: training before school, after school, Saturday matches, Sunday boot camps. The only part she was allowed to play involved putting up his packed lunches and washing his kit. She tried to talk to Greg about it but got nowhere.

'We're not all like you, Grace, content with mediocrity.' He'd spat the words at her, his mouth twisted into an amused sneer. They'd been at a dinner party and she'd seen the embarrassment on the faces of the other guests – embarrassment for Greg that he'd tied himself down to such a dull, unambitious woman.

* * *

She didn't realise she was crying until her da's hand crept up onto her shoulder. 'Don't you be thinking of all that now, hinny. You came back to the farm and thank goodness for that. Saved my bacon, you did.'

Grace sniffed back the tears and felt for his hand. She wanted to tell him how he'd got that wrong – how he'd been the one saving bacon: him and his easy ways; his shipping forecast; his need for her . . .

Gloria cranked the engine into life.

'Come on, you two. Let's get back before we all start crying. You might give me a hand with those rams before you leave, Jack . . .'

* * *

Within a mile or two Gloria and Jack were up to their knees in the merits of Bluefaced Leicester's sweetness of nature versus Swaledales' hardiness. Grace left them to it. She tuned their voices out, and tuned in to her own thoughts – or lack of them. There was a spaciousness inside her head she'd not known for years and, as she basked in the airiness of it all, Malin slipped quietly into her mind. She didn't know if Gloria was right about a pregnancy but she couldn't deny that, despite her initial alarm, the possibility had sparked a feeling of excitement in her. She knew Gloria was right about Vee, though, and that the chance of her taking such news in her stride was less than slim. The conversation was easy to imagine. A good education and future thrown away – exchanged for the tedium of toddler groups, walks in the park, home-making and *neediness*. There'd be no mention of how a child could open parts of you that otherwise remained shut; no, if Vee was involved, it would be all about making the best decision and a quick visit to a clinic. The thought of it set her heart banging.

She rifled through her handbag for her phone.

'Everything OK, Grace?' Gloria asked.

'What? Yes, yes. I'm fine. Thought I'd let Malin know we're on our way back, just to . . . you know . . .'

'What?'

'Make sure she's OK . . .'

To tell her everything will be all right . . . tell her not to contact Vee . . .

'I think you left it on the table.'

'What?'

'Your phone. I saw it on the kitchen table. There's no reception here, anyway. She'll be fine, Grace. What are you worrying about?'

'I don't know. What if she's . . . you know, and what if she leaves us?'

'Don't be daft. Why would she do that? She's only just found you.'

Grace held her breath for the last few miles, trying to look like she was interested in what Gloria and her da were talking about, but all the while worrying about Malin. *What if she leaves us?* She shouldn't have said the words out loud because she couldn't shake them out of her head, and they'd tangled themselves together with the fear of what would happen when Vee got involved. She found her thoughts see-sawing between the possibility of Malin being pregnant – carrying Michael's grandchild, her da's great-grandchild – and the thought she might disappear from their lives just as quickly as she'd appeared. She rehearsed what she might say, simple sentences that would open the conversation, that would allow her to outline her flimsy proposition before Vee took over.

CHAPTER 57

Michael

'What the fuck are you doing in my bed?'

I didn't move. There might have been something of a fairytale about the question, but not in the voice, nor in the deep ache in my chest. I pulled the damp bedclothes closer, felt the cling of them against my cold and clammy flesh and remembered my clothes, a puddling mess piled on the floor.

'I said, what the fuck are you doing in my bed?'

The voice, low and husky, definitely belonged to a woman. That was something that might go in my favour, I thought, as I turned slowly onto my back and opened one eye.

She was standing in the doorway of the caravan. Tall, dressed in army combats, her hair dyed an unnatural shade that landed somewhere between orange and red. The daylight at her back lit it up like it was on fire.

'Get up – slowly.'

'What?' The word rasped out through my torn lips.

'I said, get up slowly.'

I lifted my head from the damp pillow and the room and all its contents took off on some undulating dance. I closed my eyes.

'You've got two options here.' The woman had stepped away from the door and was standing a couple of yards from me. She had a mobile phone in one hand and a knife in the other. 'You can get out now . . .' – she raised the knife – 'or . . .' – she nodded at the phone – 'I can call the Gardai.'

The Gardai. I blew out a small breath of relief. Ireland, then – not Wales. I lifted my head off the pillow again and waited for the room to settle. 'I need my clothes,' I croaked, and pulled myself up until I was almost sitting. It was a mistake. The change of position released some pocket of air in my stomach. It was up and out before I could stop it, a loud bark that filled the small space with the smell of seawater, followed by the seawater itself.

'Oh, for God's sake . . .' The woman dropped the knife and the phone and leapt forward. 'Lie down, lie down,' she said.

I did as I was told and watched as she flitted to and from the small kitchen: she heaped my clothes onto the draining board, lit the gas beneath a small kettle, filled a bowl with water. My last memory, before I dropped into a deep sleep, was of her washing my face and neck and covering me with something clean and dry.

'I'll be back,' she said, and I neither knew, nor cared, what she meant by it, because I was already dropping like a stone. Down, down, down I fell until I landed in the arms of a dream. A dream that was set to be my night-time companion for many years.

I dropped towards the ocean bed, shedding my clothes as I went. I looked up towards the fading light and saw them strung out, like some unlikely washing line, above me: my jacket; my boots; my oilskin pants; the woollen jumper my ma knitted; my belt, rippling like an eel. I dropped until, with a sandy thud, I hit the ocean floor. In the near distance I could see a light and realised, with some relief, that it was the Laughing Girl: *that I had solved the problem as easily as that. All I needed to do was walk over to her, collect Joseph and we could be on our way. The simplicity of the solution had me on my feet and picking my way towards the waiting boat. After a short distance, though, I realised I had miscalculated the distance between us. My feet started to protest against the sharpness of the sand; my eyes blurred against the sting of salt and my lungs suddenly lost their capacity to breath and instead set up a steady burning – then throbbing – that had me pushing away from the ocean floor and thrashing for the surface. I glanced back once as I swam – my arms outstretched like a torchbearer – but the light from the* Laughing Girl *had gone out.*

CHAPTER 58

'Malin?' Grace stood at the bottom of the stairs, her voice echoing in the empty space. She went up, checked the bedrooms and bathroom, vaguely aware that somewhere, above the knocking that had started up in her head, a telephone was ringing. She got to the bottom of the stairs just as it rang off – and her da stumbled in, rubbing his hands against the cold.

'All right, hinny?'

'She's not here,' she said. It was a mistake. She realised that as soon as she saw the look on his face.

'Who's that then?'

'Malin. She's . . .'

'Malin? . . .'

'It's . . . it's all right, Da. Nothing to worry about.'

'Is that kettle on, Jack?' Gloria came through the kitchen door in a bluster of shopping bags and cold air.

'She's not here,' Jack said.

'Come again?'

He looked at Grace for a leg-up.

'Malin,' Grace said. 'She's not here.'

'Yes.' Gloria hoisted the bags onto the table and started unpacking them. 'I noticed the camper van is gone.'

'Pardon?' Grace scooted across to the window and saw she was right. There was a patch of flattened grass where it had been.

'She'll not have gone far, Grace. Have you checked your phone?'

'No.' She grabbed it off the table.

'Go on, you go upstairs and give her a ring. I'll get cracking with this lot. Right, Jack, time to make yourself handy . . .'

Grace left them to it and took her phone upstairs. There was one voicemail waiting for her. She didn't recognise the number. She lowered herself onto the bed and dialled 121.

She was glad she was on her own; glad no one was there to witness the flush of colour that scorched her cheeks when she recognised the voice. 'Oh,' she said, as if she were speaking rather than listening to a message. She played it three more times, went to the bathroom to splash her face with cold water, before going back downstairs.

'Did you get her?'

Gloria was at the sink, peeling potatoes. Her da was beside her – a tea towel wrapped around his middle – doing the cutting. He gave her a grin.

'No . . . I . . . I couldn't get through.'

'Oh. I thought I heard you talking to someone.'

'Yes . . . no. It was a voicemail. A message.'

Grace could feel it – Gloria's next question lining itself up.

'Would you mind if I popped out for a walk, Gloria? I'd not be long. Just want to stretch my legs a bit.'

'Go for it,' Gloria said. 'You never know, if Jack gets a crack on with these tatties, we might have some food waiting when you get back.'

* * *

Grace forced herself to the top of the field that rose behind Gloria's farm before stopping. She squatted down on a large rock, leaned back against the dry-stone wall and marvelled at the square tidiness of the fields below: every boundary looked intact, every gate straight on its hinges, every building well tended. She ought to have been thinking about Malin, but the voicemail had derailed her altogether. She turned her face out of the wind and played it one more time.

Grace, it's Dan. Dan Halliday. I was wondering . . . erm . . . well, I was hoping we might be able to meet up sometime? I . . . erm. Well, yes. That's it. I'll try you again.

She'd told herself it was the wind in her face that was making her eyes water, that it was the hike up the slope that had her heart charging along. He'd called her three times now – that surely meant something? She was plucking up the courage to phone him when the sound of a car engine caught her attention. She got to her feet and saw the blue camper snaking its way back towards the farm. She put the phone in her pocket and started running.

* * *

Grace cried when Gloria waved them off from the gate. She told herself it was simply the relief of leaving, because the feeling that had gripped her earlier that morning – of time slipping away – had taken hold of her again. It was the running that did it, Grace knew that, as she'd sat – tense and distracted – spooning up the soup that Gloria and Jack had made. She'd raced downhill towards the girl and not wanted to stop. She'd chivvied Jack through his meal, then left him with Malin at the kitchen table while she scooted back and forth to the camper van with their luggage.

But as they drove off down the track Grace had looked back at the farm. Gloria was standing at the gate – the wind in her face, her arm aloft against a blue and endless sky – like some young prairie wife or soldier's sweetheart – and she'd known.

ATTENTION ALL SHIPPING

It wasn't simply the relief of leaving that was making her cry, but the relief of not being the one left behind, alone and waving. Gloria had come out to the camper van and offered another invitation to stay and Grace had pretended not to hear so she didn't have to answer or defend her decision, or see the loneliness on the woman's face. She told herself she had no choice, that as rude as their departure felt, she simply had no choice, because if what Gloria had said was true – if Malin was pregnant – then now, more than ever, they needed to get to Whitby to see if Michael was there.

CHAPTER 59

Michael

It would be fair to say that my initial introduction to Vee formed a template for the friendship we formed afterwards. I was in awe and afraid of her in equal measure, but my need for her help overrode both.

When I awoke sometime later, flailing my way out of the dream, she was there. She turned from the kitchen stove, wooden spoon in hand, and surveyed my face.

'You've surfaced at last then.'

Her words put a knot in my throat.

'Hungry?'

I tried to push my way towards an answer but there was a numbness in my head that seemed to defy any attempt to think. She lifted a pan off the stove and set it on a small table. I could see she'd laid two places. Bowls, spoons, bread.

'Well, I'm planning to eat now, so if you think you can keep it down, come and join me. Here, you can put this on.'

I nodded and, with some caution, hauled myself out of bed and slid my arms into a dressing gown. The feel of it – woollen, the kind of thing my da used to wear – made my eyes well up. If she noticed, she said nothing. She watched as I knotted the cord, waited until I sat down, then held out her hand. 'Vee O'Connor,' she said, and ladled something soup-ish into my bowl. 'We'll eat first, and then,' she pushed the plate of bread towards me, 'then you can tell me what the fuck is going on.'

I sat in silence for a minute or two, listening to the tick of a clock I couldn't see.

'Is it OK?'

I knew she was referring to the soup. I was tentatively spooning it through lips that cracked and smarted with every mouthful, struggling to get it past my tongue that sat, swollen and leathery in my mouth – but her words – the unexpected kindness of them, brought tears to my eyes. She leaned over and snatched a tea towel from the counter and passed it over.

'How about we talk first and eat later?'

I wadded the tea towel against my eyes and let loose a flood of tears I thought would never stop. They coursed down my face, a salty echo of the ocean I'd somehow escaped, and dripped onto the table, into my soup.

She sat quietly through it all, her chin propped on one hand, waiting for me to finish. When I had, or thought I had, she got up from the table and took two glasses from a small cupboard.

'Brandy?' She didn't wait for my reply but simply poured out two measures. 'It's good for shock,' she said, 'and you strike me as a man who's had a shock.'

I knocked it back in one and felt it travel, like some golden solution into my belly, my chest, my brain: a warming potion that dissolved everything in its path and flooded me with a sense of calm, and an overwhelming need to talk.

Vee told me later that I didn't make total sense; that my account of what happened didn't completely add up. But she gave me free reign, she accepted my story without comment or interruption, and for that I was grateful, because, like the tears, once I got started I found I couldn't stop.

'My God,' she said when I finished. 'I wasn't prepared for that.'

'Nor was I,' I said, and the words wrenched some final sob out of me. 'It was a miracle . . .'

'Hmph . . . I don't believe in miracles . . .'

I stared at her. 'I don't know what else you'd call it then, because there I was . . .' I lifted my arm from the table, 'and here I am now, like. . .'

'Robinson Crusoe.'

'Yes. Robinson Crusoe.'

'So what happened next?'

It was the obvious question but I had no real answer for it. I remembered buckling myself into the life jacket. I remembered the cold. I remembered waking up with sand in my mouth—

I lay for a long time. The wash of whatever tide had delivered me had receded and although I could not feel it, I could hear it. The sand was rough against my cheek and tongue but I couldn't summon the will or strength to move. I opened my eyes and, unsure whether it was the sky or my head that was reeling with stars, let them close. When I opened them again the stars were gone and the sky was striped pink with the promise of a sun I could not yet feel and I realised I'd been woken by the sound of the water lapping around my feet. I lay still until it crept to my knees, then, like an emerging sea creature, prised myself out of the sand. I raised myself onto all fours, sat back on my heels and looked around. I'd been brought up in a small cove; delivered, I realised with some care, because the beach that surrounded me was strewn with large boulders. To my left the cove finished in a jut of grassy land that topped a low cliff and to my right it was half circled with tall cliffs that rose like a stony spine from the sand. I rubbed my eyes to get a better look because at the foot of those cliffs lay something blue. Joseph? The thought, the possibility, had me on my feet and staggering across.

CHAPTER 60

Malin was trying her best to concentrate on driving but her eyes kept flicking to her phone on the dashboard and her thoughts kept pulling her back to the events of the morning.

As soon as Gloria had driven off with Jack and Grace, she'd taken out the pregnancy test and studied it. She'd read and re-read the leaflet and felt the panic of the previous day suddenly turn a corner and head towards something like excitement. She hauled herself back from it – just – then drove to Sedbergh, concentrating on the muted colours of the sky and fields, stone walls coppered by the sun, the sound of the tyres against the worn tarmac – anything to keep herself from following the trail of what-ifs skidding round her head. She bought a second test, then went back to the Farfield Mill café.

She'd told herself she just needed to make sure but what she realised, as she sipped her tea, was that it wasn't confirmation she needed, but permission: permission to allow what was happening to be the miraculous, positive, life-changing thing she'd always imagined it would be. The circumstances didn't fit the narrative she'd been penning, but she could re-write the narrative. She'd left her tea half-finished, taken the test in the toilets and, after a quick glance at the result, headed back to the camper van. The test only confirmed what she already knew, what she could already feel. Life was not only blossoming all around her – she'd already found an aunt, a grandfather, maybe even a father – it was blossoming inside her too.

She got out her phone and opened Instagram. She typed in his name and considered the photograph of him. Connor Allen. It had been his name that had attracted her in the first place – some sense of familiarity in the way his name echoed hers. They'd met in the student union bar, then, at his suggestion, left the rowdiness behind and headed down to the Mumbles. They walked the length of the beach before he put his arm around her. Later, they'd gone back to her room and muddled through half an hour of sex that had been more about ticking a box than passion. He'd left soon after because – and this was something else she'd liked about him – he lived at home and his mother would be expecting him back. And then, of course, nothing. The two of them, she suspected, hopelessly paralysed by the thought of making the next move. But now . . .

She'd scrolled through her phone contacts, tapped on his number and left a message. She'd stayed awake half the night hoping for a reply but, although the two blue ticks alongside her message told her it had been received and read, Connor had not replied. His silence had initially sent her back to Instagram but there'd been nothing recent or revealing – photographs taken at a rugby match, one at a children's birthday party and a couple of seascapes. After that she'd logged into Tinder, then logged straight off because the possibility of him broadcasting his availability was more than she could manage. She'd tried to cobble together a memory of their brief encounter but it was full of holes. They'd both been on unfamiliar ground that night, too intent on covering up their discomfort to make any meaningful conversation. He was doing some sort of environmental studies course, he lived at home and he played rugby. Other than the fact he was a good deal taller than her and had red hair, it was as much as she could remember. What, she wondered, did he remember about her?

She was about to say something to Grace – an inane remark about the weather, probably, anything to take her mind off Connor Allen and the queasiness that seemed to have intensified overnight – when Grace suddenly turned to her and asked how she was feeling.

'Feeling?' Malin couldn't help herself. The concerned edge to Grace's voice and the kindness in it started tears pricking at the corner of her eyes.

'I'm fine . . .' That was as far as she got. Two minutes later, through a blur of tears, she was pulling into a lay-by.

CHAPTER 61

Michael

'So why were you drunk?'

It was my first introduction to Vee's astute mind, the way she could see behind whatever it was she was looking at, or being told.

'What do you mean?'

It was my second day in the caravan and I was nursing wounds I'd not initially noticed. What I'd taken for dirt on my feet was in fact deep bruising. So deep I wondered how I'd ever walked on them. My knees were run across with jagged cuts and my elbows grazed almost down to the bone. Worst of all was the feeling in my chest: a great pressure that carried the threat of sudden tears. It had descended as I staggered across the beach towards the swatch of blue that lay at the foot of the cliffs. I carried Joseph's name on my lips but had neither the breath nor the courage to lose it into the air.

It was a creased, flaking length of old tarpaulin, some relic that had nothing to do with the *Laughing Girl*. I sank down beside it and, to my shame, thanked God that it wasn't him.

'It's an easy enough question, Mick . . .' I'd told her my name. In the aftermath of my long crying session, she asked me, and I'd simply told her. It was a mistake but, like many others I'd made in my life, I didn't know how to undo it.

'OK. I'll guess then. It was over a girl?' She had her head on one side, sizing me up.

'No. It wasn't a girl.'

'Mmh. A boy then!'

There was mischief in her eyes but it disappeared when she saw the look on my face.

'Haha . . . a boy.' She leaned across the table and put her hand on my arm. 'Do you want to talk about it?'

'No. I don't.' I stood up and felt the lurch in my chest, the feeling of something sliding open. 'I think I might lie down again, if that's OK.'

She gave a small snort. 'Go ahead. Why don't you put your head under the covers while you're at it?'

'Pardon?'

'Or bury yourself in the sand . . . sorry, that's not funny . . .'

I turned back to face her. The low sun was angling through the caravan window. Her hair was aflame. 'I'm sorry, Vee. I'm honestly too tired to talk about it. About anything. Let me sleep for a while and then—'

And then what? I couldn't go any further. I couldn't imagine any scenario that would allow me to reveal the last portion of my miserable tale to this pushy woman. And I couldn't imagine any solution to my predicament.

But at that point I didn't know her very well.

* * *

Vee, I discovered, liked nothing better than a cause. It was the thing that had brought her to Ireland, a short contract with some third sector organisation that provided support for the rising wave of asylum seekers and refugees who were attempting a 'back door' entrance into Britain. The caravan, this small haven I'd stumbled into like a shipwrecked

Goldilocks, came with the job. The other thing that came with the job, the very important thing in my case, she said, was contacts. Vee knew everything there was to know about getting a driving licence, a passport, a bank account, about creating an identity that would allow a person to slip quietly into a new life. She could, she said, simply add me to her caseload.

But I wasn't sure. I kept putting her off because as tempting as her offer was, the thought, or fantasy, of simply staying put in the caravan, felt a lot safer. The truth was I couldn't shake Joseph from my mind. The short walks I took were nothing to do with taking the air but everything to do with searching for him. I combed the surrounding coves and beaches, trying to tamp down the fear that I would find him. That I would find him and he would not be dead, but alive. That he would grin up at me, his eyes glittering with hatred and disgust, and the thought of what he was going to tell my da. I said nothing to her about it so I wasn't prepared when she came back from her work a few weeks later with a newspaper. The *Western Mail*.

'Oh,' I said, as it slid across the table towards me. The headline took the air from my lungs.

Was the skipper drunk? I forced myself past it and scanned the text for the words I needed to see. *Lost without a trace; search called off; no survivors.* I turned the page and studied the photographs – me, at God knows what age, the *Laughing Girl* steaming out of some unnamed harbour, and Joseph, as I had seldom seen him, relaxed and smiling from a sunny wheelhouse. I pushed the paper to one side and leaned my head on my hands.

'You've no excuse now, Mick. You're dead – and no one's looking for you. You've got nothing to lose. So . . .'

She came in a week later with the small bundle that was

going to change my life. A driving license, National Insurance number, birth certificate.

'Mick Jackson,' I said.

'After your dad, yeah?'

I looked down at the papers in my hands so she wouldn't see the tears in my eyes. I squinted at the address on the driving license.

Henrietta Street, Whitby.

'But I don't know Whitby, Vee . . .' It wasn't entirely true. I had a vague memory of a day trip there when I was very young. But Joseph had hated the east coast and we'd never worked there.

'Isn't that the whole point, Mick? Besides I've got a friend up there. He'll help get you sorted, no questions asked.'

'Christ.' I sank down on the nearest chair. 'When?'

'Next week. My contract's coming to an end so I'll be out of here too.'

I gazed around the caravan, at the small space that had held me safe for weeks, at the woman who had nurtured me back to life.

'How can I ever repay you, Vee?'

She gazed back, twirled a lock of hair between her fingers, then smiled. 'Well,' she said. 'I've been meaning to talk to you about that.'

CHAPTER 62

Is this it? Jack hadn't said it out loud but the thinking of it put a sag in his knees. One minute they'd been winding their way down from the North York Moors; a tumpy landscape of heather and sheep; the sea a glittering sheet stretched from one side of the windscreen to the other – and the next they'd somehow descended into . . . this. *Whitby*, Grace had said. *Like the postcard in the envelope.* He'd been expecting boats, a harbour, a pier . . .

'Is it a supermarket?'

'No, Da. It's the park and ride.'

He gave a small nod. *The park and ride?*

'It'll have changed a lot, Da, since you were last here. Don't worry, you'll recognise it once we get to the harbour.'

He tipped her a quick smile. 'Will we have to walk?'

'No. There's a bus. Look. Over there. Park and ride, see?'

He didn't see. All he saw was tarmac, cars, people.

'Why don't I just stay here, pet,' he said. 'Maybe have a few winks? Top myself up a bit?' It was worth a shot, but the look on her face told him it wasn't going to work.

She shook her head. 'You'll be fine, Da, come on.'

Come on. It was her answer to everything. Giddy up. Like he was some reluctant nag. The truth was he needed some time on his own so he could think. Or try to bloody think. It was something that Gloria had said to him as they were leaving her farm. She'd leaned in and said something that had suddenly chinked open a door in his head, then – before he'd had the chance to walk through the damn thing – Grace had chipped in with some comment and she and the girlie had set off talking, and never shut up. He'd tried his best to close them out but it hadn't worked; the door hadn't just slammed shut, it had disappeared altogether.

'Perhaps we should go and have a quick look ourselves, Grace? We could see what's what, make a bit of a plan while Jack has a rest and . . .'

He jumped straight in. 'Oh, yes. That's a good idea, Grace, isn't it?' He detected a slight give in her shoulders, some hesitation on her face so threw in a small yawn. 'I'd be asleep in minutes, honestly, just leave me here and let me snooze . . .'

'Well . . .'

He gave the bench seat a light pat and launched on. 'Oh, yes. I'll just stay here on the bunk. You can pull the curtains round. You can . . .'

'OK, OK, Da. You can stay, but . . .'

And off they'd gone, after she'd issued him with enough instructions to fill a book, leaving him alone in glorious silence. He gave it a few minutes, then leaned between the front seats and opened the glove compartment. It was sweets he was after, but the envelope side tracked him. He slipped it out, got himself comfy and emptied the contents onto his lap. He considered them in turn – the photograph of Michael and a baby, the newspaper cutting, the postcard. He hauled himself off the bunk, swished back the curtain, then slid open the door and peered out. Tarmac, tarmac everywhere and not a boat in sight. What on earth would Captain Cook make of that then? He put the envelope in his pocket, slipped his shoes back on and climbed out of the van. He wasn't going anywhere, of course – rules number one, two and three before Grace had finally left him in peace. No, he was simply stretching his legs, getting a bit of fresh air, a change of scenery to maybe jog his memory . . .

He wandered across the car park, adding a slight jaunt to his step because he knew he was disobeying orders. A young girl with a dog fell in beside him.

'We're on our holidays.'

Jack looked down at her.

'Oh. That's nice.'

'We're staying in a cottage over there.' She paused to point beyond a line of trees that had a struggling look about them. 'It's blue and you have to bend down to get in.'

'Oh. Right. Well . . .' Jack looked over his shoulder but couldn't see anyone bringing up the rear. No sign of an adult.

'Are you on holiday, too?'

He gave this some thought. *I think so*, didn't feel like the right thing to say.

'I am,' he said, and then, because he didn't know how to follow it up, bent down and stroked the dog.

'He's a sheepdog,' the girl said. 'A blue merle.'

'Yes,' Jack said. He was starting to feel nervous. It was one thing going AWOL, but this child appearing from nowhere, chatting away like she knew him. It had him wondering if maybe she did and somehow, between getting out of the camper and walking across the car park, he'd slipped another cog. He suddenly wanted to be back on his own, lying on the bunk. Safe. He turned away from the girl and started walking back the way he'd come. Thought he'd come.

'Are you not getting on the bus?'

'What?'

'The bus,' she said and pointed at a sleek coach parked a short distance away. A long queue of people lined up beside it. He gave one last look around the rows of parked cars and, failing to pick out the van, gave her a quick nod.

'Yes,' he said. 'I am.' And set off towards it.

* * *

'I think it must be a funeral,' Grace said, as they neared the town, then, as she noticed the young couple walking ahead of them – the pair of them decked out in black velvet capes, motorbike boots and handcuffs – 'or maybe a film set?'

'They're goths,' Malin said, which didn't explain a thing, but marked the end of the conversation because the density of the crowd forced them into single file. Grace followed behind as they threaded their way through a suffocating sea of black. On and on – a tide of rubbish beneath their feet, a mob of screeching gulls overhead. The intensifying smell of fish and seaweed was the only indication they were nearing the harbour.

'Malin.'

Grace lurched forward, swerving around the couple in front of her and grabbed Malin's arm. 'Let's sit down a minute. Get started on that plan?' She pointed to an empty bench perched on the quayside, then worked her way towards it. She slid a tray of cold chips out of the way and sat down. She gazed over the boat-filled harbour, the rows of vessels anchored below them tethered up like battered old workhorses.

But Malin wasn't looking at the boats, or listening – she was at the quayside checking her phone.

Once they'd left Gayle Farm, Grace had waited for her da to doze off, then, before she lost her nerve, started *the conversation*. Gloria, it turned out, had been right – a tearful confession somewhere near Hawes that had them pulling over to the side of the road, Malin sobbing over the steering wheel as traffic streamed past them. They'd spent the rest of the journey mulling over the details – the impossibility of the pregnancy (a half-hearted pairing with a boy called Connor), the fact that Vee would go bonkers when she found out and, most importantly, the certainty that Malin was going to keep the baby. It was this that Grace needed to talk about again because the thought of it had lit her mind like some shady path had suddenly been illuminated – and she'd found herself wanting to walk down it. Now, waiting on the bench, Grace wasn't so bothered about making a plan so much as rekindling their conversation.

A baby, she wanted to say. *A baby will change everything.*

CHAPTER 63

Michael

It was our last weekend at the caravan and we were celebrating. I was opening the second bottle of wine when Vee suddenly got up and turned down the music.

'You know what we were talking about, Mick?'

'Which bit?' It seemed to me we'd talked non-stop all week: she'd set about preparing me for my new life like she was some kind of MI5 handler.

'Well . . . you asked how you could repay me?'

I have to be honest – my heart sank a little. The fear that she was going to ask me for money, that our friendship was going to end in some financial arrangement. But no.

'I want a baby.'

I put the wine bottle on the table.

'A baby? What do you mean?'

'I mean just that. I want a baby and I was hoping you might consider . . .'

'Good God, Vee. Me? A baby?'

'I know, I know, but I've given it a lot of thought, Mick. You turning up here at exactly the right time . . .'

'What do you mean, exactly the right time?'

It turned out that Vee had hankered – her word, not mine – for a long time. Her hormones, she said, would not let her alone; she was helpless to their demands. She wanted a baby, she needed a baby. It would be simple, she said. No need for *physical contact*, just a quick clinical exchange of bodily fluid and the job would be done.

'But what about . . . I don't think I'm ready for that, Vee, to be a father, to . . .'

'Good God, Mick. I don't need you for that. It's a baby I want – not a man.'

How could I object, I thought, as I poured the wine and listened to her reasoning. It wouldn't take more than a minute and she would raise the child alone with no input, financial or personal, from me. If asked, she would stick to a story that said I was dead and had no living family.

'There'd be a couple of stipulations though, Vee,' I said.

'Oh. What?'

'Well . . . the baby's name for one. I'd like to have a say in it?'

'Oh, really?' She gave an incredulous snort. 'You're telling me you've got a list of names lined up and ready to go? For God's sake, Mick.'

She had a point. Baby's names? I'd never thought of such a thing before, but now . . .

'Malin,' I said. 'If it's a girl.'

She cocked her head to one side. 'Malin?'

An image of home slid unbidden into my mind – the low hum from the late-night kitchen as I lay in my bed. 'Yeah. Ireland; the *Shipping Forecast*, you know . . .'

She shrugged and took another sip of wine. 'Well, we'll see. So . . . what if it's a boy?'

I told myself it was the photograph of him in the paper that did it. The smile on his face and the fun in his eyes that had made me go with him in the first place. But it wasn't. It was the guilt.

'Joe,' I said. 'If it's a boy, I want you to name him Joe.'

I slid my hand across the table and put it on hers. 'There's something else too, Vee. If I am going to give you a baby, then I want to do it properly.'

She snatched her hand away. 'Properly? What do you mean?'

The sudden flush of colour at her throat told me she knew exactly what I meant.

'Don't be stupid, Mick, we can't do that. We're . . . we're friends, for God's sake.'

I shrugged, but I was certain. If we were going to make a baby, then I wanted it to have a proper start in life, not the cold, mechanical transaction Vee had in mind, but something warm and loving and *intended*. I nodded at the narrow bed in the corner, then got up and led her towards it.

The warm part was easy: the wine; the woodstove; the narrow bed. The loving part came as a surprise. There was a softness about her I'd not seen before and didn't expect, some sense of giving up and giving in that filled me with tenderness for her. I stroked the hair from her face and kissed her eyelids, her cheeks, her neck and felt her fold herself into me.

Afterwards, we huddled together in the soft glow of the stove. Vee fell asleep for a while but I lay, staring up into the darkness, imagining what might be taking place inside her; the magical journey – and connection – that could create a new life.

CHAPTER 64

Grace patted the bench beside her – an invitation to sit down that Malin ignored.

'So . . . any news yet? Has he been in touch . . . erm, what did you say his name was, your . . .'

'Connor,' Malin said. 'But no, there's nothing.'

Grace tried to read the look on Malin's face.

'So . . . what are you going to do, will you . . .?'

'I've sent him another message. I'll see if he gets back.'

'Why not just phone him?'

'I'm going to. I just want to see . . . see how we get on here first.'

Grace nodded. This was more or less what she'd been thinking. She'd see how they got on in Whitby and – if they were unsuccessful . . .

She took a deep breath. 'I just wanted to say . . . for you to know . . . that whatever happens, you don't have to do it on your own. The baby I mean.'

Grace was grateful that Malin didn't hear: that her voice was swallowed up by the noise of the crowd, the gulls, the music from the amusement arcade, because she knew she wouldn't have been able to stop herself. She would have lurched on, laying out the wild plan that had been forming in her mind all day. She would offer to talk to Vee, invite Malin to stay at the farm – live there, even – Grace could help out with the baby. She would have sounded desperate and she knew it – but what other choice did she have? She couldn't bear the thought of losing her.

She'd written a poem once – another deep and meaningful schoolgirl rendition. *They are cutting down the forest, and a house that once sat in deep shade now shines, like a brooch, on the hillside . . .*

When the teacher asked her about her inspiration behind it, she'd blushed and muttered something about living on a farm rather than admit it was about Greg. It was the last line that made her smile now – *And this is where I sit, pondering the miracle of unexpected solutions* – the realisation that there she was again – almost thirty years later – doing the same thing. *Transformation*, she'd called it, thinking that's what Greg had been offering, a chance to change, reinvent herself. But it had been pure imagination, like the poem itself, because Greg hadn't transformed her, he'd modified her. But this girl, who had woven herself into their lives like some alchemical thread, this girl named for a wild stretch of coastline, for the *Shipping Forecast* that had lulled them all their lives, this girl who had brought the promise of a future she'd not thought possible – surely she was the real path to transformation.

* * *

'Would you recognise him, Grace?'

'What? Who?'

'Michael,' Malin said. 'Do you think you would recognise him?'

It was a good question, but the wrong question. Twenty years had passed, but she knew she would recognise her brother the instant she saw him. What she was not sure of was how she would react. Would she step forward, make herself known – or would she want to step back and leave things as they had been for twenty years?

'I'm not sure,' she said eventually. It was the best answer she could think of but she saw the slight drop in Malin's face. 'Would you? From the photo, I mean?'

'I think so. I . . . I like to think I would recognise him just . . . just because, you know . . .'

Grace knew: the recognition that comes from being a part of someone – or somewhere. After Harry's death she'd returned to the football field every weekend to watch from the sidelines, bundled up against the cold and the stares of other parents, her eyes seeking out the shape of him, her heart waiting for the familiar tug as he sought her out and gave a small wave.

'What about Jack? Do you think . . .'

Jack. Grace pulled back her sleeve and looked at her watch. 'Oh Christ. How long have we been?'

'It's less than half an hour, Grace. Grace . . .'

But Grace was off the bench and threading herself back into the tide of tourists. 'I didn't mean to be this long,' she shouted back. 'Come on.' And off she went, fighting her way through a crowd that had no give in it, her heart banging in her chest.

Malin had no choice but to follow: the two of them dodging and weaving until they emerged, red-faced and out of breath, near the railway station. They were at the side of the road, waiting for an opportunity to cross, when Malin took hold of Grace's arm.

'Grace, look.'

'What?'

Malin pointed to a bus idling on the other side of the road. 'Is that Jack?'

'Where? Where?' Grace was already stepping onto the road.

Malin grabbed her by the coat sleeve with one hand and pointed with the other.

'There.'

'What? Oh my God,' Grace sputtered and yanked herself free. There he was – his pale face pressed up against the bus window. 'Da, Da!' she yelled, waving her arm frantically. He saw her at the last second and gave her a cheery wave as the bus swung away from the kerb and drove off.

* * *

Jack shuffled in his seat. He was for the high jump now and no doubt about it.

'How do I get back?'

The woman sitting next to him turned and gave him a smile. 'What's that, luvvie?'

'How do I get back? You know – to the other place?'

'What other place, pet?'

He gave it some thought. 'The tarmac place.' He knew it wasn't quite right but that was all he had. 'Tarmac. Where all the tarmac is.'

The woman gave him a smaller smile, then turned to speak to the man across the aisle.

'Did he know?' Jack leaned forward in his seat and looked at the man she'd been talking to. 'Where the tarmac place is?'

'No, he didn't. You didn't, did you, Dougie? Anyway, pet –' she bent down and picked up a carrier bag from the floor '– we're here now. It's time to get off.'

Jack looked out of the window. 'Where are we?' But the woman was already making her way down the aisle. He stepped off the bus into a crowd of people who seemed to be moving in one direction. Buoyed up by some familiar tang to the air (it was fish and chips) he joined the slow-moving throng until the road narrowed into a street and the street suddenly ended. He stopped and considered his options: the way ahead led down to the beach – or onto the pier. He turned and looked back the way he'd come, scanning the crowd for a glimpse of Grace's face. She would not be pleased, but he didn't care – all he wanted was for her to be there.

CHAPTER 65

Michael

We left the next day. Vee didn't look back once, striding out like she was marching us into battle. I trailed behind, barely able to walk a straight line, struggling against the constant urge in my eyes and in my feet to turn back. I told myself it was the need to remember, to frame the picture in my mind and store it there, the jaunty angle of the caravan, the pleasing jar of its green paintwork against the blue sky. But it was more than that.

Vee had taken me through the plan several times, counting the stages off on her fingers. The drive to the ferry, the crossing, the drop-offs in Liverpool, Manchester, Leeds, and the final push to the east coast. I'd nodded and smiled and tried to look like a man who was taking it all in, but the minute we were out of the door I'd felt it, a sense of foreboding at my back, like I was some soft-bodied creature venturing out into the open. Vulnerable, unequal to the danger that lay ahead.

It would be easy, she said. She'd done it many times. There was nothing to be worried about. My paperwork was perfect, the plan was perfect. I wanted to explain that it was neither the paperwork nor the plan that would give me away, but my eyes. There was no woolly hat or beard that could disguise the guilt in them. Or the shame.

But Vee was in no mood for that kind of talk. If our closeness the night before had meant anything to her, she hid it well. She launched herself into the day with military focus and kept me at arm's length.

By the time we arrived at the ferry port I'd written an entire newspaper article. *Missing Skipper Jailed For Negligence*, a photograph of me being led away by some port official, a scathing account of me hiding out like the guilty fugitive I was. I cowered on the back seat of the minibus, looking down at my shaking hands, while Vee, all balls and business, handed over the pile of passports. I knew I wasn't alone in my fear of discovery, that mine wasn't the only heart hammering out some unsustainable beat. Half the passengers were like Vee, activist types who involved themselves with the human fallout of bad politics rather than simply shouting about it, but the other half were like me. Travelling on a raft of fear and flimsy paperwork and praying for deliverance. I felt the communal holding of breath when the sliding door juddered open and a uniformed woman climbed in. She did a quick head count and jumped back out. There was a conversation with Vee that I couldn't hear above the sound of blood banging in my ears, then, with a light tap on the bonnet of the minibus, she waved us through.

I was giddy with relief as we crossed the wide expanse of tarmac and joined the short queue for the ferry, so I simply wasn't prepared for the feeling that swamped me as Vee drove across the ramp and into the lower car deck of the ferry.

'You all right, brother?' The bloke beside me was staring at me.

'Yeah, I'm fine . . . I just . . .'

ATTENTION ALL SHIPPING

I was far from fine; I was charged by some sudden urge to get out of the minibus and run. To run through the car deck, across the ramp and back to the caravan. To run away from the smell of oil and diesel, the clanking of chains and boots on steel, the throb of the engine through the soles of my feet. To run from a sea, I realised, I could no longer trust.

CHAPTER 66

Grace set off after the bus at a half jog, then, suddenly mindful of Malin's pregnancy, forced herself to slow down. She strode as fast as she dared, craning her neck above an indifferent crowd, trying to keep the bus in sight.

'It's all right, Jack'll be fine. We know where he is . . .' Malin was all helpful smiles and soothing words but Grace shrugged them off.

'No. He won't. We don't. This road ends at the beach and then . . .' She trailed off. *Then the sea – and the pier.* 'Come on . . .'

She surged on, cursing herself for leaving him on his own, trying to haul in her imagination.

She didn't know how they managed to find him. Her homing-pigeon instinct, she might have joked, except by the time they tracked him down she was barely containing her tears. Her first glimpse of him – perched on a bench, chatting to some young woman – afforded her a moment's relief, then switched track.

'Da!'

'Aha,' Jack croaked. He avoided Grace's eye – and ignored the ice in her voice. 'You've come back at last. I was just telling this young lady . . . oh, cheerio . . .'

The young woman was already off the bench and walking away. Keen to deviate the attention from the real matter in hand, namely his absconding, he ploughed on. 'Well, I was just telling that young . . .'

'Da.'

'I got lost,' he said and pushed his hands in his pockets. He dealt her one of his hang-dog faces for good measure, but she ignored it, stuck her hands on her hips and launched into him.

'You got out of the van after you promised me you wouldn't. A snooze, you said. "Leave me here, Gracie, and I'll just have a little snooze", and what happens? You disappear and I have to spend half the day looking for you' – this was an exaggeration but he knew better than to point it out – 'and where do I find you? On a damp bench trying to chew the ear off some poor stranger.'

He waited for her to run out of steam.

'I wasn't chewing her ear off, actually, I was doing some detective work. A bit of Morse, if you like.' He pulled his hand out of his pocket and, with a theatrical flourish, pulled out the envelope. She grabbed it off him.

'What the heck are you doing with this, Da? It's . . . it's . . .'

'It's been very useful, that's what it's been. Here, sit down a minute, and I'll tell you what I've found out.'

And at that point, of course – his moment of glory where it would be smiles all round and everything would be forgiven – his own steam gave out.

'Ah. Just hang on a minute, I . . .'

He closed his eyes, willing the bloody thing back – everything he'd discovered, everything he'd had lined up to tell her.

'Da?' She was on the bench beside him now, no-nonsense arms folded across her chest. He looked at the envelope in her hand, *willing* it to give him some kind of clue.

'Hang on, Gracie. Give me a minute. I'll . . . oh, damn it.'

But she was easing him up from the bench and her voice had thawed into a gentle chivvying tone that told him he looked as witless as he felt. *Let's get ourselves back to the van, you can tell us all about it then . . .* There was no chance of that, none at all, because it was gone. The lot of it.

* * *

The campsite they booked into – the only one brave enough to stay open in winter according to the woman who took their money – was perched high above the town. Malin parked the van facing east and the three of them sat gazing out at the sea, the roiling unfamiliarity of it – no comforting hints of land to catch the eye, just a lonely expanse that didn't stop until, if Grace remembered correctly, it reached Denmark. Her first priority, after they'd finally found Jack, had been to get him warmed up and the brisk walk back to the van followed by cups of tea had done that. But it hadn't put the light back in his eyes – or quelled her fear of losing him.

'That's the North Sea, Da.'

'Mmhh. Looks a bit blustery.'

Blustery didn't cover it. There was an edge of impending menace to it. Black clouds hung low and heavy over the rearing water, a strange moon pointed its long finger across waves high enough to bury a man.

'I reckon he better be getting a shift on . . .'

Grace followed Jack's gaze to a fishing boat lurching through the trammelling swell.

'Ten-footers at least I should say. Poor bugger's going to be late for his tea.'

Grace held her breath as she watched. The boat was still a good distance out, and struggling to hold a straight course. She sent up a quiet prayer of thanks that her da was at her side and not – as her imagination had spun it – flailing around in water, unseen, unheard . . . She watched the boat labouring slowly in and allowed herself to wonder. To imagine what it would be like to find yourself on a sea like that – or *in* a sea like that; to feel the pull of the ocean floor beneath you. The awful realisation that you had misjudged, underestimated and that you were unprepared. The dreadful loneliness of gazing up into an indifferent sky, knowing there would be no one to tell you goodbye.

'You all right, girl?'

'What?' She shook the thought away and turned in her seat to look at him. 'I'm fine, Da . . .'

'Well, that's good news because I'm bloody starving.'

'What?'

'Hungry, Gracie. Hungry.' He gave his belly a little pantomime rub. 'How about you, girlie?'

'Well,' Malin raised an eyebrow, 'I think I spotted a pub on the way here.'

'A pub? But . . .'

Grace had envisaged them settling down early. It had been a long day and she was thin at the edges with the emotion of it – Malin's pregnancy, the anxiety about Michael, her da disappearing – she just wanted it over. An early night, the *Shipping Forecast*, time to settle her mind and a fresh start in the morning, that's what she'd been anticipating – not some foray out in weather that was getting worse. But she could see her da had other ideas. *A pub?* The idea had him clapping his hands like he was in the front row at a show. He nudged her in the ribs.

'Fish and chips for me, I reckon, hinny.'

'Well . . .' She wiped the condensation from the inside of the windscreen and peered out into the approaching gloom. 'I don't know. It's looking pretty bad out there . . .'

She was on a losing wicket and she knew it because the thought of the pub, the fish and chips, had done something she'd not managed to do. It had put the light back in his eyes.

CHAPTER 67

Michael

I spent the first part of the journey roaming the ferry looking for some place that would relieve the wild feeling in my head, but the bar, the cafeteria, the duty-free simply made it worse. Too many people and too much noise. I ventured outside eventually, thinking the fresh air and the view would settle me. I found a quiet space, clamped myself against the damp railings and turned my face into the headwind. I closed my eyes and concentrated on the churn of the engine, the thrum of the deck, the salt spray on my lips. I was seeking some relief in the sheer familiarity of it all, but all I found was a strain in the note of the engine, an unexpected tilt in the angle of the deck, a sudden shift in the wind. I stayed there a minute or two longer, gazing down at the water, until I was suddenly overtaken by a strange impulse that had me letting go of the rail, taking a step back and fleeing to the safety of the inner lounge.

I dropped onto the first seat I came across and rested my head in my hands. The woman sitting across from me leaned over and passed me a small bag. *Seasickness, lovey?* I answered with a weak nod, knowing that the feeling that had sent me running back across the deck was nothing to do with the sea's effect on my stomach, but its pull on my mind. There had been something magnetic and alluring about it, a feeling that all would be well if I simply slipped into its easy embrace and, before I knew it, I had imagined it closing over my head, its steady weight taking me down to the quiet peacefulness of the ocean floor.

I knew then that my seafaring days were over, that the ferry trip would be my last voyage. Not because I couldn't trust the sea, but because I couldn't trust myself.

* * *

It was late by the time we were on the final stretch towards Whitby. Late enough for me to assume that Vee would not simply drop me off, as she'd dropped off every other passenger, but would stay over. I had imagined, or hoped, that our parting would be as warm and intimate as the night we had shared in the caravan. It would be a belts and braces liaison from her point of view maybe, but would offer me some release from the anxiety that had gripped me on the ferry and had stayed, coiled tight around my chest, throughout our long journey.

I was wrong. The nearer we got to our destination, the more distant she became. She resisted all my attempts to talk about what had happened between us or what would happen next if she were pregnant. She was shutting me out. So much so that, by the time she dropped me at the end of a long and dark narrow street, I convinced myself our coupling would come to nothing. No man, especially one like me, would be able to breach the fortress that Vee had fashioned herself to be.

I stayed inside for days. A kind of hibernation, I thought, ignoring the fact that number three Henrietta Street was not the warm cosy nest the word usually conjured up. I spent most of my time sleeping or crying, padding aimlessly between my bed, the cold bathroom and the damp kitchen, thinking of everything and everyone I had lost. My life with

Joseph seemed like a dream. The years we'd spent roaming the sea, the *Laughing Girl*, Patrick. None of it real. And home; home was some lost horizon, a place I could only visit in my dreams. My ma at the stove, my da out in the yard and Grace at the kitchen table, laughing.

Eventually, my stomach caved in with hunger, and I ventured out. I was a stranger in a strange place, I thought, as I stepped out into a wind that took the air out of my lungs. I explored the warren of narrow streets, spent most of the ten pounds that Vee had given me on groceries, then slipped into a pub to spend the little that remained. I chose a corner seat, a high-backed bench that looked like it might have come from a church, or a ship, and sat, unfurling in the heat of a log fire. It was, I realised, as I nursed my half pint and a small bag of nuts, the warmest I'd been since leaving the caravan. Despite the heat, my intention to formulate some kind of plan came to nothing. I leaned back into my seat and allowed myself be lulled by the fire.

I'm not sure what drew my attention, but I suddenly became aware that the barman was watching me. I shifted in my seat, angled my face slightly away from his gaze and feigned a fascination with the painting on the wall beside me.

'I don't think I've seen you in here before . . .'

'Oh.' I looked round and there he was, hands in his pockets, smiling down at me.

Although I had a pretty good idea where his interest in me might lie, I said nothing. I was waiting, I realised, for my normal response to kick in. The reciprocated smile, the slight lift to one eyebrow, the tip of my tongue against my bottom lip. It didn't, thank God, because he walked past my table to the window that overlooked the street and taped a small square of paper onto the glass.

'It's worth a try,' he said, as he passed me again. 'But not much chance – not this time of year . . .'

ATTENTION ALL SHIPPING

I smiled, like I knew what he was talking about, and turned my attention back to the painting. It was, remarkably, one that I knew well because a copy of it hung in the sitting room back at home. It wasn't just the painting that I knew well but, thanks to my da, the story that went with it. Grace Darling and her courageous rescue mission. I sat there a while longer savouring the coincidence, the memory of home and family, then nodded to the barman and went out.

The painting, I decided later, had surely been some kind of message, a sign, even. Because as I walked away from the pub, I stopped to look at the square of paper sellotaped in the window, and the plan that had so far eluded me suddenly made itself apparent.

Staff wanted. Apply within.

CHAPTER 68

The pub had its face to the street and its back towards the harbour below. It was crouched low, as if sheltering from the wind that had buffeted them off the campsite, then bowled them, arm in arm, towards its open doorway. Bad weather or not, Grace knew the minute they were over its threshold they'd made the right decision. It was, she imagined, as she stepped through the porch into a low-lit, low-beamed room that smelled of wood smoke and cooking, exactly the kind of place she and Dan might meet up. Her da gave a small peep of pleasure, then headed straight for the log fire. He stood warming his backside, smiling at anyone who caught his eye.

They ordered straight away, which turned out to be a blessing because – just as they'd finished eating – the lights suddenly dimmed, and went out. A cheer went up as the bartender produced a torch, then did a tour of the tables with candles and matches. One of the men drinking at the bar got up and went to the door. He came back in shaking his head.

'Hope to God there's no poor bugger out in this.'

Grace was wondering whether she should speak up about the boat she'd seen from the campsite, when all of a sudden a small alarm started up. A shrill beeping that had the bartender grabbing his coat, legging it across the half-lit room and flying out of the door. Seconds later a car revved loudly and screeched away.

'Well, he was in a bit of a hurry.' Jack slurped down the last mouthful of Mackeson and banged his glass on the table. 'I was just about to ask him for a refill.'

Grace went across to the man sitting at the bar.

'What's happening?'

'He's on call-out. Ewan.'

'The lifeboat, you mean?'

'Yeah, the lifeboat.'

The man took a long pull on his beer, then wiped his mouth on the back of his hand. She could tell from his expression he had her down for a tourist – dim-witted about anything to do with fishing, lifeboats – the sea. She wanted to tell him he was wrong – that although it was a different sea that salted her blood, it was just as greedy, as unruly as the sea that salted his. Instead, she nodded and went back to the table. Malin was waiting for her.

'What's happening, Grace?'

'He's on the lifeboats. The barman. It was a call-out.'

Her da was half up out of his seat. 'A lifeboat, you say?'

'Yes, Da. A lifeboat.'

'Oh, right.'

She could almost hear his mind ticking, the cogs and wheels clicking into place. When he sat back and cleared his throat, she got up from her seat.

'Probably time we got going,' she said.

'But Gracie . . .'

She was sorry, and there was the truth of it, but she was in no frame of mind for another one of his recitals. If he got started on the Whitby lifeboat rescue, they'd be there for hours.

'Sorry, Da, but we should get back to the van.' She turned and indicated the rain lashing at the window. 'Come on, I'll take you to the bathroom, and then we'll get to the campsite.'

Malin teased the vehicle across the field towards the most sheltered-looking spot. She parked against a blasted hedge, facing away from the sea. It made no difference. The wind sought them out straight away: it howled overhead, shrieking at a demented and wild pitch, then disappeared, only to descend without warning and hammer itself against the sides of the van.

Prompted by the reluctance to undress in the cold, and the possibility of having to abandon ship in the night, they'd gone to bed with their clothes on. Grace had togged Jack up with a fresh pad before they'd left the pub, but apart from that, they'd climbed into bed wearing everything bar their boots. Malin seemed to fall asleep instantly but Grace was too tense to let herself go. Eventually, rocked by the wind, and the *Shipping Forecast*, she started to drift off.

'Well, they've got that bloody wrong . . .'

'What, Da?' The edge of sleep was beckoning and Grace didn't want to pull herself back from it; she didn't want to have to decipher what it was he was talking about either.

'This weather. No mention of it at all.'

'Oh.' The *Shipping Forecast*. She'd thought he wouldn't twig. That putting it on would help settle him rather than perk him up again.

He shuffled onto his side and took most of the duvet with him. She didn't care. Sleep was a moment away. She yawned again and lowered herself towards it and, as she let go of the day and drifted away, she heard him say something. She let his words float over her.

'Mmhh,' she said and fell asleep.

* * *

Jack couldn't sleep because he was composing a letter. *Dear Sir or Madam*, it started. *Regarding this evening's* Shipping Forecast . . . The buggers had got it wrong, simple as that:

ATTENTION ALL SHIPPING

Forties, Dogger, Fisher, German Bight – not a peep about the weather that had sent the poor chap from the pub running out into the dark or the sleeting wind and rain that was, at that very moment, threatening the very fabric of the van. And the announcement? That sombre voice that had any sailor turning up the radio volume? *Attention all shipping.* Not a mention of it. As far as the man on the radio was concerned, all was well at sea. Well, it bloody well wasn't.

He wriggled over onto his side, pulled the duvet over his head and tried to think back through the day.

'Where was I when you found me, Gracie?' His voice was thin against the noise of the storm. She was asleep or didn't hear him. Either way she didn't answer.

* * *

Malin wasn't asleep. She was resisting its pull because she didn't want to let go of the day. She wanted to keep hold of it as long as she could, to imprint it on her mind, to set it down in order, like the first page of a new chapter.

Malin slid her hands onto her belly and clasped them lightly over the place she imagined her baby to be. She'd told Grace about the baby, and Grace's eyes had filled with tears like the words – the confession – had unlocked something deep inside her. Then, as if her reaction had cast some spell over it, the day had only got better. Even losing Jack – the frantic search before they'd found him – hadn't taken the shine off it, because later, while Grace was supervising him in the pub toilet, her phone had pinged. She'd hesitated at first, worried it might be Vee, but it was a message from Connor: short, but enough to put a grin on her face. Of course, he remembered her. Could they meet up again soon? She'd played it safe with a quick thumbs up because Grace was already steering Jack towards the table. *Ready, then?* Grace said. *I'm ready*, she'd replied and, with the grin still on her face, followed them out into the howling wind.

She lay, listening to the banging and thrashing of the storm outside, unable to pull her thoughts away from him. Connor Allen, the father of her baby. If he wanted to be. If he didn't, then . . . She wasn't sure of it all, just that there'd be no repeat performance of her own experience: no lies to tidy away; no clues in hidden envelopes; no bloody *team of two*.

She could tell that Jack was still awake because she could hear him muttering under his breath.

'Everything all right, Jack?' she whispered.

'What. Oh. Glad to hear someone else is on night duty.'

'What's wrong?'

'Wrong? Nothing.'

There was a silence and she didn't fill it.

'Well, actually. You might be able to help out . . .' He gave a small cough. 'I was just wondering . . . where was I when you found me? Today I mean?'

'Oh. You were on a bench, Jack. Outside the Lifeboat Museum.'

'The Lifeboat Museum!'

The door in his head that had been so bloody obstinate slid open and there it was. He'd talked to the man at the Lifeboat Museum . . .

Jack started slowly, like he was chasing after the words, then gathered confidence and pace, until he had the whole thing spun out and in order.

'Phwaw,' he said, when he'd ground to a halt. 'That's better. Did you get it all down, girlie?'

'I did, Jack, I did.'

Malin lay in the dark, marvelling over what Jack had just told her. It was a loose blanket of a thing, full of holes but still somehow holding itself together. She stopped herself asking for more, the thirst to hear the words again suddenly outweighed by the fear that a second telling might expose the miracle of his discovery as mere confusion. Instead she rolled onto her side, quietly folded his story into her and added it to the new chapter of the day.

'Let's go to sleep now, Jack. We'll tell Grace in the morning.'

CHAPTER 69

Michael

I walked back to Henrietta Street with a spring in my step, amazed that something as simple as a part-time job in an out of season seaside pub could make me feel so happy. It wasn't simply the job, of course, although that gave me plenty to smile about. Regular money; a chance to get to know people; a free meal each shift. I was relieved to have a plan. I would, I decided, as I trotted along swinging my grocery bags, celebrate my good fortune by cooking myself a proper meal. I'd survived up till then on the supplies that Vee's friend (who I had yet to meet) had left. The Pot Noodles, tinned soup, cereal and long-life milk had somehow suited my frame of mind. They got me by, but didn't demand too much of me. But now I suddenly felt ready for more; hungry for more.

I didn't have long to wait.

A few days later the letter arrived. The flamboyant scrawl on the front of the envelope, plus the fact that no one else knew I was there, said it was from Vee. I opened it carefully and pulled out a card. *Madonna and Child.* I didn't know the painting but I knew exactly what it meant. I smiled down at the image of a young woman cradling a small baby, then burst into tears.

I hoped to hear more from Vee, I sent her a couple of postcards over the following weeks, but heard nothing back.

Although I reminded myself that this was how we'd arranged things, I couldn't ignore the growing need to know how the pregnancy was going, how she was feeling. I wanted to be involved. I placated myself by crossing off the days and weeks on a homemade calendar. It wasn't completely accurate, but it was near enough to give me a rough idea of when our baby would be born.

Her letter arrived halfway through January: an arty black and white photograph. Vee's part in it was minor. The soft scoop of her fingers at the baby's back, a loose tendril of hair, a fold of fabric. But the baby, the baby was a miracle. *Me*, I thought, as I traced the outline of her tiny head. *Me*. I did that. I turned it over and smiled. There was no message, but what Vee had written was enough.

Malin O'Connor, born January 2nd 2001

I propped the photograph on the mantelpiece and hurried out into the street. The post office was ready for closing so I grabbed the nearest postcard and penned a short message: *I trust all went well. Will you come – please?* I tipped it into the post box, and walked back to Henrietta Street, praying that she would, because what I needed most in the world was to see my baby girl.

* * *

It would be fair to say becoming a father changed me. It wasn't a visible thing, although when I looked in the mirror I fancied I saw a difference there, but something internal, integral. It felt like a new thread had been established in the world, something fine but strong, like a spider might spin, a connection that, despite the distance between us, tied Malin and me together. Consequently, when Vee eventually brought the baby to see me I approached her with the idea I'd been pondering for weeks, one that would allow me to play the part of a proper father.

'Don't be ridiculous, Mick.'

'But why not?' I looked down at Malin, asleep in my arms. I'd barely put the child down since they'd arrived.

'Because that's not what we arranged, is it?'

'We could just . . . just rearrange, then. Just . . . you know, change our minds . . .'

Vee shook her head, leaned across and took Malin from me.

'Forget it, Mick. It's not happening.'

I watched as she untucked her T-shirt and half bared one breast. The baby latched onto the nipple without waking.

'Anyway,' she said. 'I've already made other plans.'

'What do you mean?' I had a sudden and unwelcome vision of another man holding my child. 'Have you . . . have you met someone?'

'Christ, no. You think I've got time for something like that?'

'What then? What plans?'

She was going back to Greenham. Not to the Common, because the protests were over, but to the women's commune that had established itself nearby.

'Think of it as a sort of watching post,' she said, then laughed at my concerns for the baby's safety and well-being. 'She'll be fine, Mick. Think of all the mothers she'll have . . .'

'Yes, but . . . what about a father, Vee. She won't have me. She won't know who I am . . .'

She let out an indignant snort. '*Who you are*, Mick? That's a good one. I think you're forgetting you don't actually exist . . .'

'But . . .'

'And this,' she nodded down at Malin, 'this was payment for what I did for you, not some . . . some free ticket into my life. We stick to the arrangement, Mick – I get Malin and you get my silence. Right?'

I said nothing, rendered speechless by the ice in her voice and the half-disguised threat behind her words.

Later I eventually negotiated a change to our initial agreement that meant I would not completely lose touch. She was willing, she said, to send photographs, something that would allow me to keep track, but from a safe distance. It was far from enough but all she was willing to give.

'Come on,' she said. 'We might as well start now.'

When I'd got myself settled in the post office photo booth, Vee handed me the baby. I held her close to my face, breathed in the warm scent of her and smiled at the screen.

She left the next day, waving from the train window with an exaggerated cheerfulness, leaving me alone on the platform staring down at my boots and listening to the dull thud of my own heart. It was only when she'd gone and the train was nothing but a hum of memory on the tracks, I realised that although I had a picture of Malin, Vee didn't have one of me. I went straight back to the post office and watched as the woman behind the counter snipped the strip in two. *Michael and Malin, 2001* I wrote on Vee's half. I dropped it in an envelope and put the other half in my wallet.

CHAPTER 70

The morning had been a generous one; that's what Grace was thinking as they drove off the campsite. It had not only brought good weather – the sea flat and gleaming beneath a sky that seemed to have flown in from the Mediterranean – it had brought amazing news. Her da and Malin had been ready with it the minute she surfaced.

'All right there, hinny?'

She'd rolled over on the bunk to find him up, dressed in fresh clothes and holding out a mug of tea.

'Oh. What . . . what time is it?' She propped herself up in the bed, shielded her eyes against the sun and took the mug from him.

'Time to get cracking, I reckon. The girlie has looked it all up.'

'Looked it up? Looked what up?'

'Oh, the times, you know. When it opens . . .'

Grace rubbed her face, trying to unravel what he was saying. She couldn't resist a sigh of relief when Malin appeared in the open doorway.

'Morning, Grace. We survived!'

'Well, yes, but . . . do you know what my da is talking about?'

* * *

He was talking about the Lifeboat Museum, that's what he was talking about. Malin filled her in on the details as they packed the van up and headed off the field.

'Thank goodness you were there – and awake,' was all Grace managed to say, because Malin set off at a gallop, breathless and smiling as the story tumbled out of her: not only had Jack been into the museum and got talking to the man behind the counter, he'd pulled out the photograph of Michael. *And guess what?* – Malin's voice was pure joy – the man seemed to recognise him. Details beyond that were sketchy but it didn't matter, she said, because couldn't they go back there as soon as it opened, talk to the man and find out what he'd said?

So there they were, heading off towards town under a sky that bore no trace of the night's storm, heading off to speak to the man who had recognised Michael. Grace felt the anxiety of the night before melt away. Hope. She was overflowing with it, and try as she might she could not cap it. Didn't want to cap it. It had her cresting on a wave, carrying her forward at a speed that was exhilarating, not frightening. They'd weathered the storm – she'd weathered the storm – and surely now she was receiving her reward: Malin, the baby – *Michael?* She lifted her face to the warmth of the sun and dared herself to add Dan to her list.

* * *

It took longer to get to the Lifeboat Museum than they'd anticipated because they couldn't get Jack past the boats in the harbour. He insisted on inspecting every vessel tethered there.

'What you looking for, Da?' Grace was holding onto his arm as he near dangled over the quayside in an attempt to get a better look.

'The names of course, hinny. The names of the boats.'

She didn't point out to him the futility of his search. Why remind him that the *Laughing Girl* was long gone.

The museum was already busy when they got there. Half a coachload of people it seemed, crammed into the tiny space, some jaunty sea shanty playing through a set of tinny speakers. The bench outside was already taken by a row of tourists poring over a map.

'Let's give it a few minutes,' Grace said. It was the last thing she wanted to do. She wanted to be inside, finding out if her da had it right, but she wanted the moment of truth to be perfect. 'We could have a walk along the pier while we wait.' She said this mainly to Malin, an acknowledgement of her pregnancy, but realised as she spoke that, overnight, the girl had acquired a new shine. The tiredness and pallor of the previous week had gone and been replaced with what could only be described as a bloom.

'You look so . . . so well,' Grace ventured, as the three of them strolled side by side along the pier.

Malin's face lit up – a patch of red on each cheek. 'I got a message,' she said. 'It came through last night when we were in the pub? From Connor.'

'Oh. That's . . . that's marvellous.'

'Yes. I know . . .'

Later – when the excitement of the day had settled, Grace would try and piece together the moments that followed. She would try to establish the order of things that had her leaving Malin and her da for a moment, walking ahead, phone in hand and dialling Dan's number. It might have been the generous feeling of the day that had bolstered her up, or Malin's success with Connor; or the fact that she was wearing the new clothes she'd bought in Aberystwyth. However it happened, she'd found herself at the end of the pier, watching a group of seagulls skimming the water below, waiting for him to answer.

'Dan, it's Grace.' It was a bit abrupt but she had to say

something quickly so she wouldn't back out and end the call. He was busy – a lot of noise in the background.

'Grace?'

She could tell she'd caught him at a bad time. 'Yes. I . . .' She'd planned nothing – nothing beyond dialling his number. 'Yes. I got your message. About . . . erm, about meeting up.'

'What? Hang on a minute . . . Jason. He's over there . . . Grace, sorry about that. What did you say?'

She ran her finger round the collar of her shirt. 'You . . . you left me a message. Said something about wanting to meet up?' She could hear shouting on the other end of the line. 'Look – I'm sorry. I'll call another time . . .'

'No, no, it's OK. Right.' The background noise dimmed as if he'd closed a door.

'Thanks for getting back but . . . I managed to sort things out.'

She was smiling and she didn't know why. A stuck-on grin that bore no relation to anything because she didn't have a clue what he was talking about.

'Sort things out?'

'Yes. I needed a bit of advice. My own mother is going a bit . . . you know, and I thought with how your dad is, you might be able to give me some pointers. But I managed to get in touch with . . . oh, hang on a minute. Jason! Sorry, Grace, I've got to go.'

'Oh, well, that's good. I'll . . .' She still had the stupid grin on her face; her tongue was stuck to the roof of her mouth. 'I'll leave you to it then.' She waited to see if he was going to say anything else – but he was already gone, leaving a faint hissing in her ear that could have been the lost connection or the sea.

His mother. She tossed the phone into her bag. She would have tossed it into the sea if it had been possible, along with her new T-shirt and trousers – anything to distance herself from what she'd just done, what she'd allowed herself to believe. She turned her head to catch the breeze, to cool the embarrassment of it all and concentrated on what she could hear. The endless gulls, their raucous conversation, the push and pull of water against the pier, a boat engine – arriving or leaving – and, somewhere in the distance, her da calling her name. She pushed away from the railings, from thoughts of Dan, and concentrated on putting one foot in front of the other.

CHAPTER 71

Michael

The first photograph arrived a few months later. It was framed and mounted and had something of a studio look about it. Malin was propped up against a pile of colourful cushions and surrounded by a scattering of soft toys. I could see no evidence of Vee, either in the photograph or in Malin, but my own mark on the child was undeniable. Her dark hair was already spinning into soft curls and her eyes were the soft green of a quiet sea. She wasn't smiling, but laughing – some full-bellied chortle that had her small cheeks bunched up and her little starfish hands dancing at her sides. I grinned when I read the short line Vee had pencilled at the bottom of the photograph:

Laughing Girl II.

Then time, as it does, moved on, and I tried my best to move on with it. The town and the pub grew busy with tourists, each day brought another fleet of holiday coaches, another horde to roam the narrow streets in search of Whitby jet, Lucky Ducks and Dracula. I was alarmed at first, convinced that one day I would see someone who knew me. But as the weeks went by I relaxed and my days acquired a certain rhythm. A one-step-after-the-other sort of pace that had more to do with aimlessness than contentment, but granted me enough peace to get me through each day.

My nights and days off, though, were a different matter. Without the buzz of the bar I was unable to shut out thoughts of Malin. The distance between us put a crease in me I couldn't straighten out and the small voice that told me life without her was meaningless became hard to ignore. I comforted myself with romantic notions. I penned poems and letters to her and stashed them in an old shoebox beneath the bed. I pounded the deserted streets at night, further and further each time, relishing the ache in my muscles when I eventually tipped myself into bed. One night, still too restless to take myself to bed, I ran, like some eager worshipper, up the one hundred and ninety-nine steps to St Mary's Church. When I got to the top I leaned, panting, against a nameless and faceless gravestone and looked out at my old love, my new enemy, the sea. I fancied I could hear its call even from that distance: a coaxing siren wail that carried on the air between us, the offer of release, of real peace. It was a hard invitation to ignore and I felt every grain of salt in my blood keening towards it.

The following night I altered my usual route. *A test*, I told myself, as I left the safety of the streets behind and headed towards the East Pier. The moon was but a suggestion, a yellow glow behind a low bank of cloud in a dark velvet sky. When I stepped onto the narrow footbridge, the first time my feet had left solid ground since the ferry trip, my heart stumbled. A small hesitation that was neither fear nor excitement – but relief. It suddenly seemed to me that the dull thudding of the waves, the damp fret misting my face and the tangle of salt and seaweed lacing the night air were the things I had been missing, the things I needed to fill the gap in my life. I felt for the small strip of photographs in my pocket. Vee had been right: I didn't exist. I would never exist for my daughter. My life was pointless, meaningless . . .

I walked on like a man in a dream not knowing, or caring, what would happen when I reached the end, whether I would stop or simply step off and, with a small shout of surprise that no one would hear, wheel through the air into the waiting water. The lights of the town lay to my left, and the dark, roiling sea to my right. I think my hand was on the railing, my feet were lifting, some part of me was judging the drop, when the moon suddenly appeared from behind its veil of cloud. It beamed down – *like a searchlight*, I thought – as I blinked up at it and stepped away from the railings. I watched as it stretched itself along the length of the pier like some bright and gleaming arrow, then stepped into its light and followed it, like a path, back home.

I woke late the next morning, too late to think of anything other than getting myself out of the house and into work. The busyness of the bar and the kitchen allowed me no time to think about anything other than getting food to the right table and keeping a tab on who owed what. It was gone three before things calmed down and I was looking forward to five minutes with the newspaper and a sandwich when the door opened and someone came in. I fixed a welcoming smile on my face and glanced across.

Oh. I'm not sure if I said it, or simply thought it, but either way, the sight of her almost had me off my feet. I held onto the edge of the table as she walked across the room, my head reeling with some faint feeling of recognition, of connection.

CHAPTER 72

The Lifeboat Museum was less busy, but not empty. Grace left Malin and Jack to examine the various information boards and loitered at the edges of the room, watching the man behind the counter. There was something of an actor about him, something rehearsed about whatever it was he was saying. When he'd finished, she called over to Jack and Malin and the three of them presented themselves. She introduced her da, recapped on his visit the day before and pulled out the photograph, steadying herself for the big moment. The bloke shook his head before he'd even looked at the photograph. He'd not been there the day before. He made a big palaver of pulling a book out of a drawer and scanning through the pages.

'Ah, no, see . . .'

He turned the book towards her. It was a diary.

'Looks like it's Will you need to be talking to. He was on yesterday.' He looked at her da. 'A youngish bloke? Well – younger than me . . .'

And off he went, a heap of information they didn't need, that she wanted to block out – new to the town, just settling in, always wanted to live by the sea, blah, blah, blah . . . He was just getting onto the house repairs he'd had to do when Jack butted in.

'So when's he coming back then? This Will?'

'What? Oh.' The bloke reconsidered the diary. 'Ah. Not this week.'

'Have you got his number?'

'Well, yes – but no. Not allowed to do that – giving out personal information, you know.'

Grace didn't know what changed his mind – whether it was the look on their faces or the fact that a group of tourists had walked in. A fresh audience.

'Mind you . . . and this didn't come from me . . .' He glanced over his shoulder, leaned over the counter and, in a stage whisper, said, 'I reckon I know where you might find him . . .'

* * *

Malin typed the details into her phone, linked arms with Jack and set off. Grace trailed behind. Try the Endeavour, the chap in the museum had said. She'd looked at her watch: eleven in the morning and the man they were looking for was already in the pub. Somehow this information demoted him in her mind and suggested their quest might be born of fancy rather than reality. She was readying herself for the failure, the disappointment – the picking up of pieces – so the pub came as something of a surprise. The warm air that met them at the threshold was laced with a smell of fresh coffee rather than stale beer. A group of women sat in one corner, a corporate look about them that suggested a meeting. A lone man sat by the window, typing on a laptop. Grace, slightly bolstered by the unexpected sobriety of the place, led the way to the bar.

The man by the window turned in their direction, then carried on with his typing. 'I'll be right with you now this minute . . .'

Jack nudged Grace in the ribs. 'That's the fellow we're after.'

'What? That man there, you mean. Typing?'

'Yes. That's him.'

Grace studied what she could see of the man. He looked like he'd come off some advert for whisky. The rugged cut of him – a tangle of hair pushed off his face, the sleeves of his fisherman's sweater pushed up, a dog curled asleep by his feet. He typed a minute or two longer, then closed the laptop and got up. The dog didn't stir.

'Right, so . . .' He lifted a hatch at the end of the bar and walked round to face them.

'What can I get you?' He delivered a smile that showed up the weathering in his face.

Grace realised she was holding her breath. 'We're looking for someone called Will?'

'Well, consider him found.'

Her da squeezed himself round her and stuck out his hand. 'It's me. Remember?'

'So it is, so it is . . .' The smile never left Will's lips but Grace wasn't sure if he knew her da or not, until he asked, 'And who are your lovely companions, Jack?'

'My daughter, Grace . . .' her da indicated with a sweep of his hand, 'and . . . and . . .'

A minor hesitation, but it whipped the rug from under his feet.

Grace stepped forward. 'Malin,' she said, putting her hand on the girl's arm. 'This is Jack's granddaughter, Malin.'

She draped her arm across her da's shoulders and steered him towards a bar stool, trying to remember when he'd last had something to eat. Wondering if a hot drink, something sweet, might pick him up before he fell too far.

'Tea, Da?' She scanned the bar for a menu. 'A piece of cake?'

'How about a nice bit of pie?' the barman said. 'Due out of the oven any minute . . .'

Grace wanted to say no, to tell him they just needed to

ask him what he'd told her da the previous day. Instead, she nodded, and watched as he left the bar and started laying one of the tables with cutlery. When he was satisfied with the arrangement he came over and helped her da off the bar stool.

'I've been wondering how you got on, Jack,' he said. 'Did you find him?'

Jack looked back at her. 'I don't know . . .'

Grace joined the barman at the table and eased her da onto a chair. He closed his eyes as soon as his backside landed. She waited a moment, until she was sure he was asleep, then turned to the barman. 'You do remember my father then?'

'Oh, yes. I was a bit worried about him if I'm honest. On his own, you know . . .'

She might have explained what had happened, gone into the whole shebang of the thing, but it suddenly seemed superfluous.

'He . . . he gets a bit . . . mixed up. We weren't sure if . . .'

'Ah, no. He was definitely at the museum yesterday. Chatted for a good length of time, we did.'

'Yes, that's what he said. The problem was . . .' Grace felt herself holding her breath again. 'The thing was he couldn't remember what you told him.'

'OK. Well, that's not a problem. Why don't you all sit down here, I'll go and get that pie sorted, then I'll tell it again.'

Will Fletcher was a writer – *of sorts*, he said. A hobby gone wild. His job at the pub and the Lifeboat Museum were part of his research: a six-month stint he was halfway through, embedding himself into a community that could furnish him with the facts and the flavour he needed for his story. *Quiet Heroes*, short stories that explored acts of bravery and courage. That was how he started – watching, as they ate, quietly framing his next paragraph.

'So Jack told me he was looking for someone. He showed me a photograph? Well, the long and short of it – I thought

I recognised the man in the photograph, that I'd seen his face before – in a newspaper article.' Grace had put down her knife and fork at this point to ready herself for whatever was going to come next. She glanced at Jack, unsure whether she should wake him or leave him sleeping. She quietly loosened his jacket and propped a cushion behind his head. It was a ploy, a stalling tactic: some mundane task she could grab on to, to steady herself for whatever Will was going to say next. Jack muttered something under his breath but slept on.

Malin had both elbows on the table, gazing intently at Will Fletcher.

'What newspaper article?'

'It was about a man who'd rescued someone from the sea. Hang on . . .'

Grace watched as he retrieved his laptop from the table by the window. His words were looping round her head. *A man who'd rescued someone from the sea.* Rescued *who* from the sea? Her mind, suddenly loosened off its rails, went straight to Joseph, to her mother and da poring over maps, studying tides and sea currents; the story of the *Andrea Gail* . . .

'I should have it on here, somewhere. Ah, here we go . . .' Will turned the screen towards Grace and Malin.

LOCAL MAN IN HEROIC RESCUE. It was the front page of the *Whitby Gazette*. There was no mistaking Michael – despite the fact the photo was slightly out of focus, that he was older – and that he'd changed his name. *Whitby man Mick Jackson* – that's how the story started.

'That's unbelievable,' Grace whispered, not sure which part of the story she meant. That her brother had been walking his dog on the beach one February evening, or that he'd gone to the aid of a man and his son, the two of them swept off their feet and into the surf by an unexpected wave. Or how, according to onlookers, he hadn't hesitated, but plunged straight in, boots and all. He brought the young lad in first, then went back out for the father.

'When was this?' She broke off from her reading to scan the clipping for a date.

'A couple of years back, I think . . .'

'So . . .' The words took an age to come. 'He's one of the people you've interviewed? You've spoken to him? Is he still in town . . . ?' She was giddy with the thought of it.

'Oh, God . . .' Malin was still reading, her face pale from the light of the screen. 'Grace, look . . .'

Grace leaned in and read the line Malin was indicating, and pulled abruptly back.

No. It was all she could manage. Because the story went on to describe how her brother had rescued the man and boy, and then, before he could get back to shore, had been swept off his feet and, twenty years after surviving the Irish Sea, was dragged under and swallowed whole – like he was unfinished business.

'He's . . . he's dead?' Grace glanced at her sleeping da, not sure if she'd shouted the words or whispered them. She slumped in her seat trying to make sense of this thing that made no sense at all. Michael was dead. She closed her eyes and tried to erase the image that had risen up uninvited. Michael alone in the dark and dangerous sea, trying to free himself from the hammering surf, to gain some kind of foothold against the water bearing down on him. Michael crying out above the thundering waves, knowing he was outmatched, that he could not win. She could feel herself sinking as the water closed over her head, the pressure in her chest as she dropped towards the ocean floor, the invitation to simply give in, to take a final breath . . .

It was Malin's voice that pulled her back to the surface.

'Grace.' She had her finger close to the screen, following the lines of text. 'Look . . .'

Grace didn't want to look. She didn't need any more details, she was trying to work out how they were going to go forwards now, what she was going to tell her da . . .

'Grace. Read it.' Malin tilted the screen towards her.

She read quickly until she got to the last line. Eight words. She felt the breath go out of her; a noise in her head like the sea itself.

Mick Jackson leaves a wife and a son.

CHAPTER 73

Grace was walking like she was airborne. The only thing keeping her down was the hold Jack had on her arm. He was in a tailspin but she – she was flying high, soaring through the air, arms wide, ready to embrace whatever, *whoever*, they were going to find. Jack called out various insignificant landmarks as they passed: car registration numbers, street names, road signs. She'd told him nothing in the Endeavor – either about Michael, or where they were headed – she'd simply woken him up and said it was time to make a move.

Mick Jackson leaves a wife and a son.

The words had had her from empty to full in a matter of seconds. The sudden loss of Michael replaced by a discovery beyond anything she could have imagined.

'A son?' Malin had said. *A brother.*

'Oh, yes. Nice lad too,' Will said. 'I interviewed him. Joey. That's his name.'

After that it was like everything simply rolled out in front of them. A long stretch of smooth road they'd never imagined walking down. Will Fletcher had glanced at the clock behind the bar, then said, 'Anyway, I reckon he'll be coming in shortly.'

Grace had misunderstood. 'What, here? Coming in here, you mean?'

Will had smiled. No. That wasn't what he meant. What he meant was Joey Jackson, this sudden gift that had dropped in their lap – brother, nephew, grandson – would be on his way in from the sea. He would be sailing back into harbour within the hour.

'Come on, Grace, we have to go now.' Malin had got to her feet, pulled her coat on. She was almost out the door before Grace had rallied her da, smoothing out the crumpled edges of him. Will Fletcher stopped her as she turned to leave, one hand on her arm, the other holding a small card.

'I'd love to know how you get on. If you have the chance, you know . . .'

'Yes, yes. I'll . . . I have to go. Thank you . . .' She pushed the card into her coat pocket, linked herself to her da and hurried after Malin.

'What's the rush, Gracie?'

She was walking too fast for him but couldn't slow down. Her feet were in charge now and her head was too full of questions to find room for an answer. *Michael had a son. Would they see him? Would they recognise him? What would they say to him?* The street was full of people. A coach tour by the look of them, the lot of them standing still and blocking the way, their eyes fixed on the tour guide at the front. Grace kept her eyes on Malin and followed the path she was slowly carving out. They had almost reached the swing bridge that crossed the harbour when its warning lights started flashing and a loud beeping struck up.

'Oh, I don't believe it.' Grace skidded to a halt, her da clinging onto her arm. She scouted left and right for an alternative route but there was nothing.

'Grace, come on . . .' Malin sped up, like she was going to make a quick dash for it: some Jason Bourne manoeuvre, impossible but bold, that would have them hurtling across the bridge, then, in a leap of faith, off the other side.

'Malin, no. Stop!' The barriers jerked themselves loose, then rattled down, barring their way.

'What's going on girl?' Jack said. She could feel him shaking, and the sharp clutch of his fingers on her arm told her she needed to calm down, to explain, to reassure, but she was too het up: their way ahead suddenly obstructed; stopped in their tracks when they needed to be moving, to be readying themselves.

'Oh. What's that . . . ?' She felt him take a couple of steps back as the bridge slowly ground into action.

'It's the bridge, Da. It's opening.' It was all she could manage as she watched the ancient mechanism, thick with grease, slowly crank into action.

'Gracie. Those railings . . . are they moving?'

She couldn't answer. Her feet were treading the ground beneath her like some runner on the blocks, ready to fly at the sound of the starter's gun. She needed to go. Go *now*. Find the boy *now* – not risk being in the right place at the wrong time again . . .

* * *

Jack let go of her arm and put his hands over his ears to block out the dreadful noise. The ground in front of them was moving and Grace was acting like there was nothing wrong. He took a step away, then another, and pushed himself through the crowd of people gathered behind them until the high-pitched beeping sound receded and was drowned out by a different noise altogether: the noise of an engine. There was something settling about its low thrum, something that pulled him deeper into the crowd. He saw it in quick glimpses as he made his way through shoulders, bags, children. It was a boat; a red fishing boat, heading lazily towards him. He pushed past a couple with three dogs and stationed himself by a low wall to watch it pass. The sun was mirrored in its wheelhouse windows, the deck was wet and rippled with the reflection of the sky. He could hear the crew but he couldn't see them. It was the colour of the thing that got his brain ticking. A far-off hint, at first, then a steady beat that had him squeezing closer and squinting his eyes against the slant of sun. He leaned over the wall as far as he could and scanned the prow for a name. And there it was: white lettering, painted with a flourish like a signature – like something he'd seen before. He hoisted one knee onto the wall as the boat pulled alongside and concentrated on the words. The three words.

'Gracie . . .' His voice was lost in the din of the water, the clanking of metal, the thrum of the engine. 'Gracie . . .'

'Da, where are you?' Her voice was a million miles away. He looked back at the boat. Rubbed his eyes again – but he was right.

It was the *Laughing Girl*. It was Michael's boat.

'Ahoy there,' he shouted. 'Ahoy there . . .'

* * *

'Malin. My da. Where is he?' She'd heard his voice, turned round and found him gone. She swallowed down the wash of acid that hit the back of her throat and scanned the crowd behind her. 'Da? Da. Where are you?'

The bridge was almost fully open, she could hear a boat's engine nearby, preparing to come through.

'Grace. Look.' Malin was tugging on her arm, pointing towards a shopfront. 'He's there. Jack's there. Oh my God, Grace. He's on the wall . . .'

Grace ran, fighting her way through the crowd. Malin was at her side. 'Is he still there? Is he still there?' She couldn't see him. 'Da! Da!'

After that the world went into slow motion. Malin was

ahead of her, craning her neck as she ran; she could hear the slow grind of the bridge, the low hum of a boat engine, the blood pounding in her head. The crowd thinned and then, it seemed, simply parted before them – and there he was. Her da. Standing on the wall, his two arms in the air, shouting . . . She launched herself forward and grabbed him round the waist. 'Da . . .'

It wasn't until her breathing settled and the banging in her head faded that she realised what he was shouting.

'Michael, Michael!' He was yelling it at the top of his voice. People were turning to look at them. He was oblivious. His arms were a mad flail, his face was lit like a Christmas morning. 'Gracie, look. It's him. It's him!'

Grace looked down into the boat idling below them; at the white scroll of a name across a red prow; at the young boy looking up at them from the deck: laughing eyes, a head full of curls. Her da loosened himself from her grip and snapped off a smart salute – and the boy sent him a smile and saluted back.

CHAPTER 74

Grace's first attempt to explain that the boy on the boat wasn't Michael had gone straight over Jack's head. They'd crossed the bridge at a lick, the three of them arm in arm, and Grace had tried to line the words up in some order he would understand. It was impossible because he was *alight*. His feet were barely touching the ground. He was, she knew, on a fast road to agitation. So, despite the fact the *Laughing Girl* was sailing away from them, she'd slowed things down. As soon as they regained solid ground on the other side of the bridge she cast around for somewhere to sit. To pause a moment and come up with a plan.

'What the hell are you doing now, girl?' She steered him towards the bench, cleared a couple of cans out of the way and sat him down.

'I need a breather, Da . . .'

'A breather? What are you talking about, Gracie? We don't need a breather, we need to be up and . . .' He was off the bench, on his toes.

She pulled him back down beside her and pointed to the harbour. 'He's there, look, Da. See the boat? He's tying her up. We'll watch for a minute. We'll not lose him, don't worry.'

We'll not lose him. The thought swelled her heart.

'You all right, Grace?'

She didn't have to look to see the smile on Malin's face. It was there in her voice. Had been from the moment they'd seen him – and he'd seen them. *Recognised them*, that's what Grace liked to think: that the sight of them had stirred something in his blood, some rising up, some helpless clamouring.

Hiraeth. There'd been a time, steeped in the grief of Harry's death, she'd held that word close to her heart, grateful to be part of a nation that understood what she was feeling. *A pull on the heart that conveys the feeling of something missing, something irretrievably lost. A sense of yearning for a home, a place, a person...* There'd been comfort in it – and reassurance, maybe – but she'd never, until now, felt the hope in it. She'd never imagined that the longing could be answered; that the yearning could be satisfied.

She wiped her eyes and watched as the crew took leave of the boat, the tidy closing down of the day. They hadn't found Michael, but they'd found another part of him. No matter what was going to happen next, one thing was certain: she had been dealt a new deck, one with more aces than she'd ever hoped for. There'd be no more losing from now on. Just living.

She was right. They'd rested a moment or two on the bench, then, unable to restrain Jack any longer, the three of them made their way towards the *Laughing Girl*. Grace tried to harness her thoughts, to formulate something that might sound like a sane introduction, but it was as much as she could do to put one foot in front of the other. By the time they reached the quayside Joey was off the boat and, as far as she could tell, waiting for them. Ten minutes later they were following his broad frame back across the swing bridge and through the narrow streets of old Whitby.

Michael's wife – his widow – was waiting at the door of the shop. Joey had phoned ahead, an attempt to pave the way for what was about to land at her feet. Grace had overheard snippets of their conversation: *they're asking about dad... three of them* : . . . *I think so* . . . She'd welcomed them in, dropped the latch on the shop door and ushered them through to a back room – more of a glassed-in courtyard – that let out onto a steeply rising garden.

'Sarah,' she'd said, holding out her hand. 'I'm Joey's mother.' There was something about the woman – some quiet calm – that had Grace suddenly lost for words. The account she'd given Joey had been garbled and confusing, her da colouring in the edges every time she paused for breath and they'd been at the shopfront before she'd had time to formulate anything better. She needn't have worried, because at that point Malin had stepped forward into the sunlight spilling down through the glass roof and stood beside Joey.

Sarah put her hand to her mouth. 'Oh my God,' she said, reaching out to touch Malin's arm. 'It's you.'

They'd stayed there the night, the three of them lined up in an attic room that groaned and rattled like an old ship. Grace had lain awake, unable to tear herself away from the marvel of the evening, the feeling she'd had – once she'd settled Jack in bed and they were sitting at the kitchen table – that they were each holding separate strands of the same rope. They'd told their parts in no particular order, but by the time they'd finished the frayed ends of Michael's story had been wound back together, each tangled thread and fibre of it smoothed out until, nearing midnight, they had it braided before them.

Sarah had met Michael in 2001. She was studying in Newcastle at the time, almost at the end of a two-year course in silver smithing, and had travelled to Whitby in search of material – and inspiration – for her end of year exhibition. She'd spent the day combing the beach for jet, then settled into a quiet corner of a pub to eat and sketch out some ideas. She didn't know who noticed who first, only that once they'd got talking they'd found it difficult to stop, and once she'd got back to Newcastle, she'd found it difficult to stay there. *There was something magnetic about him*, she'd said and Grace had nodded. He'd charmed her with tales of hard fishing grounds and stormy seas, casting himself as some seafaring vagabond, entranced and run aground by her silver bangles and her beauty. *Pure baloney*, she'd said, because she never saw him go near a fishing boat. Everything happened quickly – she moved in with him within weeks of finishing her course – and six months later she was pregnant.

'Mick was over the moon,' she said. 'Like really over the moon. And that was when he showed me the photographs . . .' She got up from the table and left the room.

She came back with a framed picture in her hands. She gave the glass a gentle wipe, then passed it to Malin.

'That's you, isn't it?'

'Oh my God. Yes . . . I . . . we have one like it at home . . . but . . .' she pointed to the pencilled caption at the bottom edge, 'yours is slightly different to mine. *Laughing Girl II*?'

'It's the name of my boat,' Joey said. 'I named my boat after you.'

CHAPTER 75

Grace spent much of the night trying to thread the story together in a way that Jack would understand. She was awake long before he was, ready to get him up and out of the bedroom before Malin woke. She led him quietly down from the attic, the windows at each turn of the stairs painted in pink and gold – a sailor's warning. She'd made tea, then guided him through to the glass room.

'Where is everyone, girl?' The agitation of the previous day had burned itself off and left its usual mark: the heaviness in his eyelids; the slack drape of his cheeks as he gazed down at his hands clasped loosely in his lap.

'Still in bed, Da. It's early.'

What she'd planned to say now seemed confusing even to her. Nonetheless she launched in.

'We were talking last night, Da. After you'd gone to bed . . .'

* * *

Jack could have told her then, eased a line or two off her face; explained how he'd not fallen asleep straight away the night before, but arranged himself under the duvet, not so much tired as *full*; knowing that if the door in his head were to suddenly spring open, the contents of his brain would fly out and maybe give him some relief. But for once, he didn't want it to. There was so much to think about and he didn't want to lose any of it.

He'd thought the boy was Michael. And who wouldn't? Squinting up at him from the deck, his eyes creased against the sun, smiling back like it was the most normal thing in the world. Grace had grabbed hold of him just in time because every fibre in his body had urged him forwards – some magnetic pull that seemed to narrow the space between them, to invite a short leap and jump that would have his lost boy safe in his arms.

It was all wrong, of course. There was some part of him registered that, even as they crossed the bridge, Grace trying to chivvie the mistake out of him, to calm him down. But he'd wanted none of it. He'd wanted to run and keep running towards his beautiful boy, to outpace reason and logic and keep the flame inside him burning. It had gone out of its own accord, of course: the sudden switching off that always took him by surprise, that left him on the floor, in the dark, trying to remember his own bloody name.

It wasn't the look of the boy that did it because, as he clambered off the boat and hoisted himself up the harbour ladder, he *was* Michael: the strength in his back, his arms, the mischief in his green eyes. No – it was the boy's name that had the rug from under him. He didn't know what Grace had said to the lad, but at some point he'd nodded and said, *Joey. Joey Jackson.* The flame had flickered brighter for a few seconds – throwing light in some dark corner of his brain – a slanting ray that had ignited a single realisation. This was not Michael, but Michael's boy. And then, before the flame inside him had sputtered and gone out, a final thought that had taken the strength from his knees: Michael might not have come home, he might have left them wondering, but the name he had given the boy said he'd never forgotten them.

* * *

When Malin opened her eyes Jack and Grace were gone. She shifted in bed and angled her face into the pink and gold glow coming in through the attic window.

How easy it would be, she thought, to simply stay here, to abandon the life she already had and start afresh – just as her father had done. Perhaps it was the miracle of survival – of being given a second chance – that had allowed him to do it: that his brush with the Irish Sea had washed away a past he needed to let go of. A baptism of sorts, she thought, knowing she was adding a romantic edge to the man, because whatever miracle had saved him hadn't saved Joseph. Nonetheless he'd been given the chance of a new life and he'd embraced it. She rested her hands lightly on her belly, and knew – no matter what Vee had to say – that was exactly what she was going to do.

It had been obvious the evening before – as she listened to Sarah and Grace knitting the two ends of their stories together – that there was a gap in the middle of it: neither of them knew how Michael had survived; how he'd gone down in the Irish Sea and magically reappeared in Whitby. There had been so much else to tell – and to listen to – that they'd all been content to move on swiftly, let the mystery lie.

It resurfaced, though, the minute she got into bed. She had lain awake until the early hours formulating a list of questions: questions only one person could answer – her mother. She'd worked her way through the obvious ones – the *hows* and the *whens* – it was the *why* that stuck in her gullet, stuck fast and convinced her that, as tempting as turning her back on her current life might seem, she couldn't. She'd never stood up to Vee before but knew she needed to do it now because, somewhere in the missing chapters of Michael's story, her own story had begun.

She was engrossed in packing her bag and didn't hear Sarah's tap at the door.

'All right if I come in?'

'Oh, yeah. I'm . . . just getting ready for off.'

Sarah closed the bedroom door behind her and held out a tatty shoebox. 'I thought you might like this,' she said.

'Oh.'

'It was your . . .'

'My dad's?'

Sarah nodded.

Malin sank down onto her bed and sat the box on her knee. The cardboard was soft and furred with age – or maybe use.

'You don't have to open it now . . .'

'No, I know . . . but . . .' She hooked her finger under the elastic band that held the battered lid in place and slid it aside.

'Your mother sent them,' Sarah said, as Malin sifted through the collection of worn photographs – a small catalogue of her childhood. Sarah sat down on the bed beside her. 'He thought about you all the time, you know. Wondered about you.'

Malin couldn't speak. She was looking at the card that lay beneath the photographs: it had a painting of the Madonna and child on the front, and a sheaf of loose papers – letters or poems, perhaps – tucked inside. She set it aside with the photographs and considered the folded sheet of paper that lay at the very bottom of the box. There was some familiarity in its rough texture and torn edges. She scooped it out, opened it up and burst into tears.

My Family. The drawing she'd done at school. Vee with her violets, flanked by a ballerina child on one side and a laughing, dark-haired man on the other.

CHAPTER 76

'So. Da . . .' Grace set it all out carefully for him, pausing frequently to make sure he'd absorbed each part of it. She explained how Michael had been in Whitby a long time, that he'd married and had a son. Then she recounted the story in the *Whitby Gazette*: the beach rescue, his bravery . . . and his death. He looked up when she'd finished and asked her the one question she had no answer for.

But how did he survive Milford?

She'd tried to imagine it, of course, conjuring up confused accounts of what happened: the *Laughing Girl* morphing into the *Andrea Gail*, the Irish Sea into the Grand Banks. She'd had him picked up by a passing boat, or clinging to floating debris, floating semi-conscious on waves that miraculously delivered him to shore.

'I don't know, Da. I don't know . . .'

She got no further because Sarah had come down the stairs, followed soon after by Joey, then Malin, and before she knew it the five of them were eating breakfast and exchanging phone numbers, addresses. Despite the revelations of the night before there was an edge of self-consciousness to their conversation: an awkwardness that Grace struggled to push past. Part of her wanted to leave straight away – to put some distance between herself and this miracle that had been served up – and find some quiet corner where she could get her thoughts in order. She was wondering how soon she might broach the subject of leaving when Jack suddenly clattered down his spoon and wiped his mouth on the back of his hand.

'So where is he?'

It would have been easy to pretend she didn't know what he was talking about, to put the colour that rushed to her cheeks down to the heat of the room rather than the embarrassment – the mortification – of having not asked the question herself. Never mind not asking it – for some reason she'd not even thought of it. She looked at Sarah and saw the woman's cheeks were as flushed as her own.

'I . . . we . . .' Sarah said, and stopped. There were tears in her eyes.

Grace, eager to steer away from what seemed to be the obvious conclusion – that they didn't know where Michael was because the sea had never returned him – started in buttering a slice of toast for Jack. He shook his head and pushed it away.

'Where is he? Where's Michael?'

'Da. Leave it. Sarah . . .' She couldn't bring herself to look at the poor woman. 'I'm so sorry, my Da's confused.' The meanness of saying it stung, but his arms were folded over his chest now, and she could see he wasn't going to stop until he'd got himself an answer.

'No, really. It's OK. It's just, you know . . .'

Still too fresh, Grace might have said, except Joey suddenly leaned forward and put his hand on Sarah's arm.

'Perhaps we should just show them, Mum.'

* * *

'What's happening, girl?'

Grace didn't know what to tell him because she didn't rightly know. *Perhaps we should just show them*, Joey had said and Sarah had wiped her eyes on her sleeve and simply nodded. So she'd obeyed the instructions to wrap Jack up in something warm and the five of them had filed out of the shop into a morning tinged with pink, and cold enough to make her nose run. The narrow street, despite the early hour, was not deserted. Shop owners were out, winding down awnings and mopping doorways; a couple of men strode past, cupping cigarettes against the wind; a young woman rattled by with a sleeping child in a buggy.

'Keen this morning,' a bloke shouted, as they approached the swing bridge. Grace didn't know if he was referring to the wind – or the fact they were up and out so early. Joey simply raised his hand in reply.

'Where is it we're going, girl?'

Grace pretended not to hear. The metal surface of the bridge rang and reverberated as they hurried across. She could feel the drag of him on her arm and was suddenly worried that wherever it was they were headed, it was going to be too far. Malin was up ahead, walking beside Joey. The two of them were chatting. Sarah walked alone with her head down. It was hard to tell if she was deep in thought, or avoiding the sting of the cold.

They veered left as they came off the bridge, passed the bench they'd rested on the day before and set off along the quayside.

The *Laughing Girl* lay in a slant of sunlight, like she was warming herself up for them. When Joey jumped down onto the gleaming deck, Jack let go of her arm and stepped forward, squinting against the sun as he leaned down to check the name painted along the boat's side. He gave a small nod, then held his hand out and let the boy help him aboard.

Ten minutes later – minutes that had kept Joey busy at the helm, Sarah silent and pale faced beside him – they were heading out of the harbour and onto the open sea. Grace watched and waited, wondering how it was going to play out: a marker buoy perhaps, that bore her brother's name, or a rockface or piece of coastline that somehow commemorated him. This is what she was thinking when Joey, prompted by a nudge from Sarah, slowed the engine and turned to face them. He smiled at his mother, then reached up to a shelf above the window. He brought down a tin – and for a moment Grace imagined he was going to put some unseen kettle on and offer them biscuits. But no. He handed the tin to Jack.

'We had dad cremated,' he said. 'I keep him here on the boat with me.'

For safe-keeping, that's what the boy said next, then pushed the throttle in a notch and off they went. Her da said nothing. He bent his head towards the tin and cradled it in his arms like he was holding a baby. 'My boy,' he whispered. 'My boy.'

CHAPTER 77

Malin drove slowly, turning her head from time to time to admire the stretch of sea to her left. It was impossible to describe the colour of it, the seamless meeting of water and sky. It was impossible to describe how she was feeling. *He thought about you all the time.* Sarah's words still had tears pricking at her eyes.

'So where to now, hinny?'

Jack was in his usual place, wedged on the back seat between the soft bedding.

'Back home, Da,' Grace said. 'Back home to the farm.'

'Good move,' Jack said, shuffling back in his seat. 'And what about the girlie?'

Malin glanced across from the driver's seat and smiled.

'Well she's going to drop us off, Da and then . . .'

Grace didn't know how it had happened, but somehow it had. The talk of the past had turned into talk of the future, of Malin staying at the farm a bit longer, of Sarah and Joey coming down to visit . . . of contacting Will Fletcher to let him know what had happened . . .

Grace swivelled in her seat and looked at Jack. She'd not asked what 'a bit longer' meant, but the pictures it had conjured up were all happy: the three of them in the kitchen, the kettle ticking on the Rayburn, a tray of scones cooling on the side, a bunch of daffs on the windowsill – her da on the armchair in the corner with the baby on his knee.

'I'm looking forward to getting back home, Da, are you?'

'I most certainly am,' he said. 'I can't feel my backside any more.'

Back home. Grace wiped the window with her arm and peered out. She wound down the window and let the air in. They'd been gone for days – mere days – and here she was with the world turned on its head, anticipating a future that, two weeks earlier, hadn't existed. There was still ground to be gained, she knew that, but what ground it was.

His call had been completely unexpected. They were just pulling back onto the road after a service station stop when her mobile rang. The screen told her nothing other than it was an unknown number. *Hello?* She'd heard the uncertainty in her voice; she listened for background clues – a police siren, maybe – knowing her face was already flushed.

Just catching up, was how Will Fletcher started, followed by a short burst that sounded rehearsed and left him slightly out of breath: he'd got her number from Joey, he was sorry for disturbing her, he was just curious as to how they'd got on and he'd be back home by the end of the month so maybe they could meet up to talk about it?

Back home? She'd fished in her coat pocket for the card he'd given her.

'My God.' She held it up to the window and smiled at the marvel of it.

'Well?' Malin was grinning at her.

'It was Will Fletcher. From the pub? He got my number from Joey. You won't believe this but he lives in Saundersfoot. Can you believe that? Saundersfoot. It's only down the road from the farm . . .'

'And?'

'And he wants to meet up when he gets back home. Find out what happened, you know . . .'

'And?'

She'd said yes: said it without thinking or wanting to think; no deliberation or what-ifs, no backing away before she was even over the threshold. Her heart was still pounding with the boldness of it.

She shifted the road atlas off her lap and onto the floor. She'd been travelling with one finger on the page, loosely tracing their route, keeping track of their location, remembering how Greg had ridiculed it, this need of hers to know where she was, to be able to see it on a map and lay it down in her head. It wasn't keeping up with the times or being smart, it was small-minded and old-fashioned. Unnecessary. But it had stood her in good stead. It had kept her on the right road when she needed it. The same road they were on now – the one that led home.

'He was on his boat after all.'

'He was, Da.' Grace swivelled in her seat and smiled at him. He was almost asleep, his dentures adrift. But Michael was on his boat and all was well with the world. They'd seen him, held him and then tucked him back where he belonged.

Jack yawned loud and long. 'Just wait till I tell your mother.'

EPILOGUE

Eight months later

Grace was at the kitchen sink, rinsing the first picking of lettuce. Everything else was in place – her da's birthday cake safe in the pantry, the bunting strung up across the porch and house front. She glanced at the clock to check the time – half an hour before everyone would arrive – and parked herself on the chair by the window and picked up the newspaper.

LOCAL FARMER REUNITED WITH FAMILY. The headline had pleased her da no end, but the story, when she read it to him, had set him off crying. It wasn't the part that had described their journey to Whitby, nor the account of how they tracked down Sarah and Joey, but the closing paragraph. An apology of sorts, she thought. A setting the record straight despite the number of years that had passed. He was a hero, the journalist had written. Michael James of Velindre Farm, Nevern, had died a hero.

Grace folded the paper away and glanced at the framed photograph on the kitchen windowsill. *The Aberyswyth Photograph*, she called it. She'd cried when Malin had taken it out of Michael's battered shoebox and passed it over, cried at the hopefulness of their waving arms and smiling faces as they watched Michael steer the *Laughing Girl* out of Aberystwyth harbour and out of their lives forever, cried at the two words written on the back. *My family.* Now though, it made her smile. She let her gaze drift beyond the window – at her da in his summer jacket and flat cap, Malin decked out in a vibrant cotton smock Vee had brought back from Indonesia – and Michael. Three weeks old, clamped against his mother's chest like he was still part of her. She watched them – this new family of hers, this miracle that her brother had bequeathed her, this chance to live a life that took her forwards, not backwards, a future she wanted to embrace.

She watched as her da took Malin's arm and leaned his face towards the baby. He cupped his free hand against the small curve of its back. Smiling. He was always smiling these days. And who wouldn't smile? His family suddenly swelled before his very eyes – Malin and the baby living at the farm, her *young man* visiting every weekend. She'd caught her da deep in thought one morning, counting on his fingers.

'Am I right, girl?' he'd said. 'Me and you, the girlie and the baby. That's four generations, isn't it?' She'd nodded and he'd gazed off into the distance. *Imagine what your Ma would have said.*

* * *

Two hours later the party was in full swing. They were gathered round the table she'd rigged up by the barn. The cake was cut, the singing done and her da was starting to fade. Will smiled over at her and nodded. *Now,* he mouthed and she nodded back, felt in her pocket and got to her feet.

'A few words,' she said, and looked round the table. Vee was holding the baby, Connor and Malin leaned side by side, her da was sandwiched between Sarah and Joey and Gloria Kavanagh was perched at the end, petting the two farm dogs. 'Well, a poem actually . . .'

ATTENTION ALL SHIPPING

The newspaper article had been Will's idea, but reading the poem had been hers. 'It's called "Transformation",' she said, and paused. The catch in her throat told her best to forget the explanations – how she'd written it years back, unearthed it in the pages of some old schoolbook and – although it was probably rubbish – felt it was nothing but a prophecy, like her young heart had always known where she was heading. She glanced around the table, at the new hand she'd been dealt – then took a deep breath and, through a blur of tears, spoke the words out loud.

> *They are cutting down the forest*
> *and a house that once sat in deep shade*
> *now shines like a brooch on the hillside*
> *Decades of damp rise from its walls*
> *as it bathes, like a convalescent,*
> *in the light and warmth of a long forgotten sun*
>
> *Its windows squint disbelieving at the view as*
> *crows clamour for front-row seats on the roof ridge*
> *and buzzards detour for the pleasure of perching*
> *on the telegraph pole by the track.*
>
> *Small streams, once soaked up by larch and spruce*
> *now run together to form a lively pool*
> *Which is where I sit now*
> *gazing out*
> *and celebrating the miracle of unexpected solutions*

Grace couldn't remember afterwards exactly what happened next, or the order in which it happened because, just as she was about to raise a toast to the people no longer present – her mother, Michael, Harry – her da got to his feet and pointed up at the sky. She followed the line of his arm and there they were.

'Oh,' she said, as a molten cloud of starlings steered towards them in a dancing, loose weave. She was off the chair and by his side as they approached. Then they were all on their feet. Malin and Connor, Sarah and Joey, Vee, Will and Gloria, laughing as the birds sailed overhead – the thrum of their wings like a steady heartbeat – and veered off towards the Irish Sea.

ACKNOWLEDGEMENTS

Special thanks go to my agent Sara O'Keeffe whose vision and belief in the novel took me further than I ever dreamed I would go. It has been an amazing journey and she is the best of travelling companions.

Thanks to my editor, Ann Bissell. It was a privilege to find myself – and the book – in such capable hands. Her skillful and thoughtful insights were invaluable and her enthusiasm for the book was priceless.

Thanks to the teams at The Borough Press and HarperCollins, particularly Jabin Ali, Megan Smith and Elinor Fewster.

Thanks to the teams at Andrew Nurnberg Associates, and to Vanessa Kerr and the team at Aevitas Creative for securing a publishing contract in Germany.

I am indebted to Honno Press – for their encouragement and belief in my work and for setting me on this marvelous path.

I owe huge thanks to my family, friends and the wonderful communities of Llanwrtyd Wells and Mid-Wales, for their generous and ongoing support.

Thank you to my long-standing writing friends – Nicola Clifford, Rachel Bulbulia, Ciaran O'Connell, Jan Newton and especially to Peter Barker, who believed in this novel from the get-go.

Thanks to trawler man Trevor Annetts (*The Sharon Vale* out of Waterford) and to Llyn Peninsula Lifeboat man Lee Oliver for their real life knowledge and accounts of life at sea.

Lastly – but always first – thanks to my lovely husband, Paul. How lucky I am to have you by my side.